Courting Shadows

Jem Poster

Courting Shadows

SCEPTRE

Copyright © 2002 Jem Poster

First published in Great Britain in 2002 by Hodder and Stoughton
A division of Hodder Headline

A Sceptre Book

2 4 6 8 10 9 7 5 3 1

A CIP catalogue record for this title is available from the British Library

ISBN 0 340 82257 0

Typeset in Sabon by Palimpsest Book Production Limited,
Polmont, Stirlingshire
Printed and bound in Great Britain by
Clays Ltd, St Ives plc

Hodder and Stoughton
A division of Hodder Headline
338 Euston Road
London NW1 3BH

Courting Shadows

I

I had expected bones, of course, though not in such abundance. Just a few at first, but by the time the trench was waist-deep they were being brought to the surface with each shovelful. The men would place them reverently on the trodden turf at the edge of the trench, a little apart from the mound of upcast soil, and every so often one or both would clamber out and carry them over to the porch wall, carefully adding them to the growing pile. Each night, after cleaning their tools, they would cover the bones with sacking.

I am by no means an insensitive man, but as architect my first concern was naturally for the fabric of the building. Those who specialize in church restoration tend to make something of a mystery of their vocation, but generalists such as myself know that the fundamental principles of this kind of remedial work are simply a matter of common sense. The wall is already vulnerable – that is, after all, why the job is being done – and the risk of collapse increases with every minute the trench stands open. Once you have begun your trench you finish it as quickly as you can. You underpin immediately; then you backfill and consolidate. Delay is dangerous.

'Think about it,' I said, crouching at the trench edge one morning towards the end of the first week of work. 'This section of the wall is over three feet thick and twenty feet high. It's footed on lumps of chalk which seem, as far as I can see, to have been bonded with nothing more substantial than a slurry of red clay. If you look at the wall from inside, you'll see a crack nearly as wide as a man's hand running from floor level to the corner of the window. Think about that, and you'll have some sense of the urgency of the job you're doing.'

Jefford gave a nervous cough.

'I think about it all the time, sir. We need shoring and props.'

'We'll start shoring as soon as you're deep enough. But the work's going very slowly.'

'We're working as fast as we can, sir.'

I felt it unnecessary to contradict him directly. I reached out my hand and touched the neat stack of longbones. 'Just leave them in the upcast,' I said. 'We'll throw most of it back when we've finished.'

Harris leaned back on his shovel and stared up at me. 'That's not how we treat our dead here,' he said quietly.

I had already noted a kind of insolence in Harris, recognizing it as the result of a slightly more extensive education than is good for men of his status and temperament.

'I'm afraid the job has to be done,' I said firmly, 'and as quickly as possible.'

'So you tell us. But some of us don't see the need.'

I was on the point of remarking that his doubts had not prevented him from taking on the job or precluded a rather indelicate interest in the level of pay associated with it, but I decided against it. I had had dealings with Harris's type before.

'Do you think we'd do better to let the church crumble and fall about our ears?'

'That crack was there in my grandfather's time. And no doubt before that.'

'That may well be so. But there comes a stage in the life of any building when its decline must be arrested if it is to continue to stand. That's the situation here. And when I say so, I'm offering a professional judgement based on ten years' training and experience. What kind of training and experience can you lay claim to?'

That stung, as I had intended it should. His neck and face reddened, and he lowered his gaze in what I took to be tacit apology. There was a moment's silence before he spoke again.

'Even if we do what you say with the bones, we'll still be held up by this.' He scuffed his boot along the bottom of the trench.

'What do you mean?'

'Look.' He took up his mattock and began to work it gently across the trampled floor, levering up long flakes of clay to reveal a dull greyish surface.

I leaned forward. 'What's that?'

'Lead. We've come straight down on to a coffin. Listen.'

He stamped twice. The earth rang hollow beneath his feet.

'Clean it off. I want to see exactly where it lies. We may be able to work round it.'

He glanced up, his eyes bright with malice.

'I doubt it,' he said. 'Sir.'

Harris was right. Aligned, predictably enough, with the wall and dug in surprisingly close to its footings, the coffin proved on further excavation to occupy a substantial proportion of the trench's total area. There was no question of working round it.

'It'll have to come out.'

The men exchanged glances.

'We'd rather not, sir,' said Harris.

'We'd all rather not,' I replied, 'but the job has to be done. An extra two shillings apiece if you get it out by this evening.'

3

'It's not a question of money,' said Harris. But I noted with a certain satisfaction that both men turned back to their task immediately. They worked, moreover, without resting, so that by late afternoon the floor of the trench had been lowered by a good two and a half feet, except where the coffin stood isolated on a neatly trimmed plinth of soil.

'We'll undercut most of that,' said Jefford, following my gaze, 'so that we can pass the ropes underneath. But first we need to extend the trench. You see how the foot of the coffin's bedded in there at the corner?'

'Yes, I can see that. But you don't need to cut back the whole trench to release it. There can't be more than a few inches of the thing left unexposed. Just hollow out the trench wall around it.'

'I shouldn't advise that,' said Harris. 'Even as it stands, the trench is unsafe. If we start hacking away at it—'

'I didn't ask for your advice, Harris. The risk is minimal. And I want that coffin out by nightfall.'

He looked up at the sky. 'It can't be done, sir. Not safely. You shouldn't ask.'

'I'm not asking, Harris. I'm giving instructions.'

'If you like. But they're unreasonable instructions.'

'For God's sake! I'll do the job myself.'

I admit that I was impelled primarily by anger, but it was in any case clear that Harris's challenge to my authority demanded a forceful response. I leaped into the trench, snatched up the mattock and began to gouge out the soft fill, picking and raking until the whole thing lay exposed; then I clambered back up the ladder, trembling with rage and exertion.

'Now clear that up and prepare the coffin for lifting.'

As I walked away I was aware of one of the men climbing out of the trench behind me. I turned.

'Where are you going, Harris?'

He looked at me, his eyes wide with exaggerated surprise. 'Going, sir? Nowhere. At least, only to fetch the ropes.'

He cleared his throat, spat and moved off towards the porch. I strode out of the churchyard and down to the stream, where I stood for some time gazing at the water, trying to calm myself. By the time I returned, Jefford had cut away most of the earth from beneath the coffin, leaving only its ends supported. He was working with feverish haste, breathing heavily as he shovelled up the last of the loose soil. Harris stood above him, uncoiling a length of stout rope and paying it over the edge of the trench. Jefford looked up as I approached. 'I'd meant to show you this, sir.' He straightened up and thrust his hand into his jacket pocket.

'What is it?'

He held out a small greenish plaque. Two copperplate initials and a date: E.S. 1792.

I took it from him and examined it closely. 'Did you find this with the coffin?'

'Yes, sir. Directly above it.'

'But not attached to it?'

I was struggling with an acute sense of unease. Jefford shook his head.

'It would have been fixed to the wooden casing. That's rotted and gone. But I'm sure the plate belongs with the coffin.'

He glanced round quickly for corroboration. Harris laid down the rope he had been holding and wiped his hands on his breeches.

'No reason to doubt it.'

'But if that's so, the body we're dealing with has been in the ground for less than ninety years. I was expecting . . .'

I am not sure exactly what I had been expecting; but this was certainly, historically speaking, rather too close for comfort.

'There's some in the village will know who this was,' said Harris.

'I'm well aware of that.'

I handed the brass rectangle back to Jefford.

'Get rid of this.'

'Get rid of it, sir?'

'Lose it. Bury it. I don't want it lying around where it might be seen.'

He touched his cap and slipped the object back into his pocket. He peered up at Harris, who was now uncoiling a second length of rope.

'Give me that.'

Harris handed him the frayed end. Jefford squatted down and passed it beneath the coffin; then he knotted the rope securely and reached behind him for the other.

I think I registered the expression on his face before I understood what was happening. Nothing dramatic: just a widening of the eyes, a slight dropping of the jaw. No cry. He made as though to stand and, as he did so, the hand which had been feeling for the rope went up to the back of his neck. And then the trench wall hit him.

It struck him just above waist height, a dark wedge exploding on contact into a shower of clods and bones. His legs buckled and he lurched sideways and a little forward, groping at the edge of the coffin as he fell. Then he was under it all, winded, gasping for breath on the wet floor of the trench.

Harris was down there before I had even thought to move, wrestling his shovel from the tumbled clods. He began to dig furiously, flinging the spoil into the far corner of the trench, grunting as he worked. Jefford, whose head, shoulders and right arm were clear of the fallen earth, was grimacing horribly, opening and closing his mouth like a landed fish. Beads of blood welled from a small contusion just above his eye.

'Where's the other shovel?' I shouted.

Harris muttered what might well have been an obscenity, though I gave him the benefit of the doubt.

'Jefford's shovel. Where is it?'

'Under this lot. Go and find another.'

I ran to the porch, my feet slipping on the wet grass. Dusk was falling and the interior was so dark that I spent several minutes fumbling around the walls before I could be sure that, as I had already obscurely surmised, there was no third shovel. By the time I returned to the trench, Harris was helping Jefford up the ladder, one hand beneath his arm, the other gripping his leather belt. I put out my own hand for Jefford to grasp, but he simply stared at it with the fixed gaze of a sleepwalker and then pitched forward at my feet. Harris scrambled up the ladder, dragged him – rather roughly as it seemed to me – from the trench edge and propped him in a seated position against a headstone. He made a strange convulsive movement and attempted to rise to his feet, but Harris pushed him back down.

'Bide still. You're safe now.'

Jefford's face was extraordinarily pale and almost completely devoid of expression. Lolling there in the twilight, his sunken eyes fixed on nothing, he might have been a graveyard ghost. He breathed deeply and irregularly, with long, shuddering sighs. Harris took a dirty scrap of cloth from his pocket, then stooped and wiped Jefford's glistening face before passing the rag over his own sweating forehead. The action struck me as peculiarly distasteful, though I hardly had time to consider the matter, my immediate concern being naturally for the welfare of the injured man.

'Are you all right, Jefford?' I asked.

Harris gave an abrupt snort of impatience or contempt. 'Let him be,' he said. 'Your meddling's done enough damage for one day.'

'I admit I misjudged the situation.'

Harris stared at me with an expression of such malevolence that I wondered if he were about to strike me.

'Misjudged? What price your ten years' training and experience now, Mr Stannard? Misjudged, you say. But I'll tell you what I think. I think you knew the risks as well as we did, only you chose to ignore them. A trench six foot deep and more, the soil cut and cross-cut with graves, not so much as a stick by way of shoring; and you go and undermine one of the walls to save a couple of hours' work. It's bad enough having to lift one corpse; it's lucky for you we're not dealing with two.'

It was evident that the man was not entirely rational. He was working himself into a frenzy as he spoke, the sweat starting out again on his forehead, his voice unnecessarily loud. I was about to reply when Jefford put out a hand and tentatively touched his companion's knee. I saw that he was trembling violently, like a sick animal.

'Let's drop it,' he said quietly. 'I've got to get home.'

I would have accompanied him and, indeed, offered to do so, but Harris brushed aside my suggestion.

'I can look after him,' he said.

He reached out a hand, gripped his companion's wrist and hauled him to his feet. Jefford stood like an old man, his shoulders hunched, his breeches soaked and clinging to his thin legs.

'You're sure there's nothing I can do?'

'We can manage,' said Harris.

The two men turned and made off through the churchyard, Jefford stumbling a little as he walked.

It was almost dark. The wind was rising, sweeping in across the marshes, laden with sleet. I retrieved Harris's shovel and placed the boards carefully across the top of the trench. Then I closed up the church and returned to my lodgings.

2

I had ample opportunity, during those early days in the village, to examine my reasons for taking on the commission, but each time I returned to the matter it was with a faint sense of perplexity, as though the decision had not been entirely my own. The Dean's initial letter had been flattering, certainly, recalling his long association with my father and reminding me of a meeting in my twelfth year at which, he assured me, I had convinced him that I was marked out for future eminence. But flattery alone could hardly have persuaded me to commit myself for an estimated two to three months to a place of such deadening mediocrity. Subsequent reflection has convinced me that my decision was, in part at least, a throwback to the earliest phases of my interest in architecture.

Always, in those days, ecclesiastical architecture. I was obsessed. Until relatively recently I kept, in a stiff folder tucked away in my desk drawer, a record of that early obsession: drawings of tapering spires and elongated windows; designs for a pulpit, memorial plaques, a traceried font; and, again and again, those spacious interiors, vaults of – as I was later to understand – impossible proportions springing from the slenderest of columns. The drawings missed the essence of the vision, of course, but for many years they served as a reminder of my aspirations. No grotesques, no stained-glass martyrs, no shadowed corners, but light passing unimpeded through clear windows, striking the whitewashed walls and the gilt and polished surfaces of the spare furnishings; and the eye drawn through the luminous space of the nave and the raised chancel to an altar draped with a plain white cloth. Behind that, the marble reredos which, in my early youth, I had supposed I might carve myself, though I came to realize long before the vision itself had lost its lustre that I should never possess the necessary skills. I can still see it, dimmed a little now by time and disappointment, a tripartite crucifixion in high relief, the two side-panels filled with mourning figures, their faces lifted to the sky; and towering above them, in the central panel, the crucifix itself. I spent hours imagining that Christ: not the pitiful, suffering creature of so much medieval church art, but a hero assured of his own salvation and of the ultimate redemption of all mankind; the brow smooth, the lips gently parted, the eyes already lit by knowledge of a place beyond pain.

Nothing could have been further from that juvenile vision than the ugly hodge-podge of a building which was to serve as my introduction to the practicalities of church restoration. St Mary's sits awkwardly between the open marshland and the insignificant village it serves, oddly marginal to the small cluster of shabby houses and separated even from its own rectory by a broad strip of grazing. It is, as the guide-books never tire of informing us, a building of considerable antiquity: the round-headed lights of the tower clearly define that part of the structure as Norman, while the clustered piers in the nave suggest a significant phase of rebuilding and expansion within a century of the church's foundation. A little later still the aisles were widened and a chancel added, but the development was a half-hearted affair, hampered by the existing structure and, no doubt, by lack of funds. What we are left with – whatever the antiquarians may tell us – is a monument to a rather unappealing type of human enterprise, a piecemeal assemblage of botched fragments.

Did I imagine that I could transform the building into something approximating to my vision? Obviously not. Its ugliness was irremediable, and my brief was in any case inhibitingly mundane: I was to carry out such consolidation of the fabric as seemed strictly necessary; to install a stove and heating-pipes; and to replace, subject to detailed approval from the Dean, any unserviceably worn or damaged furnishings. But I think I felt – yes, I know I felt initially – a faint tremor of excitement at the mere thought of working on a church; and I suppose that can be traced back to those early projects and the powerful but suspect emotions once aroused in me by the abstract contemplation of ecclesiastical architecture.

I could hardly avoid reflecting on such matters as I sat among the congregation at what was to be the last service held in the church prior to its closure. Once we moved indoors – and my intention was to begin stripping out the pews during the following week – Mr Banks and those of his parishioners who wished to continue with their weekly devotions would have to make the three-mile journey to the neighbouring parish each Sunday pending completion of the works. Perhaps it was the imminent disruption of the regular patterning of their lives which accounted for the sombre mood of the worshippers that morning, but even in the normal course of events their surroundings could hardly have been conducive to emotional or spiritual uplift. The windows – some of which, as I had explained to Banks at our single, rather constrained meeting, would undoubtedly have to be replaced in their entirety – were cracked and holed; and the cold airs seeped through them and wandered around the nave, chilling our hands and faces. How, I asked myself, should such a place provide inspiration? So much meaningless clutter, so little coherence of design; everything tending to drag the gaze and spirits downward, so that even when the organ roared out the triumphant strains of 'Rejoice, the Lord is King', and I threw back my head and raised my voice in a deliberate attempt to lighten the almost palpable sense of oppression created by the dark surfaces of the pews and pulpit, I simply found myself appraising, with a cold professional eye, the bulging plaster to the right of the chancel arch, wondering whether I might have underestimated both the extent and the seriousness of the problem it represented.

Banks made strenuous, perhaps over-strenuous, efforts to compensate for the drabness of his surroundings. His sermon was delivered apparently extempore yet with remarkable rhetorical control. He had the trick of repeating particularly significant words or phrases with an almost passionate emphasis, leaning forward over the edge of the pulpit, his pale eyes searching the faces of his parishioners with a peculiar and compelling intensity; or he would break off for several seconds at a time, still holding us with that unsettling stare, creating a silence so highly charged as to induce in his congregation a quite unusual state of nervous receptivity. His choice of subject was, perhaps, a little disappointing – I have heard too many sermons preached on the stock themes of compassion and neighbourly behaviour – and I was unable to dispel the suspicion that the high polish of his performance indicated a degree of self-regard not quite appropriate to a clergyman; but I was left with the strong impression of a man who might justifiably have aspired to higher office or, at least, to office in a less remote and backward community.

There was little evidence of comparable distinction among those members of the congregation visible to me from my admittedly unsatisfactory vantage-point, the single and obvious exception being a man of about my own age who sat alone in the low-sided box-pew in the south aisle. Even in his case, it would have been difficult to deduce breeding from the face alone, which was rather weakly proportioned and, in every sense of the phrase, lacking in resolution; but his upright bearing, coupled with the discreet elegance of his dress, left me in no doubt of his social standing, and I determined to make his acquaintance at the earliest opportunity.

It was not until the end of the service, as we rose to leave, that I discovered that the pew immediately behind mine had been occupied by a figure in some respects even more remarkable. I have always prided myself on my measured response to feminine beauty, but this young woman struck me as quite exceptional, appearing to stand out from her surroundings with what I can only describe as a kind of radiance. Despite the unusual darkness of her hair and eyes, despite the sobriety of her clothing, that was the impression she gave as she turned, one hand on the pew-end, and looked me full in the face for a second or two before moving slowly down the aisle towards the door. What was it? The clear lines and tones of her pale face, perhaps – but the effect of light seemed relatable to something deeper. Attempting later that day to isolate and define its source, I found myself unable to get beyond the tired, familiar abstractions – beauty, refinement, nobility, grace – and abandoned the attempt as futile.

I emerged into the watery sunlight to see her standing beneath one of the yew trees, adjusting her bonnet, the ribbons whipping about her face in the stiff wind. The woman at her side was evidently her mother: the same accentuated cheekbones, the same open gaze, though the older woman's skin was lined and her features generally of a sterner cast. As I looked, a young man strode towards them, apparently with the intention of engaging them in conversation; but they barely acknowledged him before turning and walking away, leaving him staring after them, his face and awkward stance betraying an acute awareness of his humiliation. That, I thought to myself, observing with a certain satisfaction his foolish, crestfallen expression, is what happens when a man presumes to approach his betters on terms of false equality. As the pair left the churchyard, both moving with the same upright dignity, the younger woman glanced back over her shoulder. It seemed to me that she was looking in my direction; but the sun was in my eyes, and I might well have been mistaken.

It would have been wiser to have gone straight back to my lodgings, but I had time on my hands and my mind was running on my work, and it seemed natural enough to stroll over to the trench to examine in fuller light and in a calmer state of mind the effects of the previous day's mishap. I had had a troubled night and had woken early from a dream in which the tumbled soil seemed to churn and swell, rising like a yeasty dough above the edge of the trench; and I was relieved now, lifting the end of one of the boards, to see how little had actually fallen. Enough to floor a man, of course, but not so much as to hold up the work for more than an hour or so.

'I hope you'll not be working today, sir.'

I started and dropped the board.

'With respect, sir. We are enjoined to remember the Sabbath, to keep it holy.'

I disliked the man's sanctimonious tone and, straightening up and turning to face him, disliked even more what I saw. A thin, sallow face, the mouth twisted up at one side in what I took to be a smile; the eyes watering slightly, rimmed with red; lank grey hair hanging over the collar of a dark jacket. I drew my handkerchief from my pocket and wiped my fingers.

'No,' I said. 'I have no intention of starting again until tomorrow.'

'I'm glad to hear it. You'll forgive me, but there are those in the village who feel the job shouldn't be done at all. We've had our say and we've not been heeded. The best we can do is to see the work is carried out in as seemly a manner as possible.'

'You'll find nothing unprofessional about my conduct, Mr . . .'

'Starkey, sir. James Starkey. Maybe not, but – he moved over to the wall and, with a slightly theatrical flourish, placed his hand on one of the buttresses – 'a church isn't like an ordinary building. Each and every stone is sacred. And we shouldn't meddle where there's no need.'

'Well, you can take my word for it, Mr Starkey, that in this particular case there's a demonstrable need. And think for a moment about the building's history: like almost every other church of its age, it has been modified over the years, sometimes dramatically so. If you'd been here in the thirteenth century you'd have had to watch as they tore off the roof and dismantled the walls of the original nave. My own proposals are in fact extremely modest; certainly in no sense comparable with developments of that order.'

He shook his head slowly.

'I'm not a learned man, sir, and I can't say anything about that. But I know there'll be damage and disturbance in the Lord's house while you're at work here. And tell me this: if it's good work you're about, why would William Jefford have been hurt in the doing of it?'

That question, posed not so much aggressively, it seemed, as with a genuine perplexity, made it clear that I was dealing with attitudes too primitive to be susceptible to rational argument. I was considering how best to terminate the conversation when I saw Banks approaching, stepping towards us between the gravestones, lifting the hem of his cassock above the wet grass as a woman might lift her skirts. Starkey seemed suddenly anxious to be gone. He gave a brusque nod and stalked off, scarcely acknowledging the rector as he passed him.

Banks himself seemed a little abstracted, greeting me with a firm handshake but a perceptible coolness of demeanour.

'That man,' I said, watching Starkey out of the gate, 'seems to have got it into his head that I'm here to wreak havoc in the church.'

'James Starkey is a man of strong opinions and very little tact. He exercises a certain influence over some of the older villagers, but I shouldn't imagine a man of your sophistication would have much difficulty in dealing with him or with his arguments.'

'No difficulty at all. But I hope you won't mind my observing that there's some correspondence between those arguments and the views you appeared to be promoting when I mentioned the matter of the windows last week.'

Banks smiled weakly. 'Some correspondence, yes. The irony is that while you recognize and perhaps exaggerate the relationship between my views and Starkey's, Starkey himself holds me personally responsible for having laid the church open to what he regards as an act of desecration. His stance is actually rather simple if, in practical terms, untenable: he is opposed to change of any description. My own position is far more complex: I believe that change is inevitable, and often desirable. I want my parishioners to sit comfortably in their pews on Sunday mornings. I want warmth, I want light. But I have to square this with a belief in the immeasurable value of all that has been passed down to us. I see the church as an ark, a repository crammed with treasures, visible and invisible. Sometimes when I'm alone here, early in the morning it might be, or at dusk, I walk up and down the aisles almost reeling beneath the weight, beneath the richness and density of it all. All this, I think, gathered together within these walls; and I reach out to touch something, anything – the worn stone at the lip of the font, perhaps, or the polished rail of the pulpit – and think of the hands before mine, and the hands to come. There's exhilaration in the act, but also a sense of responsibility. I'm not a prisoner of the past, Mr Stannard, but at such moments I see with extraordinary clarity that our progress towards the future must be informed by a deep respect for the lives and works of our forefathers.'

I suppose it must be difficult for a man of Banks's calling to know when to refrain from preaching, or even to recognize his own tendency to turn a conversation into a sermon. I stepped in quickly as he paused for breath. 'Tell me, Mr Banks, how do you manage for company in a place like this?'

'You've seen my congregation. Ours is a small community, but not a negligible one.'

'I'm aware that there must be several dozen families here; but few, unless I'm greatly mistaken, of any social or intellectual standing. My question should perhaps have been more precisely phrased. Where in such a place do you find company suited to your own accomplishments and status?'

'This place suits me very well, and I can truthfully say the same of its inhabitants. I try not to discriminate – not, at least, along the lines you suggest – sincerely believing myself to be no more highly exalted in my Maker's sight than any man, woman or child in the parish.'

'Oh, I know we're all equal in the sight of God. But—'

The penetrating severity of Banks's gaze seemed to me to constitute a subtle breach of decorum. I value directness in a man, but that searching stare suggested a culpable disregard for the niceties of social intercourse.

'But what, Mr Stannard?'

'I suppose I mean simply that we can't be expected – we are not permitted – to share the divine perspective. We live in a world that requires us to make certain distinctions; a world, I would go so far as to say, in which certain distinctions are inescapably apparent. Is it so unreasonable of me to observe that your congregation consists largely of men and women with whom I should be unable to sustain a conversation for more than a minute or two? Or that, with very few exceptions, your parishioners visibly lack the refinement of men such as ourselves? I admire your idealism, but the facts stare you in the face.'

'What we call facts are often little more than loose impressions, buttressed by a heterogeneous body of prejudices and assumptions. What do you really know of the merits of these people after a week in their community? I've been here for a good ten years but I wouldn't presume to judge them in the way you appear to do.'

'I think you may have misunderstood me. These are not moral judgements, but social observations. For all I know, every member of your congregation may be a living embodiment of all the Christian virtues. I'm not, I agree, in a position to evaluate these people's moral worth. I simply want to insist on the rather obvious point that only a very small handful of this morning's worshippers might appropriately be invited into our drawing-rooms.'

'My own drawing-room is perhaps a little more accessible than yours, Mr Stannard. But who are your favoured few?'

'I imagine you know that as well as I do. Apart from ourselves there appear to be three: the well-dressed gentleman in the box-pew to your right; the young lady who was seated immediately behind me; and her companion, whom I take to be her mother. You might wish to propose other candidates but not, I'm prepared to wager, more than another two or three.'

'You're on safe ground with Mr Redbourne. His family has occupied Anstone Hall for more than a hundred and fifty years, and I've no doubt at all that you'd be happy to invite him into your drawing-room. Given your sensitivity to questions of social status you might, however, experience a certain anxiety as to whether a man of Mr Redbourne's eminence could, with propriety, accept such an invitation.'

Banks was half smiling, but the gibe was clearly intended as a form of reproof. I decided to ignore it.

'And the ladies?'

'I imagine you mean Ann and Enid Rosewell. Both are striking figures, Ann particularly so, but I don't suppose you'd – look here, Stannard, is there nothing you can do about this business?'

He gestured with more than a hint of irritation towards the heaped bones. The wind was tugging at the sacking which covered them, exposing one end of the stack to view.

'I'm not responsible for that. The bones might more conveniently have been left in the upcast and shovelled back into the trench on completion of the work. I think I've managed to dissuade the men from adding to the pile, but if you want it moved, I suggest you discuss it with them.'

He stepped forward and pinned down the flapping sackcloth with a lump of limestone. Then he straightened up, ran his fingers through his thinning hair and gazed into the distance as though lost in thought.

'I must apologize,' he said at last. 'I'm not quite master of myself this morning. The last few days . . . all this disruption, you understand; and then Jefford. The man has hardship enough to bear already and might well have been spared more.'

'You've heard about yesterday's accident?'

'Of course. I visited him last night.'

'Has he recovered?'

'Hardly, though I understand that there's unlikely to be any permanent damage. His chief concern at the moment is that any period of convalescence may result in a loss of income.'

'I shouldn't normally expect to pay my labourers for days not worked.'

'I wonder, though, whether you might regard this as a special case.'

'As any employer will tell you, Mr Banks, all such cases are special cases, or can be made to appear so. In my time I've had to listen to any number of stories – ailing wives, starving children, impending evictions – many of which, I have to say, have been completely fictitious.'

'And some of which, almost certainly, have been largely or entirely true.'

'Perhaps so. But once you start admitting special cases, you lay yourself wide open.'

'Wide open to what, Mr Stannard? To compassion?'

'To exploitation. The moment an employer shows himself to be in any way manipulable, these people will take advantage of him. I don't blame them – that's the way the world works. But anyone who wishes to thrive in such a world would be well advised not to drop his guard.'

'It's a bleak philosophy, Mr Stannard, though one that the age seems to endorse. But to come back to the case in hand. Jefford does in fact have an ailing wife, as well as four children who, if not actually starving, are visibly undernourished; but even if we disregard those facts, the specific circumstances of his accident would seem to give him some claim on you.'

'I don't quite follow you. You're surely not blaming me for Jefford's injuries?'

'Not blaming you, no. But I want to suggest that you have a certain responsibility to an employee injured in your service – the more so since his injuries appear to be the result of an error of judgement on your part.'

'An error of judgement? Who says so?'

'According to both Jefford and Harris, you yourself admitted as much at the time of the incident.'

'I may have said something of the sort. I was naturally in a rather agitated state. Allow me to remark, Mr Banks, that you need to keep your own guard up. These people will not scruple to use you for their own ends; and when you tell me, as you did a moment ago, that you are not master of yourself, I'm tempted to ask whether that observation reflects an awareness, however oblique, of the hold they have over you.'

'That wasn't my meaning, and my understanding of the situation differs radically from yours – not least because it's based on fuller knowledge than you can lay claim to. Jefford is actually scrupulous to a fault, and I can assure you that he never so much as hinted that I should make representation to you on his behalf.'

He paused briefly, fixing me again with his discomfiting stare.

'May I make a suggestion? I shall be visiting him again tomorrow afternoon. I should like you to come with me.'

'I'm afraid my work—'

'Just an hour of your time. I ask no more. I believe that would be sufficient to alter your view of the matter.'

I could not see that such an alteration was either likely or desirable. But I was cold, and unwilling to prolong the discussion, and it seemed easiest, all things considered, to accept the unwelcome invitation.

3

I have seen some desolate landscapes in my time, but there is usually a compensatory romance to be found in such places – in the rugged grandeur of the Highlands, for example, or the more surprising wildness of the Devonshire moors. My new place of work offered no such compensation. The low hill behind the village seemed to stand simply as a barrier to vision, while eastward the eye was led away across tracts of impoverished grazing and flat marshland to where the sky and the estuary merged in a leaden haze. A stroll in that direction shortly after my arrival had confirmed the landscape's elemental dullness while at the same time sharpening my sense of my own entrapment. Less than a mile from the village, the lane gave out, and though I pressed on down overgrown footpaths, I soon found my way barred by a drainage ditch, too wide to leap and choked with sedge and rushes. I stood there for several minutes, taking it in – the seeding rush-heads, the abandoned farm-cart rotting beside the path, the dull shine of the malodorous silt, the grey sky pressing down on it all like a lid; then, with a queasy shudder, I turned and made my way back to the village.

My lodgings were no more inspiring than my wider sur-roundings – an overfurnished living-room on the first floor and an attic bedroom too small for any furniture apart from the bed itself, a wicker chair and a blanket-chest which served additionally as bedside table and washstand – but they suited my purposes well enough. Mrs Haskell was quite absurdly apologetic about the bedroom, though the truth is that I had expected nothing better for the very modest amount I was paying. I told her so when I first took the rooms, but she continued for some time to raise the subject on a daily basis, as though in perpetual need of reassurance.

'Please believe me, Mrs Haskell,' I said in response to yet another anxious enquiry at the beginning of the second week of my stay, 'there's nothing whatever the matter with my bedroom. If there had been, I should have moved out by now. I wonder if we might find another subject for our conversations in future.'

She evidently took this as an invitation rather than a reproof. She placed my breakfast tray on the table in front of me and proceeded to give me such a comprehensive account of her life – her parents' poverty, early marriage to an ageing master-mariner, widowhood, the death of a daughter, the virtual loss of two sons, both now in Canada and, as she bitterly put it, not troubling to write from one year's end to the next – that it was nearly nine before I was able to stem the tiresome flow and get away.

Harris was already at work when I arrived at the churchyard, clearing the fallen soil from the trench. I was pleased to see that the coffin still stood intact on its plinths of compacted earth.

'You've done well,' I said. 'It looks as if it's just about ready for lifting.'

'Near enough. But we need another pair of hands.'

'We may have lost Jefford,' I said, nettled by what I took to be his suggestion, 'but I should like to think that I'm man enough to take his place.'

He set aside his shovel and stared up at me.

'Take his place? With respect, sir, this isn't a job for two. The third rope – there, coiled up by your heel – that's yours. As I said, we need another pair of hands.'

Having just offered my assistance, I was poorly placed to

challenge his casual assumption of my availability for the task, but I was not going to be pushed into hiring unnecessary labour.

'The coffin's not an unduly large affair,' I said. 'I think our combined strength should be equal to it.'

'Take my word for it, sir, it's heavier than it looks. But it's not simply a matter of strength. With only two of us on the job there's no room for mistakes, if either of us should stumble or lose his grip, the whole thing goes. A third rope – a third man – gives us an anchor in case of trouble.'

'I don't think we'll have any trouble. Let's try lifting the thing. If we then decide it's too much for us, we can always lower it again and bring in additional labour at that stage.'

I am not sure that this satisfied Harris, but it certainly silenced him. He stooped and picked up the end of the rope which Jefford had been about to attach at the time of his accident. He passed it under the shoulders of the coffin and tied it firmly before retrieving his shovel and clearing the last of the debris from the corner of the trench. Only when he had finished the work and joined me at the trench edge did he speak again.

'I shall have to ask your help, sir, fetching one of those poles from the far side of the church.'

'What for? We need them all for the scaffolding.'

'This is only temporary. You'll see.'

I followed him round, irked by his reticence and obscurely aware of having been placed at a disadvantage. He selected one of the sturdiest of the scaffold poles, lifted one end and motioned me to take the other.

'Listen, Harris, I think you'd better tell me what you're up to.'

'It's obvious. We can't drag the coffin straight up the side of the trench. This will hold it clear as well as giving the ropes a smoother run.'

I should have thought of it myself. It was a good point, and I conceded as much.

'It's only common sense, sir.'

The pole comfortably spanned the length of the trench. Harris aligned it immediately above the coffin, about eighteen inches in from the trench edge, and drove in four wooden pegs to hold it in place. Then he climbed down and checked the knots, inspecting them carefully, tugging at the ropes.

'All safe?'

'Safe isn't the word I'd use, sir. But the knots should hold.' He flung the ropes over the pole and clambered back up the ladder.

'Are you ready?' he asked.

It occurred to me that he was rather relishing his own dominance of the situation. I nodded and picked up the nearer of the two ropes.

'Perhaps I should take that one,' he said. 'The foot of the coffin will be lighter.'

'I can manage, thank you, Harris.'

He shrugged. 'As you like. But I want to say something before we start.'

'If it needs saying, say it.'

'Supposing we can lift the coffin at all, we're going to exhaust ourselves within a few minutes, so we need to work fast. But steadily; remember, it's important to keep it on an even keel as it rises. If it once unbalances itself, we'll have the devil's own job of it.'

'Only common sense, isn't it, Harris?'

I had intended the comment to be playful rather than malicious, and slightly surprised myself by the acerbity of my own tone, but Harris gave no sign of offence. He spat on his hands and picked up the end of the second rope.

'Most things in life are a matter of what we call common

sense. The trouble is, in my view, it's not so common as it ought to be.'

I thought, as we started to pull on the ropes, that the coffin was going to be too heavy for us; then it broke free of the two plinths, scattering soil, and began to rise. Not easily, but steadily, swaying slightly as it came but essentially under control. It was not until it reached surface-level and hung there, hard against the pole, that I felt myself to be in any kind of difficulty.

'What now?' I asked, suddenly and uncomfortably aware of my quivering thigh muscles, the tension in my back and shoulders. 'It's jammed.'

'Just put a turn on the rope. Hitch it around the pole.'

I kicked the free end into the space between the pole and the trench edge and dropped to one knee.

'That's it. Now you'll need to reach across the pole with one hand and bring the rope – easy now, easy!'

'I can't do it. I need both hands to hold the thing.' My voice was unsteady now, my whole body trembling.

'Hold hard. I'm coming over.'

I looked across and saw that he had braced one foot against the pole and was letting down the loose end of his own rope. He lunged forward and downward, seized it as it swung away from him and, with deft, economical movements, wound it several times around the pole before fastening it with a couple of half-hitches. Then he scrambled to my side and leaned out over the trench.

'I've got it.'

He was taking some of the strain now, his left hand grasping the loop of my rope just below the knot, the fingertips of the other hand hooked under the flange where the lid lapped over the coffin edge.

'If you can tie the rope now, we're home and dry.'

I could see he was right. Once secured, the coffin could

hang there for as long as it took us to recover our strength. It would then be an easy matter, each of us taking one end of the pole, to lift it clear. I edged round him and braced myself as he had done.

I felt it in my hands and wrists before I saw anything happen. Just a subtle premonitory tremor, something slipping, catching; and then the loop slid over the angle of the far shoulder so that the coffin twisted in the air and lurched heavily inward. It would, I think, have fallen at once had Harris not held it steady against the side of the trench, pulling hard on the rope with his left hand, tightening his grip on the lid with his right. I remember the strained gape of his mouth as he threw back his head, eyes tightly closed, the veins standing out in his neck and on his sweating forehead.

'I can't hold this. Tie the rope quickly and get your hands to it.'

I started forward and, as I did so, felt the coffin shift again. I heard Harris gasp and saw him scrabbling with both hands now at the lid. Then the weight was gone from the rope.

The impact of the coffin on the trench floor seemed oddly subdued, a muted smack or thud reverberating through the ground beneath me. As I struggled to regain my balance I looked across to see Harris on his knees, staring over the edge, clutching a large sheet of lead to his heaving chest. The expression on his face was extraordinary, disgust warring for a moment with what I could only interpret as a terrible fascination. Then he was on his feet and stumbling away, casting aside the lead as he hurried towards the gate.

In this respect, at least, I proved myself to be made of sterner stuff than Harris. Although the smell that rose from the trench as I leaned over was undeniably repulsive and might well have overpowered me in a more confined space, I was able to cope both with that and with the thing itself. The coffin had fallen right way up, though tilted a little towards my side

of the trench by the crushed plinths of earth beneath it. The
section of the lid which had peeled away in Harris's hands
had left exposed the upper part of a body so astoundingly
well preserved that for a second or two I imagined that I was
looking at an effigy rather than a corpse.

I know men who have worked extensively on church restoration and I have heard several of them speak in general terms
of the remarkable preservative properties of a well-sealed lead
casing, but I was not prepared for anything so disconcertingly
complete. I was astonished by the surviving detail of the
graveclothes: the scalloped edges of the stained sheet which
enfolded the body, the gathered cloth of the garment visible
where the sheet fell open around the breast, the delicate
drawstring tied in a neat bow at the throat. The woman –
for the body was unmistakably female – stared up at the sky
through half-closed lids from beneath a lace-fringed cap, her
lips unevenly drawn back from her teeth in what might have
passed for a wry smile. The brown skin of the lower part of
the face appeared slightly crusted or cracked, but the brow
was smooth and the hair still lay in thick dark drifts on the
pillow that supported the head.

Searching my memory, I can find only one parallel to the
curious intimacy of that moment. I am a child, small enough
to have to stretch upward to see, sleeping on the high four-
poster in the guest-room, a middle-aged woman. She lies on
her back, one arm hanging over the edge of the bed, breathing
noisily through her mouth. I have stumbled in unknowingly
and now I hesitate in the half-light, snuffing a faint unfamiliar
perfume, wanting – absurdly, since the woman, as I now
suppose, can know nothing of my presence – to apologize
for the intrusion. But the parallel, I realize, is inexact. The
childhood experience speaks to me of embarrassment, even
of trespass; but standing there at the edge of the trench I
experienced something more. Not terror exactly, for the

emotion was firmly under control; but some sense of the way in which a mind of a more primitive or superstitious cast than my own might be overset by sudden confrontation with the enigmatic lineaments of the dead.

Banks was almost upon me before I became aware of his approach. As I turned, he stopped and looked at me enquiringly, narrowing his eyes against the pale sunlight.

'What's going on, Stannard? Is Harris all right?' He nodded towards the gateway where Harris stood, one hand on the wicket, staring at the ground as if he were lost in thought.

'I think so.' I lifted my head and called out across the graveyard. 'You're not hurt, are you, Harris?'

'No, sir.' He shambled towards us. 'No. It gave me a turn, that's all. I was expecting bare bones, not—'

He broke off with a nervous shrug of his broad shoulders, moved to the edge of the trench and looked in. Banks, following his gaze, started visibly.

'What's happened here?'

'An accident. Nothing serious.'

'You're rather prone to accidents, Stannard. Or, rather, those who work with you seem to be having more than their share of them. And I'm bound to say, too, that the matter may be more serious than you think. If certain members of the community were to find out about this—'

'I'm aware of the problem. But there's no reason why anyone other than ourselves need know. Once we've got the coffin out, we can rebury it temporarily in the upcast, and it will be easy enough to slip it back in when we refill the trench. What is it, Harris?'

'Nothing, sir. I was just thinking that the lifting will be even more difficult now. We shouldn't try again until we've found someone to pull alongside us. I can vouch for George. My brother, sir, strong as an ox; and he'll keep his mouth shut.'

I glanced across at Banks. He seemed to hesitate briefly before giving me a discreet nod.

'Very well, Harris. Would he be free to come over at once?'

'He might be persuaded, sir.'

I saw where the conversation was tending.

'You can tell him he'll be more than adequately remunerated. But I want this thing out of the way by the end of the morning.'

'Thank you, sir. I'll fetch him over.'

Banks watched him go, waiting until he was out of earshot before turning to me.

'This is a troublesome business,' he said, indicating the damaged coffin. He shifted uneasily and stared into the trench, his mouth pinched as though clamped on some unspeakable grief.

'I'm not unduly troubled myself. I regard this as a trifling setback. We'll be back on course by this afternoon.'

'I hope so. The Dean was optimistic that the work would be completed by early spring.'

'I shall do my best not to disappoint him.'

'He thinks highly of you, Stannard. I gather you've known one another for some time.'

'Mr Vernon is an old friend of my father's. He took some interest in my progress when I was young, but it's a good few years since I last saw him.'

'You must have made a considerable impression. He was adamant that the contract should go to you.'

'I'm very much indebted to him.'

'As is the parish, of course. I think it's fair to say that none of this would be happening if it hadn't been for his intervention. I had mentioned the condition of the church to him early last winter, pointing out the difficulties we faced, as an isolated and impoverished community, in finding subscribers for even the most modest programme of restoration;

but my observations had been made casually and without expectation. The Dean's response, on the other hand, was far from casual: shortly before Easter I received a letter informing me that subscriptions were being raised from other quarters, that he had approached an architect and that we could expect work to begin in the late autumn.'

'The answer to a prayer?'

'I suppose so, yes. But the tone of the letter seemed ominously high-handed, and when I wrote to suggest that we might more conveniently wait until spring to start the work it was made very clear to me that, as recipient of a substantial gift, I was in no position to challenge the wisdom of those who had placed it in my hands. I'm not ungrateful, Stannard, and I know better than to jeopardize a programme designed to prevent the building from falling into ruin, but I've had ample reason over the past few months to regret my own impotence in these matters.'

He turned aside and wandered slowly away towards the gate. I watched as he lifted the latch and stepped out into the lane. He stood there for a few moments, head bowed, before suddenly straightening up and motioning to me.

'They're on their way,' he called.

Harris was by no means a small man, but his brother was a good three inches taller and even heavier in build. A little too heavy, I thought as he approached, moving with the slight hesitancy of a man not entirely easy with his bulk, breathing deeply as though the walk to the church had been an effort. But once he had seen what needed to be done, he set to work immediately, easing himself into the trench to rope up the coffin and ordering Harris about in a manner which left me in no doubt as to who had ruled the roost in their boyhood home. There was no doubt, either, about his physical strength. Between them the brothers hauled up the coffin with such ease and speed that I barely had time to take up the strain on the third rope. Within seconds they had lashed their burden to the pole and lifted the whole thing clear of the trench.

'You're sure you want it buried here?' asked Harris as they manoeuvred it towards the spoil-heap.

'Yes. It's not an ideal solution, but there isn't a better one.' I paused, wondering whether Banks might intervene, but he said nothing. I decided that his silence might reasonably be construed as acquiescence.

'About here,' I continued, indicating a point a little over half-way up the mound. 'Don't spend too long on it. It just needs to be properly covered.'

'Nothing very proper about any of this,' murmured Harris, just audibly. I ignored the remark and turned to his brother. 'I shall be in the church,' I said. 'Come and see me when you've done.'

Banks's claim to find satisfaction in the company of his parishioners was compromised by the tenacity with which he clung to mine, and it was growing increasingly apparent that he was likely to become something of a nuisance to me. I had expected him to get back to his own business but he accompanied me into the church, evidently hoping to pick up the thread of our earlier conversation.

'The fact is,' he said, holding back the door for me, 'a project of this kind needs to acknowledge the views of all parties involved. As rector, I might reasonably have expected to have had considerable influence on the fate of what, rightly or wrongly, I have come to regard as my own church, but I've not been allowed my say.'

His preoccupation was no doubt natural enough, but none the less irksome for that.

'I'm sure Vernon has worked with everyone's best interests at heart,' I said. 'Perhaps you'd be good enough to help me with this ladder?'

That silenced him for a moment. Together we manoeuvred

the ladder towards the chancel wall and set it up just to the right of the arch.

'I don't like the look of that at all,' I said, indicating the area of bulging plaster above us.

Banks smiled. 'I, on the other hand, take great delight in it. I know what you mean, of course. As an architect you naturally regard a patch of uneven plaster as a blemish. But I imagine you'll have some sympathy with my own view: for me, these irregularities are part of the building's charm.'

'It's not the unevenness that troubles me but its probable cause. My guess is that the entire section has more or less parted company with the wall beneath. Would you mind holding this steady?'

He set one foot against the bottom rung and watched as I climbed. I mounted as high as seemed safe, then reached up and rapped the plaster smartly with my knuckles.

'As I thought. The whole lot's blown. It'll have to come off. Not a major addition to the works, but not an insignificant one either.'

'Perhaps you could simply ignore it and save yourself the labour?'

'Unwise. It may hold for a year or two yet; maybe for a decade or more. These things are unpredictable. But there's no doubt that at some time in the reasonably near future the affected area will peel off and fall away. I should also point out – without wishing to overstate the case – that the rendering seems to be quite substantial, and the weakened section therefore poses a certain danger to your congregation. It would obviously be sensible to address the problem as part of the current restoration programme rather than risk having to deal with it as an emergency at some later date. I shall mention the matter to the Dean, but I don't anticipate objections.'

Banks stepped back as I rejoined him at ground level.

'No,' he said. 'I'm sure there'll be no objection from that quarter. Nor from me, of course – your argument's eminently reasonable, and I can see that the job needs doing. But even that small and doubtless necessary alteration to the fabric of the building will touch me with a sense of loss. You see how the light falls on that plaster now, striking the bumps and ripples from the side? I remember noticing that as I sat here one afternoon shortly after my arrival in the village. It was a cold spring day and I was huddled in my cloak in that pew over there. There was a blackbird singing just outside, the sound entering very pure and clear; and I was suddenly struck by – if I may put it this way – the sheer extraordinariness of the ordinary. I don't think I could quite describe it as a visionary experience, but it was certainly a kind of revelation. Sunlight and birdsong, the intricate textures of the building, all inalienably themselves, all undeniably more than themselves.'

'I'm not a man for paradoxes, Banks, and I don't believe there's any particular value in the practice of contemplating everyday objects until they become distorted by the intensity of our focus.'

'Or clarified by it. But you must have felt such things yourself.'

There have been moments. One quite recently. The day I came to make my preliminary survey of the church. I had climbed up to check the roof of the south aisle and was crouched on the leads examining the guttering. As I lifted my head I experienced a kind of dizziness, an almost intolerable sense of the world's immensities rushing in upon me, or of my rushing out to meet them. Yes, that was where I was, squatting behind the low parapet, but out there too, out where the willows lined the riverbank, the pale undersides of their leaves turned to the light wind; and beyond that again, lifted and borne away – and as I looked a heron rose from behind the trees, mounting slowly on broad wings – to where the sky and the estuary merged in a radiance as blindingly seductive as that of any of my childhood visions. These are the moments when anything seems possible: the perfect edifice, an ideal society, knowledge of God. They are the moments we have to guard against.

'No,' I replied, 'I can't say that I have.'

Banks would undoubtedly have pursued the matter had George Harris not entered at that moment. He stood in the shadows, tapping his folded cap against the palm of his left hand, until Banks motioned him forward.

'It's all right, George. I'm just leaving. I'll call by for you at two o'clock, Stannard.'

'Call by?'

'I'm visiting Jefford this afternoon. I hope you're still planning to join me.'

'It had slipped my mind; but yes, of course.'

'I look forward to continuing our conversation. Excuse me, George.'

The man stepped aside to let him pass, then ambled up and stood directly in front of me, a little closer than I found comfortable.

'The work's done,' he said. 'More or less. My brother can finish it off.'

I heard the door scrape shut as Banks left; heard the latch fall.

'I'm grateful to you,' I drew my purse from my jacket pocket. 'I don't believe we actually discussed your remuneration, but I imagine half-a-crown would be acceptable?'

'I'm afraid it wouldn't, sir.'

I was taken aback by the bluntness of his response and the direct challenge of his gaze.

'But you've worked for less than half an hour. My offer's an extremely generous one.'

'Generous enough for the work, sir. But I believe you're asking something more of me.'

'Meaning?'

'I think you understand my meaning.'

I understood perfectly, of course, and found some difficulty in containing my anger.

'This is a form of extortion,' I said.

'I don't mind what you call it, sir. You're asking for my silence on the matter, and that's an unwelcome burden for an open-hearted man. I'll take it up, but you'll need to pay me for my pains.'

'How much do you want?'

'I'll settle for five shillings.'

I laughed out loud, partly with relief, partly at the contemptible scale of his aspirations.

'Five shillings it is. You drive a hard bargain.'

The irony of my remark was evidently lost on him. He held out his hand and I counted out a florin and three shillings.

'Thank you, sir.' He pocketed the coins, gave me a brusque nod and made off, his nailed boots clicking on the flags. He turned at the door, one hand on the latch, and called out to me with the casual effrontery of his kind: 'Let me know if you need my help again. I'd be glad to oblige.'

I felt it unnecessary to reply.

4

Banks arrived punctually on the stroke of two. As we left the churchyard the rain began, a dull drizzle at first but gathering force as we walked, so that by the time we reached Jefford's cottage we were drenched. It was Jefford's wife who opened the door. The warmth with which she greeted Banks gave place to confusion as she registered my presence.

'This is Mr Stannard, Laura, come to enquire after your husband's health. I hope this doesn't inconvenience you at all.'

'No, of course not, but I should have . . . if I'd known . . .' She was visibly agitated, nervously plucking at the collar of her blouse with one hand and pulling the strands of loose hair away from her face with the other as she stepped back from the doorway. She gave a bobbing half-curtsy as I entered and held out her hand for my hat and coat. I sensed from her manner that she had been in service.

'You'll have to forgive us, sir,' she said, turning to me as she led us through to the back room. 'We're really in no fit state to receive visitors at all, let alone . . . well, Mr Banks knows how it is with us, he understands; but if I'd realized he was bringing you—'

'Please don't concern yourself, Mrs Jefford. I've simply called by to express my heartfelt wishes for your husband's speedy recovery.'

'It's very good of you, sir.'

She pushed back the door and ushered us in. Jefford was propped in a chair beside the fire, his head tilted back at an awkward angle, his body shifting uneasily against the grubby cushions. His eyes were vague and unfocused and he seemed not to see us at first; then he started forward, like a man struggling from a dream, and attempted to get to his feet. Banks stepped towards him, holding out a restraining hand.

'You mustn't disturb yourself. I've called to see how you are, as I promised I would; but it's important that you continue to rest.'

Jefford sank back in the chair. There was a moment's silence before he spoke, his voice small and unsteady.

'You didn't say you were going to bring Mr Stannard.'

Just the faintest hint of reproach. Banks smiled gently, leaned over and laid a hand on his arm.

'How are you feeling now? Any better?'

Jefford forced an answering smile. 'Much better, thank you. I should be back at work now if it weren't for . . .' He flapped his hand vaguely across his abdomen and looked helplessly in my direction. 'When I breathe deeply; so I can't—'

'Of course not,' said Banks reassuringly. 'There's no question of your returning to work until you're fit to do so.'

'Yes, but when will that be? Will there still be a job for me then?'

Banks glanced at me. I avoided his eyes.

'Mr Stannard sympathizes deeply with your predicament. I'm sure he—'

'I shall do what I can, Jefford, though I have to say that we're already falling behind and, as you'll appreciate, I can't hold the job open for you indefinitely. For the moment, however, you may regard yourself as being on sick-leave. Perhaps we could review the matter towards the end of the week.'

'Thank you, sir.' A tear ran down his cheek and he turned his head sideways, at the same time passing his hand across his face. His wife felt among the cushions, drew out a small square of frayed cloth and handed it to him. I expected him to wipe his eyes but he simply sat there, clutching the fabric, while the tears gathered and fell.

'He's been this way since he was brought back,' she said. 'Forever crying. It's not like him, sir. He's never been very strong in body, but he's always had a firm mind. Such a support to me in my own illness – Mr Banks will tell you. Seeing him in this state . . . it's like having another child in the house.'

'How many children have you?' I asked, knowing the answer but ready to snatch at any opportunity to lighten the conversation.

'Four, sir. A girl and three boys, one still a baby. The two older ones are at school.'

'And the other two?'

She seemed momentarily to lose concentration, her eyes flickering towards her husband as he turned stiffly to adjust the cushion behind his shoulder, her long fingers resuming their agitated play about her neck and hair.

'The other two children, Mrs Jefford?'

As if on cue, there was a muffled wail from upstairs. I heard footsteps crossing the floor overhead. There was a moment's silence and then the wailing began again. Mrs Jefford went to the door and opened it a crack.

'Bring him down, will you, Alice?' she called out. She appeared to wince, or grimace; and then she was coughing uncontrollably, doubled up, groping her way back towards us, fighting for breath. Banks took her by the arm and guided her towards a chair. She fell into it and slumped forward over her thin knees, pressing the back of her wrist against her mouth in a hopeless effort to stifle the racking spasms. And as she gasped and struggled, the door shuddered back on its hinges and a small girl burst in, half carrying, half lugging a yelling baby, bumping it along in front of her as if it had been a sack of meal. She stopped in the middle of the room, her gaze wavering uncertainly between Banks's face and my own; then she heaved the child over to Mrs Jefford and attempted to lift it on to her lap. Banks leaned towards her.

'Your mother can't take him now, Alice,' he said. 'Give him to me.' He reached out and pulled the writhing infant from her grasp.

I try as a rule not to dwell on such things, but that scene continues to haunt me: the bewildered girl, the baby screaming in the rector's arms, the woman rocking convulsively in her chair while her husband stares into vacancy with the tears running unheeded down his gaunt face. All in a day's work, no doubt, for a conscientious clergyman but, speaking for myself, I should be unable to sustain regular or prolonged contact with such disquieting manifestations of human misery.

At last Mrs Jefford stopped coughing and leaned back, her face flushed, swallowing hard. Her lips and wrist, I noticed, were smeared with blood. She drew a stained handkerchief from her blouse and, with a slightly furtive, apologetic glance at me, wiped herself clean. Then she took the baby from Banks and began to jig it mechanically up and down on her lap. Its cries became less insistent but it continued to squirm between her hands, reaching intently towards her breast, its small red mouth working vigorously. This, I felt, was the last straw.

'I'm afraid I shall have to leave now, Mrs Jefford. I'm needed back at the church.'

She looked up, her eyes widening in what might have been interpreted as silent entreaty or even a kind of panic; but she said nothing, and the expression faded almost before I had time to register it. She tried to rise but fell back, jolting the baby's head against her shoulder so sharply that I wondered, in the momentary hush that followed, whether she had stunned it. Then the unfortunate child drew a deep breath and began squalling again.

'I'll see Mr Stannard out,' said Banks, taking me firmly by the arm. Mrs Jefford gave me a wan smile as I left the room. Her husband seemed scarcely to notice my departure.

The rain had stopped but the wind was up again, buffeting me as I stepped out, tugging at the sodden skirts of my coat as I fumbled with the buttons. Banks stood in the doorway, his right hand gripping the jamb tightly at head-height, his face dark with what might have been construed as either grief or anger though his words, when he spoke, were determinedly casual. 'I shall be here for another half-hour or so. Shall I find you at the church?'

'I'll be there until dusk.'

He closed the door gently and I set off down the lane, shaking my head and shoulders vigorously and drawing the damp air deep into my lungs. I was, I freely admit, relieved to be clear of the cottage and the suffering it held. I am not unsympathetic to the problems of others but it has never seemed to me particularly sensible to brood on them, and I was pleased to find my spirits appreciably lightened by the time I reached the churchyard.

Harris was squatting in the trench, putting the finishing touches to the shoring. The job had been carried out with absurd meticulousness; scarcely a gap between any of the boards and the whole thing held in position by an unnecessarily elaborate system of cross-bracing. He squinted up at me between the struts.

'Did you see him?'

'Jefford? Of course.'

'Is he improving?'

'I think he'll be back at work by the end of the week.'

Harris looked doubtful. 'I saw him yesterday morning,' he said. 'He seemed poorly to me. Like a man who's lost the will to go on, I thought. I talked to him for a while but he wasn't listening, I could tell. It's the pain perhaps, or the worry of it all.'

'He's feeling a little sorry for himself, that's all. Look, Harris, do you realize how difficult it's going to be to move about in this trench with these struts in the way?'

'A small price to pay for a man's safety, sir.'

The accusation hung in the air, unspoken, unmistakable. I turned to go but Harris seemed anxious to detain me.

'Another thing, sir. I was thinking about the next stage. When we cut back beneath the foundations, we'll need props. The whole weight of the wall bearing down . . . You said as much yourself.'

'I was urging haste – I wasn't suggesting the likelihood of imminent collapse. And I should perhaps make it clear that we shan't be undercutting the whole of the exposed area at once. We shall construct the underpinning in sections, a couple of feet at a time, ensuring that each phase is begun and completed on the same day. That way there'll be no need of props.'

He looked doubtfully at the footings, shaking his head almost imperceptibly from side to side.

'Don't worry about it, Harris. These matters are my concern, and you can safely leave them to me.'

Not a word; just a fleeting glance in my direction as he turned back to his work. But I read his thoughts as clearly as if he had articulated them.

'Harris.'

'Yes, sir?'

'I don't want the matter of Jefford's accident to dominate our dealings with one another. Do you understand?'

'Of course, sir. I've been very careful not to mention it. I know how troubled I'd be if I were in your place.'

Perhaps I was wrong to let it rest there, but the obliquity of the insolence left me uncertain how to respond and, as I hesitated, Harris changed the subject.

'Those bricks against the wall on the other side of the porch – are they for the underpinning?'

'Yes. When you've finished what you're doing I'd like you to bring them over and stack them at the edge of the trench. Not too close, and not too high, but they need to be ready to hand for tomorrow. When that's done you can go home.'

He looked as if he were about to object, but I moved quickly away. I had measurements to take for the joiners and had left my tape and notebook in my lodgings. I hurried across the meadow, reaching the far side a little out of breath.

No doubt it was foolish to attempt to vault the gate. I still think of myself as a young man, but I am already beginning to feel something of the rheumatic stiffness of the upper back which has afflicted my father for much of his adult life; and as I thrust down on the top bar a stab of pain went through my shoulders and up the left side of my neck, throwing me off balance. I cleared the gate but landed heavily, stumbled, and fell face forward in the rutted lane.

I have always been peculiarly sensitive to any blow to my self-esteem. I still bear on my right forearm a reminder of an occasion on which, attempting to demonstrate my prowess, I caught the tip of one of my blades on some unevenness or obstruction and went sprawling, hurtling across the ice until brought up short by collision with another skater. Nearly twenty-five years on, the raised white cicatrice says nothing to me of pain or fright (though I recall the pressure of a tourniquet around my upper arm and the bright splashes of blood on the trampled snow as I was carried home) but is still capable of reviving the embarrassment of my long helpless slide from grace beneath the eyes of the schoolfellows I had been so anxious to impress. I squirm now as I think of it; I squirm as I think of myself raising my head from the gritty surface of the lane to see the woman running towards me, one hand outstretched, the other hitching her heavy skirt above her ankles. I was on my feet before she reached me, brushing down the front of my coat with my sleeve, trying to ignore the dull ache in my knee.

'Are you hurt?'

The expressive lilt of her voice was to some extent compromised by a surprisingly strong rural burr.

'Not seriously.' I examined my grazed wrists and palms. 'Hardly at all, in fact.'

'Let me see.' And with a brisk impulsive movement she took my right hand in her own and examined the broken skin.

'You should get this cleaned,' she said. 'All that dirt and grit. If you don't get rid of that—'

'I was on my way back to my lodgings. I'll do it there.'

'I could help you if you want.'

I think she herself recognized the extraordinary impropriety of the suggestion, for she blushed faintly and released my hand. I felt that an explicit rejection of her offer was probably unnecessary.

'Thank you for your concern,' I said. I bowed stiffly and would have walked on if she had not reached out again and laid her hand on my arm.

'I saw you at church yesterday,' she said, blurting out the words, flushing more deeply now. Her gaucheness, and indeed her sheer lack of breeding, astonished me. That dignity of bearing which had struck me so forcibly on the previous morning had vanished completely; had perhaps never existed. This, I realized, was a woman scarcely beyond girlhood, seventeen or eighteen years old at most, possessed, admittedly, of considerable beauty and a certain naïve charm but not –

emphatically not – the imposing figure I thought I had seen. I stepped back a pace, breaking her hold on my sleeve.

'I was there with my mother. Did you see me?'

'Not to my knowledge. There were so many people in the congregation, and their faces are all new to me.'

'Of course.' She smiled dazzlingly, unexpectedly. 'I suppose you'll have written us off as a dull lot.'

'Not at all. What makes you think that?'

'Your life must be very different from ours. The people you meet, the places you go.'

Her conversational strategies were transparent, as childishly unsophisticated as her demeanour. I was not going to be drawn.

'I'm afraid I have work to do,' I said.

She seemed to miss the point of the remark.

'Important work, Mr Banks says. I suppose it will keep you here for some time.'

'For several months, certainly.'

She stood looking at me for a second or two, her head on one side, before resuming with a kind of stumbling eagerness.

'We have so few visitors here. Almost none. Nobody worth speaking of anyway. And to have someone like you among us – well, I don't know you of course, but just seeing your face – I mean, seeing you there in church . . .'

Her words died on the damp air. And I was flattered – flattered and not a little intrigued – by a discomposure which seemed to reveal more than the girl could possibly have intended. I narrowed the space between us again, at my ease now and rather more inclined to indulge her evident hunger for company and conversation.

'But surely,' I said, 'you can see the advantages of seclusion. Yours is a simpler world than mine, certainly, but there are many who would envy you your simplicity.'

She appeared to find something unpalatable in the observation. I saw her body stiffen slightly, her gaze harden.

'And you?' she asked. 'Do you envy me? Would you change places with me, or with anyone here?'

I judged it advisable to change tack. 'I presume,' I said, 'that you've always lived in the village?'

'Just outside.' She waved a slender hand towards the hillside. 'Over there.'

'With your mother?'

She nodded.

'Brothers? Sisters?'

'I have a brother. He doesn't live with us any more.'

'And your father? What's his trade?'

'All these questions,' she said uneasily, tossing back her head so that I caught the fragrance wafting from her thick hair. 'You can't expect to find out everything about a person at your first meeting.'

I was later to examine the remark more closely, but at the time I simply laughed – yes, laughed out loud with a sudden and not entirely explicable sense of exhilaration – at what I took to be its artlessness.

'So you anticipate further meetings?'

She stared at me, wide-eyed; clapped her hand to the side of her face.

'Oh,' she said, visibly flustered, 'you mustn't think I meant . . . only that we're bound to meet again, you being here in the village for so long and me—'

'Don't trouble yourself about it,' I said quickly. And then, surprising myself with my own *galanterie*: 'A man might be forgiven for wishing you had meant a little more.'

There was a long silence. I could see from her expression that I had made insufficient allowance for the literal-mindedness of an unsophisticated country girl. Time, I thought, to bring the conversation to a close.

'You must forgive me,' I said. 'I really must be getting on.'

She stood aside to let me pass.

'Of course. Your work.' And then, abruptly, with an odd nervous movement of her head: 'My name's Ann. Ann Rosewell.'

'I know.'

I recognized my own stupidity almost before the words were out. She said nothing, but I saw her expression change. A slight narrowing of the eyes, lifted suddenly to mine with a confidence bordering on audacity; and then that smile again, more prolonged this time, disturbing in its suggestions of power and awareness. If I had begun the interview on a stronger footing I should no doubt have found some way of reasserting my own authority, but as it was, I turned and moved off in confusion, mumbling a clumsy farewell, my knee throbbing painfully as I went. I imagined her gaze on me as I limped down the lane towards my lodgings, careful not to look back, careful not to stop.

By the time I got back to the church the light was beginning to fade. I had expected the stacking of the bricks to keep Harris busy until nightfall and was surprised and a little put out to find that he had already finished the task and gone. There was no sign of Banks, either in the graveyard or in the church itself. I stood uneasily for a moment in the hushed nave; then I took my tape and notebook from my pocket and set to work.

I was unable to identify the noise at first: a faint whirring in the air somewhere above me; a bump, a scrabbling, a light fluttering rustle. Then silence. I looked up.

I rather dislike starlings as a rule – their swagger, their jostling vulgarity – but for an instant I saw this specimen quite literally in a new light. The bird hung there, motionless against one of the clerestory windows, its claws gripping the buckled leads, its wings heraldically outstretched, the fanned primaries lit from behind, delicately translucent. Only for an instant; then it was off again, crossing and recrossing the darkening nave, hurling itself with what looked like increasing uncertainty of judgement from one window to another.

I was so intent on its erratic movements that I did not register Banks's presence at my back until he spoke. 'Once they've found their way in here – I'm sorry, I didn't mean to startle you – once they're in, it's surprisingly difficult to get them out. Eventually, of course, they exhaust or injure themselves and can be caught, but by that time it's usually too late.'

'Too late?'

'Too late for the birds, I mean. Where there seems to be any hope at all, I tend them, but very few survive.'

He was silent for a moment, staring into the gloom above. Flutter and bump; and, from the tower, the steady ticking of the clock.

'*Ita haec vita hominum ad modicum apparet.* Bede's sparrow, you'll remember, has an altogether cleaner trajectory: swiftly in at one end of the hall and straight out through the other. I wonder, though, whether this poor creature, flinging itself hopelessly against incomprehensible barriers, may not be the fitter emblem of the human condition.'

'The germ of a sermon?'

'No. Just a private observation arising from a particular state of mind, a particular preoccupation.'

'You're thinking of the Jeffords?'

'Of course.'

'I think we've done what we can for them.'

'If what we've done is insufficient – as it clearly is – then we must ask ourselves whether we can do more.' He paused, his eyes fixed on mine as though he were waiting for a response. I said nothing, and had the satisfaction of seeing his gaze falter – just a flicker, but an unmistakable acknowledgement of my own force of character – before he returned to his theme.

'Mrs Jefford was naturally grateful for your visit, but was concerned that she might have failed to give you the welcome you deserved. I told her you'd understand the situation, but she was troubled by your rather abrupt departure.'

'I found the circumstances oppressive.'

'Indeed. So, no doubt, do the Jeffords. The difference is that they don't have the option of leaving.'

'You make it sound as though that were my fault.'

'That's not my intention. But it's perhaps salutary to remind ourselves that we – you and I, Mr Stannard – are privileged beyond the ordinary, and far beyond the wildest hopes of people like Will and Laura Jefford. And we cannot – I mean we must not – turn away from suffering, least of all when we find it on our own doorstep.'

'Your doorstep, Mr Banks, not mine. It has already been made abundantly clear to me that I don't belong here.'

He looked at me sharply, even, it seemed to me, a shade aggressively; then his expression softened and he laid a hand on my arm.

'These matters are difficult,' he said quietly. 'Indescribably difficult. For me as well as for you.'

'No doubt your faith sustains you.'

'I'll be truthful with you: Mr Stannard. My faith is severely tested by such scenes as we witnessed this afternoon. In common, I imagine, with most of mankind, I look for evidence of pattern and meaning in the universe; but what design is revealed to us by the sufferings of the Jeffords and others like them? Good people, by and large, caught in the mire of poverty, disease and despair, battered by forces which seem to know nothing of their virtues and deserts. Oh, I know the stock response, but even a clergyman may be permitted a certain scepticism, a little bitterness, hearing for perhaps the thousandth time that God's plan is developing along lines as orderly as they are inscrutable. It may be so; but I shouldn't feel inclined to argue the case very forcefully, certainly not in the presence of a man prevented by injury from earning the wages his family so desperately needs and a young consumptive oppressed by the not unreasonable fear that she may not survive the winter.'

'Yes, I'd be worried about Mrs Jefford if I were her doctor. I'm less sure about her husband, though. What exactly is the extent of his injuries?'

'Well, there's nothing broken, but he's bruised and quite severely shaken. Dr Barratt tells me it's the shock to the system in general, rather than any specific injury, which has brought him so low.'

'There's no possibility that he's malingering, is there?'

'Out of the question. Look, Stannard, I thought I'd made it clear: Jefford's as scrupulous and plain-dealing a man as you'll find in this village or several dozen round about. And what in any case could he hope to gain from such a strategy?'

'Nothing at all – unless, of course, he had been led to expect that I should continue to support him while he sat at home.'

'I can give you my firm assurance that the matter has never been so much as hinted at in our conversations. Nevertheless, I'm appealing to you now. You've seen these people's circumstances; please do what you can to alleviate their distress.'

'I've agreed to hold his job for him until the end of the week.'

'I don't imagine that Jefford would have dared hope for more, but you must forgive me if I express my own disappointment. The family is desperately short of money and your continuing to pay Jefford – no, listen to me – your continuing to pay him during the period of his convalescence would remove one of his more immediate worries. The situation is stark and simple: either he receives those wages or his children go hungry.'

'Wages? This sounds more like charity.'

'If you like, yes. And charity, St Peter tells us, shall cover the multitude of sins.'

I resented Banks's coercive rhetoric, and should perhaps have made my feelings plainer. I might quite reasonably have challenged his melodramatic analysis of Jefford's predicament or taken issue with the offensive suggestion that such assistance as I might be prepared to offer could be viewed as a form of expiation. In the event, however, I did neither.

'To the end of the week, then. I shall hold his job open and pay him his full rate until then. Beyond that point he must either return to work or fend for himself.'

Banks's face lit up as though he himself had been the recipient of my generosity.

'Thank you, Stannard. I know that Jefford will be greatly relieved. Would you like to tell him or shall I?'

I pictured again the dingy room, the sick woman, the man weeping as though he would never stop.

'You may tell him,' I said.

5

I arrived at the churchyard next morning to find Harris hunkered down against one of the gravestones, staring at the spoil-heap. He looked up as I approached.

'Someone's been at the coffin,' he said, rising clumsily to his feet. 'Look at this.'

The slippage might conceivably have occurred naturally, but the bootprints around the site of the disturbance suggested otherwise. One side of the coffin had been completely exposed, and some attempt seemed to have been made to clear the soil from above. The smell of decay hung in the air around us.

'The rector's already been over. He wants a word with you.'

'Is he coming back?'

'Just now, sir.' He nodded towards the gate.

Banks's greeting was perfunctory to the point of rudeness: a grunt, a slight inclination of the head. He came up beside me and stood looking at the coffin for a moment before speaking.

'All this damage,' he said at last. 'All this disturbance. And I can't help asking myself how much more we'll see before you're finished here.'

'I hope you're not suggesting that I'm responsible for this.'

'Not directly responsible, no. I suspect it's the work of one or more of the villagers. Curiosity, I should like to think, rather than outright vandalism.'

'Rather a sinister form of curiosity, I'd say.'

'Perhaps so.' He looked across at Harris, then took me lightly by the arm.

'I wonder if we might speak in private, Stannard?'

'Just a moment, please. Could you deal with this, Harris? See if you can consolidate the area around the exposed edge. I'll be back in a few minutes.'

Banks walked me over to the porch and stopped with his back to the angle of the wall, out of the worst of the wind.

'I've just been to see Jefford again,' he said.

'How is he?'

'Much as he was yesterday afternoon. Still very unwell. But he was anxious that I should convey his gratitude for your generosity.'

I shrugged. 'As long as he doesn't imagine it to be bound-less.'

'You can be sure I've impressed that upon him.'

The tone of the remark seemed faintly offensive, but perhaps not calculatedly so. I let him continue.

'There's something else. Jefford gave me this.' He held out the brass coffin-plate.

There was a moment of uneasy silence.

'He said you'd asked him to dispose of it, but that he hadn't liked to throw it away. At the same time he had an obscure sense that his accident might have been the result of what he thought of as wrongful possession of the object. He eventually resolved his dilemma by giving it to me.'

'I hadn't intended to burden the man. It's a very small scrap of metal to have weighed so heavily upon him.'

'With respect, Stannard, your instructions to Jefford sug-gest that you had already recognized it as something rather more than that. An object such as this has a certain potency. Whether we're dealing with primitive superstition or with sophisticated forms of antiquarian curiosity, the fact is that many people find it difficult to jettison these fragments of their history.'

'More's the pity. What hope is there for the future while we remain encumbered by the debris of past ages? I'm not speaking of the great achievements of previous generations, of earlier civilizations; but these insignificant leavings . . .'

'I've come to believe that nothing is insignificant. Everything around us resonates with meaning, whether we're attuned to it or not. Holding this plaque in my hand, I have some sense of the anxiety Jefford appears to have experienced. But I also feel somehow privileged, as if the fragment were a means of access to a hidden world, a kind of key.'

He was leaning towards me with something of his pulpit manner; eager, animated, a shade too intense. I should have liked to return to my business, but felt compelled to respond.

'A key of sorts, yes; but supposing you were now able to track down the coffin's occupant in the parish register, what then? Access to what? Parentage perhaps, a date of birth, spinster of this parish or wife of this or that gentleman. The barest facts. And even supposing your researches were to take you further, what pettiness you'd be likely to lay bare, what numbing ordinariness. Most human lives are profoundly uninspired and uninspiring. We might rake them over for ever without discovering anything of value.'

'Let me offer you this possibility, Stannard: that our blindness to the value of other lives is a curable condition. It is, moreover, the condition I most wish to cure, both in myself and in those to whom I minister. I should like to be able to celebrate those lives, in all their supposed ordinariness. I should like to be able to acknowledge – and to make you understand – the worth of each one of them.'

He was holding the plaque out towards me, his arm quivering slightly.

'Take it,' he said suddenly. 'Take it.'

'Really, Banks—'

'Go on. Take it in your hand.'

It seemed easiest to comply. He stared into my face for a moment, his eyes searching mine. I shifted uneasily beneath his gaze.

'I don't know what I'm supposed to—'

'I want you to experience the active presence of the past, to know this object as it really is, charged with the energies of other lives. Your hand around it connects you with others: hands bearing down on the burin, engraving this date, these initials; hands tying the drawstring at the girl's neck or smoothing the pillow around her head; in some shaded room, perhaps, a hand hammers home the two brass pins which hold – held – the plaque in place. And behind those hands, bodies and minds, lives of unimaginable complexity ... Standing here yesterday, looking down on that poor blind face, I found myself, almost without thinking about it, reaching back across the years to encompass – yes, really to embrace – the living creature. It's a desire for knowledge, of course, but so far beyond mere antiquarianism as to require another name. I understand it, quite simply, as a form of love.'

I was not inclined to regard Banks as entirely imperceptive, either of his own failings or those of others, but it occurred to me that he must be unable to see how close his particular brand of sentimental enthusiasm brought him to the boundaries of conventional decency. It was, I thought, one of the hazards of sequestration in a small rural parish; or perhaps the man's superiors, recognizing certain tendencies or inadequacies in him, had deliberately placed him where he could do least harm. I handed back the plaque.

'You have a vivid imagination, Banks. I'm afraid my own concerns must seem rather mundane to you, but they need to be attended to. Will you excuse me?'

'Of course. But you may have to attend to your visitors first.'

I turned, following his glance. Harris was deep in conversation with two men, one of whom I recognized immediately.

'What's Starkey doing here?'

'Checking on progress, I should imagine. But the timing's unfortunate.'

Unfortunate indeed. Harris had begun to build up the soil around the exposed edge but had by no means completed his task, and I could see, as we approached, that the coffin was the centre of attention. Starkey assailed me at once, his voice high and querulous.

'What's this, Mr Stannard? What do you think you're up to?'

'As you know very well, I'm carrying out necessary repairs to the aisle wall. We've already had some discussion of the matter.'

'Nothing was said about grave-robbing.'

'Don't be absurd. We've lifted the coffin simply because it was in the way. As soon as the work's completed, we'll replace it in its original position.'

'That may be so, but in the meantime we're here to see that the remains are treated with the respect due to them.'

'You already knew about this?'

He looked into my face with a grimace which might have passed for a smile.

'We know more than you might think, Mr Stannard.'

'Then perhaps you know who was responsible for last night's exploratory excavations in the spoil-heap.'

There was a long silence. When Starkey spoke again there was a new note in his voice, harsh and subtly threatening.

'You shouldn't have raised the coffin in the first place, Mr Stannard. Not without consulting with Jack.'

'Jack? Who's Jack?' I felt my grasp of the situation slipping. Banks seemed to be about to speak, but before he could do so, Starkey's companion stepped forward.

'That's me. Jack Elsham. What Mr Starkey says is right. You should have asked me before you opened the grave.'

He stood squarely in front of me, a dark, thick-set young man, rather red about the cheeks and throat. His stance was aggressive but a certain timidity in his eyes and a corresponding slackness in his full lips convinced me that I was in no immediate danger of assault.

'I'm sorry,' I said. 'I really don't understand what this has to do with you.'

His gaze flickered like that of an actor who has forgotten his lines.

'Jack's mother was a Sutton,' said Starkey. 'One of three daughters. And Eleanor Sutton was her mother.'

'Eleanor Sutton?'

'E.S., Mr Stannard. Those were the initials on the coffin.'

'Where did you get that information?'

'That's our business. Let me tell you something: when you disturb the dead, you disturb the living too. Jack's grandma died before he was born, but she's no less kin to him for that; and he feels it as an insult to himself and his family that you should have taken her body from the ground – yes, and I know something of the circumstances of that too, though you might have thought you could keep your doings to yourself – and left it lying here with no more soil above it than would serve to cover a dead cat. And it's not just the insult to Jack's family, but the offence to the whole village.'

He was working himself into a fury, his face contorted, his thin lips flecked with spittle. Banks raised a placatory hand.

'It's an unfortunate situation, Mr Starkey, and I understand your concern. But the most sensible course of action would be to allow Mr Stannard to complete this part of the job as quickly as possible. Any disruption to the works will simply delay the reinterment. In the meantime, please be assured that the remains will be treated as respectfully as circumstances allow.'

'But they've not been treated as respectfully as they should have been, Mr Banks. How do you think Jack feels, knowing his grandmother lies out here above ground? How would you feel? Or you, Mr Stannard?'

He was leaning towards us, jabbing the air with an arthritic forefinger. I was struck again by something artificial in his manner, a kind of theatrical self-consciousness. It was time, I felt, to bring the ridiculous scene to a close, and I cut in quickly as he paused for breath or an answer. 'Tell me, Mr Starkey, how old is your friend?'

Elsham gave a little start and looked at me with an air of bewilderment.

'Me? I shall be twenty-four come February. What's that to you?'

'I'm interested in facts, Mr Elsham, and I have to say that the idea that the occupant of the coffin is your grandmother is – to say the least – highly implausible.'

I saw him stiffen, his throat and face flushing a deeper red.

'Don't tell me what's what about my own family. Mr Starkey here can vouch for it: Eleanor Sutton was my grandmother.'

'No doubt she was. But there's no evidence that this is your grandmother's body. On the contrary, the date of the burial suggests—'

'I know nothing about any dates, but I know when a man's calling me a liar.'

He screwed up his eyes and peered into my face, breathing heavily through his mouth, distinctly menacing now. It occurred to me that I might have misjudged his character. I took a pace backwards and, as I did so, Banks stepped nimbly between us and took my arm, steering me aside with the adroitness of a dancer.

'Mr Stannard and I have business to discuss,' he said. 'If you have anything more to say, you're welcome to call on me at home this afternoon.'

'I'm not in need of protection,' I said, shaking my arm free as he guided me back towards the porch.

'Possibly not, and protection's not exactly what I'm offering. I'm simply putting some ground between your anger and theirs.'

'I've a right to be angry. These fellows descend on us with their spurious tale and their manufactured grievances. They abuse me, they disrupt our work. One of them comes within an ace of assaulting me. I'm angry, yes, and I see no particular reason to disguise it.'

Banks twisted round as the gate slammed back on its hinges. Elsham turned to us with an abrupt gesture which might have been intended as farewell, but Starkey strode out without a backward glance. Banks sighed.

'Starkey's a strange figure,' he said, 'and, in some respects at least, a rather unattractive one. He's narrow-minded, manipulative and occasionally vindictive. But he has what he imagines to be the interests of the village at heart. As for Elsham, he's a simple young man – something of a child really. A little hot-tempered, perhaps, but fundamentally sound. I think, too, that what you understandably refer to as a spurious tale may actually represent a kind of truth for these people.'

'A kind of truth? What do you mean by that, Banks? Things are either true or they're not. This grandmother business is a complete fiction, and you know it. Think about it. Elsham was born less than twenty-four years ago. His supposed grandmother was dead by 1792. That would mean that his mother – well, work it out for yourself. The dates don't tally.'

'Of course they don't, but that's not the point. Like any community – like any individual for that matter – this village constructs and reconstructs its history partly on the basis of interpretations which are, strictly speaking, erroneous. Fictions, if you like, but fictions to which we must nevertheless give some form of assent. I'm no more convinced than you are that the remains you've uncovered here are those of Eleanor Sutton, but I recognize the reality of Elsham's sense of outrage.'

'I don't know what you mean by reality. The emotion is clearly not justified by the facts.'

'The emotion is perhaps the essential fact, far more important than mere historical detail. The body you've brought to light is not simply itself – whatever that might be – but a focus for some of those unhoused passions which hunt through our lives for something – a person, an object, an event – to which they can attach themselves. I believe that we need to be particularly attentive to those passions. It's arguable that they constitute the primary reality of our lives.'

'Rather a suspect line of reasoning, if I may say so.'

'I'm not sure that it's a line of reasoning at all. I'm trying to articulate a half-glimpsed truth, and I can only approach that truth through a series of indirections. Let me tell you something. My father was a clergyman – far more eminent than I am – and a scholar of considerable distinction. I admired him extravagantly and wanted, from a very early age, to follow in his footsteps. And for some years I did so. Almost literally. Winchester and then Oxford where, like him, I gained something of a reputation as a meticulous and lucid exegete. There was talk of a fellowship.'

'Is that what you wanted?'

'The fellowship? Oh, yes. It was part of a carefully formul-
ated plan; the first rung of the ladder.'

'But you didn't get it?'

'I'm coming to that. One night I was studying late, working
on an essay which linked the life of Christ – rather cleverly,
it seemed to me at the time – with contemporary Jewish and
Roman history. I was staring at the lamp, lost in thought,
when the room . . . I've never found a satisfactory way
of putting this: it was as though someone were turning
up the wick, but turning it up to a point of impossible
brilliance, so that the room and everything it contained
blazed and shimmered around me. The desk, the inkwell,
the books on the shelves, even my own hands, all seemed
to be refining themselves out of existence, dissolving in an
intensity of light which fell – but that's wrong. It didn't fall,
because there was no external source. Everything burned with
its own astonishing incandescence. But not exactly its own
either, since the outlines separating one thing from another
were attenuated almost to the point of invisibility . . . I'm
afraid I'm missing the mark, as I always do when I try to
explain this. I'm looking for words that don't exist. It's love,
I remember saying to myself as the radiance began to fade;
but the term seems hopelessly inadequate. I can shuffle the
counters as I like – love, light, peace, fulfilment – but my
phrases never vibrate with the incontrovertible rightness of
the moment itself . . . I'm sorry, I'm boring you.'

'Not at all. I'm rather cold, that's all. Please go on.'

'There's not very much more to say, though the experience
radically altered the pattern of my life. I continued with
my studies, of course, reading as diligently as ever, often
working late into the night as I had done from the beginning
of my undergraduate days. I attended lectures, I sat my final
examinations—'

'But without distinguishing yourself?'

'On the contrary. I did exactly what was expected of me. I got a first, as my tutors had predicted, and I was left in little doubt that the fellowship would follow in due course. No, the alterations took place at a deeper level. I went to bed that night in what I can only describe as a state of luminous tranquillity, the light softer by that time but still flowing around and through me, sometimes smoothly, sometimes in slow, pulsing waves. I lay and watched it – listened to it too, if that makes sense, as though it were music, and with an apprehension so clear and complete that I seemed to be audience, player and instrument rolled into one. Sleep was out of the question, but I lay without fatigue or fretfulness, waiting for nothing, content simply to be – or, more than that, brimming with joy at the bare fact of my being. Needless to say, it didn't last. Sometime around dawn I became aware that the experience was, in a certain sense, finished; but I also knew that my life would never be the same again.'

'A kind of conversion?'

'I suppose so. At least, I realized that certain avenues were now closed to me. What the experience revealed was the inadequacy of the life I'd mapped out for myself. In particular – and this is the point of my telling you the story – I came to see that the careful sifting of material evidence was irrelevant to the essential truth which had been so unexpectedly revealed to me, and that what I had felt during those few hours eclipsed every intellectual discovery I had ever made. That much was clear. But I had no sense of any practical alternative to the course I was now obliged to relinquish. I mean, there was no discernible route by which that truth might be approached again. I tried, of course. I would sit at my desk at the appropriate time, staring at the lamp, attempting to re-create the conditions which seemed to have given rise to the experience. But the vision had been a gift, not an achievement, and once I had recognized that,

I was also forced to recognize the futility of my efforts to recapture it. Sit quietly, I said to myself at last; just sit quietly and wait.'

'Which is what you're doing in this backwater?'

'I don't consider it a backwater but yes, this is the place I've chosen to wait. No longer with any particular expectation, but not entirely without hope.'

There are forms of irreticence which make me uncomfortable and not, I think, without reason. If quasi-mystical experiences of this kind have any meaning at all, that meaning is, it seems to me, a private one, and I see a certain impropriety in making a display of such matters. It wasn't quite clear to me whether Banks's narrative had run its course or not, but I felt justified in steering the conversation towards firmer ground.

'I'd be interested to hear more,' I said, 'but on some other occasion. I must attend to Harris. He works well enough under supervision, but he can't be relied on to do the same when I'm not standing over him. There's also the matter of his indiscretion. I shall have to speak to him about that.'

'Indiscretion?'

'Starkey and Elsham knew about the coffin. More significantly, they appear to have known that the body is that of a woman.'

'Either brother might have mentioned that.'

'Yes, but only one of them knew – or should have known – about the inscription on the coffin-plate. Besides, I paid George Harris – not handsomely, I admit, but at a level commensurate with his expectations – to keep quiet.'

Banks gave me a pained look.

'Nobody can buy silence in a place like this, least of all – forgive me – an outsider like yourself. You have to remember that this is a close community with its own loyalties and a network of family relationships intricate enough to perplex the most expert genealogist. I'm aware, for example, that

Laura Jefford has connections with the Starkeys through her mother's side of the family and with Elsham's wife through her father's. Whether she could have known anything about the coffin's occupant I'm not sure, but she's certainly seen the inscription. I'm not necessarily pointing the finger in that direction, you understand – nor, I might add, am I rejecting your assumption out of hand – but I think you should acquaint yourself with the range of possibilities before confronting Harris with an accusation which may prove in time to have been misdirected.'

'In that case I might as well drop the matter completely.'

'That would be my counsel.'

Dubious counsel, I thought; but I held my tongue.

6

Harris made a good job of reburying the coffin, piling the soil above and around it and stabilizing the heap with turves taken from the stack against the wall; but the smell of decay still hung about the place the following morning, pervasive as the fine drizzle drifting in from the west. He must have caught my expression as I joined him at the edge of the trench.

'It clings to everything, sir. You can't get clear of it. My wife smelt it on me last night when I got home – on my clothes, on my skin. You'll wash yourself down before you lie with me, she said; and even though I did as she bid me – and my skin red with scrubbing – she turned from me as I got in beside her. And it might have been my imagination, but I woke in the night with the stench as strong in my nostrils as when I'd been kneeling here by the trench with the thing cracked open below. Sweating too, sir, my nightshirt soaked. And the dreams – I can't get at them now, but they had to do with the woman. Yes, and I remember dreaming, or thinking as I woke, that we have a pact with them – with the dead. Don't trouble us, I think they say, and we won't trouble you. That's the bargain, and if we break our side of it . . . I'm not a superstitious man and I don't believe in ghosts – not in the usual way at any rate. But we've set things awry here with our meddling and I don't reckon to see them put to rights until you've packed your bags and gone.'

I should have responded, and with justifiable asperity, if Banks had not emerged at that moment from the porch, head down and with his hands cupped close to his chest. As he approached, he extended them to show us what they held.

The bird had closed its eyes, but they flickered open as I bent to examine it more closely. The feathers of the crown were spiked, matted with blood; blood was crusted, too, around the nostrils and at the corners of the gaping bill. Banks shook his head.

'Too far gone, I think.' He half opened his hands, but the bird simply lurched sideways and keeled over, its exposed wing trembling slightly, its left leg stiffly outstretched, claws tightened in spasm. As I watched, the lid slowly closed again over the lustreless brown eye. Harris leaned over.

'All the caring in the world won't save that one,' he said. 'Better to put an end to its suffering now.'

'You're probably right,' said Banks. 'I've thought about it on other occasions but could never quite bring myself to carry it through. Partly, I suppose, because I always nurse the hope, right up to the last minute, that even those *in extremis* might somehow recover.' He looked up at us with an apologetic smile. 'It's an optimism fostered by my reading of the gospels rather than by the harsher teachings of experience.'

'Take my word for it, sir, the bird's dying.'

'And partly because the calculated decision to kill a fellow creature seems such a serious matter.'

Harris held out a soiled hand. 'Give it to me. I'll do it.'

Banks appeared to hesitate.

'It seems cruel, sir, but it's the kindest way.'

Harris took the bird from him with surprising gentleness. I had expected him to wring its neck, but he placed it carefully on the ground and then, almost before I had time to register what was happening, brought down the heel of his nailed boot on the small head, crushing it as a gardener might crush a snail. The body quivered briefly and relaxed. I saw Banks wince but, speaking for myself, I felt nothing but relief. Harris took up his shovel and dug a small slot in the spoil-heap. He scooped up the body and slid it in, then scuffed the loose soil back into place with his foot.

'As close to a Christian burial as a bird is likely to get,' I remarked lightly, turning aside. 'Laid to rest in consecrated ground with a clergyman in attendance.'

Banks did not smile.

'I wonder if we might have a word,' he said.

He touched my elbow, nudging me towards the porch. I stiffened against the coercive pressure of his hand and swung round to face him.

'A word about what?'

He gave an almost imperceptible nod in Harris's direction. 'A word in private,' he said quietly, edging away but with his eyes fixed on mine. I followed reluctantly.

It seemed colder inside the church than out. Banks pushed the door shut behind us and stood for a moment in silence, staring into the gloom.

'I've been thinking further,' he said at last, 'about your proposals for the nave. In particular, the matter of the pews.'

'The matter has already been addressed, Banks, and a decision reached. I had no difficulty in convincing your superiors of the desirability of removal, and I'm under no obligation to recapitulate my arguments for your benefit. What I told you last week about the windows applies equally to the pews.'

'But the whole lot, Stannard—'

'The situation's quite simple. The majority of the pews are riddled with wormholes, and those against the north wall are, without exception, rotting from the base up. We might conceivably get away with replacing a little over half of the total. But think about it: do you imagine our heirs would thank us for bequeathing them a patched vessel when we might have left them a sound one? From a practical, an aesthetic and – if we take the long view – even from an economic standpoint, complete replacement is the only sensible solution.'

'Oh, it all sounds simple and sensible enough.' He paused, holding me with his gaze for a second or two before continuing.

'There's something else. When I raised the matter with the Dean, he told me that your correspondence suggested that you had some moral objection to retaining the old pews.'

'That's an additional consideration, yes. I imagine you'll be in broad sympathy with my views. The impact of a barbarous iconography on susceptible minds—'

'Sympathy? I'm not sure that I even know what you're talking about.'

'I can easily enlighten you. Come with me.'

I led him up the aisle to the pew that had particularly attracted my attention on my first visit to the church.

'Have you ever looked closely at this bench-end?' I asked. 'I mean the carving.'

The figure had been worn to a glossy smoothness by the hands of generations of worshippers, but one could hardly fail to recognize the essentially pagan nature of its inspiration. A young girl, her forehead crowned with what appeared to be a floral wreath, was tossing back her head with wild abandon. Her mouth was open; her snake-like tresses tumbled loosely about her shoulders. The lower part of her body was largely concealed by the crudely carved folds of a long robe or gown, but where the garment fell open above the waist it revealed a bodice stretched tightly over the unmistakable contours of the breasts. The right hand had been smoothed almost out of existence, but it was still possible to see how its slender fingers cupped the left breast in a gesture at once self-absorbed and lascivious. The left hand, partially entangled among the curls, held what appeared to be a flute or pipe.

'Of course,' said Banks. 'I often look at her.'

'With a certain amount of unease, I would imagine.'

'On the contrary, with a great deal of pleasure. I imagine her singing, in a kind of ecstasy. Between you and me, Stannard, I sometimes wish I could see a little more of her spirit in the faces of the occupants of some of these pews.'

'This animation is of the flesh, Banks, not of the spirit. It belongs to an art less refined than our own, an art still struggling to purge itself of the qualities so disturbingly evident in this woman's attitude and features. Take a good look at her. She's low-life – fairground, bar-room, slum. Surely you can see that?'

He gave me a strange sidelong glance.

'Your interpretation is your own affair, Stannard. For myself, I confess I'd taken her for a member of the heavenly chorus.'

He appeared to be entirely serious. I was struck, not for the first time, by the astonishing naïveté of the man, and it was with something approaching exasperation that I broke away from him and made for the door. He hurried after me.

'Wait a moment, Stannard.'

'What is it?'

'I feel we should continue this discussion. If not now, perhaps later in the day, at your leisure.'

I kept walking.

'There's nothing to discuss,' I said.

As I emerged from the church, a clod struck the porch wall, followed by a hail of small stones. I looked up to see two boys leaping up and down on the spoil-heap, grimacing like monkeys. One of them stooped as I stood there, picked up another stone and let it fly. I heard it whizz past my left ear and strike the downpipe behind me with a dull clang.

They must have thought themselves safe enough, and certainly I had little expectation of catching them when I started to run. The taller of the two was off and over the wall in seconds, but the other stumbled in the loose earth and fell sprawling. I was on him before he could recover, dragging him from the mound and hauling him to his feet, my finger and thumb closing on his right ear. He gave a sharp grunt and kicked out at me, striking my shin a glancing blow with his muddy boot, but I tightened my hold and twisted his ear firmly enough to bring the tears to his eyes.

'Let me go,' he shouted, pawing ineffectually at my hand, his neck hunched into his shoulders.

'Not until you promise me there'll be no more stone-throwing. What do you mean by it?'

'You're digging up our ancestors. You've no right.'

I think in retrospect that I might have applied a little too much pressure, though I remain unconvinced that the boy's response was entirely genuine. He began to sob, a dry obstructed panting, his stooped back shaking. I shifted my grip to his collar but the sobbing continued; and then, without warning, he threw back his head and uttered a loud wailing cry.

The noise brought Harris running from the far side of the tower, and at the same moment the door shuddered back and Banks came hurrying out of the church. As they approached, Banks half stumbling on the wet grass, the boy began to duck and twist, evidently in the hope of breaking my hold. I seized a tuft of hair with my left hand and, winding it around my fingers, quickly brought him under control.

'What's going on, Stannard? What was that cry?' Banks was pale, breathless, visibly agitated.

'Pure histrionics. The calculated response of a young ruffian worried that he might be about to get what's due to him.'

'What do you mean by that?'

'He attacked me. Stoned me as I came out of the church.'

Harris came up behind Banks and peered narrowly at the boy.

'Is that so, Davy?'

'I never, Mr Harris. I was throwing at the church wall when the gentleman came through the door.'

I gave a half-turn to the thick curls in my hand. Banks winced.

'You're hurting him, Stannard.'

'No more than he deserves to be hurt. It's a preposterous story. The attack was deliberate.'

'What makes you so sure?'

'He's as good as admitted it.'

'Has he? When?'

'When I caught him. He suggested that the reason for the attack was my disinterment of his ancestors.'

'It's not true, Mr Banks. I don't even know what that word means.'

'Ancestors?'

'No, the other one.'

'Did you mention your ancestors, Davy? Did you say anything about Mr Stannard's digging them up?'

'I might have. But I never said I threw stones at him on account of that. I never said I threw stones at him at all.'

Banks looked from me to the boy and back again as though weighing our contradictory claims. I felt absurdly compromised by his handling of the situation.

'For goodness' sake, Banks,' I said, rather more heatedly than I'd intended, 'you're not adjudicating between a pair of scrapping schoolboys. I've told you how it was.'

Harris leaned towards me with just the faintest hint of aggression in his stance.

'The lad's got a right to be heard too,' he said.

'Liars forfeit their rights, Harris. And this is none of your business. You've work to do – would you mind attending to it?'

He moved off, but his intervention had clearly encouraged the boy, who twisted in my grasp and stared up at me.

'I'm no liar,' he said. 'And if I did say that about our ancestors, where's the wrong in that? You have dug them up. Everyone in the village knows it. You've dug up Jack Elsham's grandma.'

'That's a story put about by fools,' I said, 'and you're as big a fool for believing it.'

He muttered something under his breath. I tugged at his collar, drawing his thin body so tightly to mine that I could feel his heartbeat against my ribs.

'What was that?' I asked. 'What did you say just then?'

'Let go, sir. You're choking me.'

'Nonsense. Tell me what you just said.'

Banks reached out and touched my wrist.

'I think you might ease off now, Stannard. There's no need for that.'

His misaligned sympathies had placed me a delicate position, and my embarrassment was compounded by the arrival of Redbourne, who came down the lane at that moment: an altogether more dashing figure on horseback, I thought, than he had appeared in his pew a few days earlier. He dismounted at the gate, tethered his horse and strode up the path towards us. I let the boy go, half expecting him to make a break for it; but he simply took a pace back and stood there glowering at me, fingering his reddened earlobe. Redbourne looked at him for a moment, evidently sizing up the situation, before turning to Banks.

'I take it young Farr's in trouble again?'

'He's certainly got on the wrong side of our architect. May I introduce—'

'It's a pleasure to meet you, Mr Stannard.' Redbourne peeled off a glove and held out a white, rather feminine hand. 'A great pleasure. It was partly in the hope of making your acquaintance that I rode out this way.'

I was flattered by the remark; but as I began to frame an appropriate reply he turned aside, addressing himself to the boy.

'This isn't what I'd hoped for, Davy. What did I say last summer when we spoke about the poaching?'

'You said I should watch my step.'

'What I actually said was that you should try to become a more useful member of society. You're a clever lad, and I believe you might do well in the world. You owe it to yourself to mend your ways, and you owe it to me too. Do you remember what I gave you at the time?'

'Threepence, sir.'

'And what was the point of my giving you the money?'

'I can't remember the word you used.'

'Inducement, Davy. The money was an inducement to good behaviour. And I can't help feeling it was money ill-spent.'

'You don't know the truth of this, sir.'

'I can guess.'

'Guessing's not knowing.'

Redbourne was silent, toying with the fingers of his glove.

'It's not the same thing, is it?' the boy persisted.

'I think you should run along now, Davy. I want a word with Mr Stannard.'

The boy looked up at him slyly from beneath his tousled fringe.

'You said there might be more to come, sir. Another threepenny piece.'

'On certain conditions. But I see no evidence that you've met those conditions. On the contrary.'

'I have met them, sir. I've kept clear of trouble since the summer. And it's not my fault if the gentleman thinks I was throwing stones at him.'

He was looking at me as he spoke, staring rudely into my face as though daring me to respond. I should have done so, and sharply too, but Redbourne forestalled me.

'That's enough, Davy. Now go away. And you're to stay out of the churchyard until the work's finished. Do you understand?'

The boy nodded and moved off, limping slightly. Redbourne watched him out of the gate before turning to me.

'Davy's not a bad lad, Mr Stannard. A little wild, that's all. I keep an eye on his activities and occasionally attempt to steer him clear of mischief. He's an intelligent youngster and might well make something of himself if he chose. Isn't that so, Mr Banks?'

Banks shrugged. 'I suppose he has a certain native shrewdness; and of course every one of us has the capacity for self-improvement. There may be grounds for optimism in this particular case, though I have to say that none of your *protégés* has so far lived up to your high expectations.'

Redbourne flushed faintly. 'Hardly *protégés*,' he said. 'Just boys in whose welfare I've taken some slight interest. And now' – he made a brusque half-turn away from Banks and took me by the arm – 'if you'll excuse me, I'd like a word with Mr Stannard.'

Banks stepped forward suddenly, stretching out a hand to detain me.

'I still need a few more moments of your time, Stannard. These pews—'

'Just two minutes. That's all I ask.' Redbourne's fingers tightened around my arm and he drew me gently towards him. 'Just two minutes and then' – he flashed Banks a mocking smile – 'you can have your architect back. Does that sound reasonable?'

Banks made no reply. Redbourne, either ignoring his tense silence or taking it for assent, swung me round and guided me between the headstones to the lower end of the churchyard.

'No great secret,' he murmured, 'but there's a certain delicacy . . .' He looked back over his shoulder at Banks, now standing disconsolately in the doorway of the porch. 'Quite simply, I came to invite you to dinner. Would you be free this evening?'

I thought I detected a trace of irony in the question, a subtle acknowledgement, perhaps, of the unlikelihood of my having, in such a backwater, any more pressing or pleasing engagement.

'I'm free every evening,' I said. 'My social diary has been a blank ever since my arrival here.'

His laughter was subdued, even a little nervous, but not without warmth.

'Shall we say seven o'clock? I'll send the groom over with a horse.'

'I'm no horseman, Mr Redbourne. I should prefer to walk.'

'As you like. In that case your quickest route will be the path across the hillside there – do you see? It's not very clear from here but it's easy enough to follow. Once you're on it, there's a walk of just over half a mile. Keep the beechwood on your right all the way. After the second stile you'll see the Hall a couple of hundred yards ahead. You'll be approaching from the wrong side, but I'll see to it that there's a light in one of the back rooms to guide you. You'll find a small gateway in the wall: go through it and follow the paved footpath round to the front of the house. I look forward to seeing you there.'

He waved away my thanks, turned on his heel and strode

towards the gate. He had barely reached it before Banks was upon me again, fretful, obsessive, repetitive; like a child, it occurred to me, obstinately seeking assurances the adult world knew better than to offer.

7

'I don't say they're mermaids,' said Mrs Haskell, whipping the tea-tray from under my nose before I could pour myself a second cup, 'but they're certainly not human. They can stay under the waves for hours; and they gather together around the rocks like seals, gripping the kelp with their hands and calling to one another above the noise of the wind and water. Nowadays you hardly ever meet anyone who's seen one, but they were common enough around these shores in our grandparents' time. In those days people would sometimes find the young washed up by the spring tides. Dead, usually; but when Cassie Adams' grandmother was a girl she once came across one in a rock pool, still very much alive, mewing like a kitten. She kept it for a week or more, in a milk-pail she topped up with brine every morning. It would lie there on its back, wheezing and sighing, holding out its arms as if it wanted to be picked up. But if you held it, even for a moment, it would writhe and scream like a colicky baby. And it wouldn't eat. She tried milk; she spent hours tempting it with chopped crabmeat, herring-flesh, shellfish, holding the stuff to its mouth on a saltspoon. It would turn its head away like this' – Mrs Haskell twisted her neck sideways and compressed her lips – 'while its eyes filled up with tears. One evening she decided she couldn't stand it any longer. She took the creature down to the shore and slipped it into the water, hoping it might swim away. It didn't, of course; I suppose it hadn't been taught how. It just rolled about in the breakers, helpless as a lump of driftwood. In the end she pulled it out and took it home again, but it seemed to have been shocked or injured, and it died during the night.'

I was already growing used both to Mrs Haskell's loquaciousness and her astonishing credulity, and knew her to be capable of spouting such nonsense for hours on end. I rose to my feet and reached down my coat; but she was clearly reluctant to let me go.

'After that she became a little crazed. She wanted the thing buried in the churchyard. The rector at that time was a kindly man but of course he'd have none of it. It's not a human child, he said, and it can't lie among us. So on the second night she wrapped the body in a scrap of sailcloth, took it down to the bottom of the garden and buried it under a pear tree. And that should have been the end of the matter; but it wasn't.'

'Even so, Mrs Haskell, it's all I have time to hear at the moment. Would you excuse me?'

'They say she was like a girl bewitched. She grew pale and thin, spending her days at the graveside, staring at nothing. And she'd have spent her nights there too if her father hadn't dragged her in each evening and locked her in her room. Yes, and he had to nail up the sash, otherwise she'd have been out through the window. But then she'd pound on the door till her knuckles bled, keeping the whole lane awake with her thumping and howling. After a week or so the family was in a terrible state – you can imagine – and the neighbours at their wits' end. It was the rector who came up with the idea of reburying the thing somewhere outside the village. Tell her what you're doing, he said, but don't let her know where you're putting it. I think he was afraid she'd try to get to the body if she knew where it was. They took it out at night, Cassie's father and the sexton. And neither of them were what you'd call imaginative men, so people were the more inclined to listen to their story.'

'I'm afraid I can't—'

'There's really not much more to tell. They took the body down to a field at the edge of the village, laid it in the grass and began to dig. But they'd barely turned the first turf when a cry went up from the marshland beyond, a wailing or keening, quite soft at first—'

'I'm sorry, but I have a dinner engagement. Some other time, perhaps. Let me carry that downstairs for you.'

She stiffened, her fingers tightening around the rim of the tray.

'Thank you, I can carry it myself. Would I be right in thinking you won't be wanting supper tonight?

'Absolutely right, Mrs Haskell.'

She made an irritable huffing sound.

'You might have told me earlier,' she said.

Supper being more often than not a slice of cold ham and a slab of buttered bread, she could hardly claim to have been inconvenienced, but she clearly felt herself affronted. She hooked back the door with her foot and swept out of the room and down the stairs. I waited until I was sure she was safely out of the way in the kitchen before following her down and letting myself quietly out of the house.

I found the path easily enough but the walk took me longer than I had anticipated and I arrived at the Hall, a little breathless, nearly ten minutes after the hour. I had actually envisaged something rather more elegant than the brick-built Jacobean structure which faced me, but I was left in no doubt that its owner was a man of substance as well as breeding.

The door was opened by an elderly manservant who took my coat and gloves and ushered me directly into a large, ill-lit dining-room. I had wondered earlier whether I might expect to meet any of Redbourne's social circle, but there was no sign of other guests or, indeed, of my host.

'Mr Redbourne was expecting me?'

'Of course.' He gestured towards the long table laid, I now realized, for two. 'He will be down in a few moments.'

He inclined his head briefly and withdrew. I heard the shuffle of his footsteps across the boards and then the click of a door-catch from the other side of the hall.

I have always held that one finds out more about a man's character from close examination of his house and its contents than from any amount of conversation with him, but what I could see of Redbourne's dining-room seemed puzzlingly equivocal. Certainly the room was opulently, if rather eclectically, furnished. The table, clearly intended for far larger gatherings than the intimate *tête-à-tête* provided for on this particular evening, was a superb piece, finely crafted in richly coloured mahogany, while the dining-chairs, though of an earlier period and fashioned of a lighter wood, were similarly impressive. Ranged around the walls were a number of portraits and landscapes, several of apparent distinction; and from above the doorway descended a double swag of carved flowers and fruits, disproportionately large but of quite outstanding design and execution.

Yet at the same time there was evidence of an unusual degree of neglect. Although the top end of the table had obviously been recently polished – and the smell of beeswax was strong in the air – the job had been abandoned less than half-way through, leaving the remainder of the surface coated with a thick film of dust; the upholstered chairs at either side of the fireplace proved, on examination, to be mildewed, the delicately embroidered fabric half rotten; and when I stood in front of the heavy gilt-framed mirror which so imposingly surmounted the mantel, I found myself staring not at my own reflection but at an incomprehensible patchwork of stains and blotches. And added to this was the effect of the room's pitiful illumination – apart from the firelight, only a lamp perched precariously at the corner of the sideboard and a group of

four candelabra haphazardly arranged around the table place-
ments, so that the eye slipped continually from the half-lit
surfaces of things to the wavering shadows beyond them.

I had just grasped the lamp and was raising it to one of
the portraits when the door opened again and Redbourne
entered. There was a momentary awkwardness as he held
out his hand in greeting, obliging me to set the lamp hurriedly
back on the sideboard.

'I was trying to see—'

'Not a Van Dyck, I'm afraid, though I believe it was once
attributed to him. I'm told it's a good collection, but not of
the highest order.'

'You certainly have some interesting work here. I only wish
I could see it a little more clearly.'

It was not quite what I had intended to say. There was a
long pause, punctuated by the slow ticking of a clock from
the far end of the room. Redbourne seemed oddly ill at ease,
fidgeting with his watch-chain, shifting unsteadily from one
foot to the other.

'I should perhaps have mentioned,' he said at last, 'that I
have no other guests. I'm temperamentally averse to social
gatherings, especially in my own house; and intelligent company is, in any case, hard to come by in these parts.'

'I appreciate that. But what about Banks? Surely—'

'You might have noticed,' he said stiffly, 'that I deliberately
excluded Mr Banks from our brief conversation this morning.
But I understand the point of your question. When Banks first
arrived in the parish, I was delighted, and for two or three
years he was a regular guest at my table. No doubting the
man's intelligence or, indeed, his articulacy. And in those
days there was a boyish openness about him – he was quite
unlike any clergyman I'd ever met – so it seemed the most
natural thing in the world to share certain confidences with
him . . .'

He trailed off, staring into the shadows for a moment before reaching out and tugging sharply at the plaited bell-pull that hung above the sideboard.

'I think we might sit down,' he said, motioning me towards the table. 'Dinner will be brought directly.'

We took our places in silence. It was not until after the soup had been served that he returned to his theme, and then only at my prompting.

'Banks? Oh, there was a change, a cooling. I don't want to make too much of it. But I came to feel that I represented a test for him, a challenge to his humane convictions. No one, I've heard him say time and again, is beyond our love. Look compassionately at your fellow-man, with a heartfelt desire for understanding, and love will follow as surely as day follows night. That's his text, his sermon, and by and large I've no doubt that his practice is consistent with his preaching. But the more he discovered about me and my weaknesses, the less – I'm sure of it, Stannard – the less he was able to love me. And on my side, I suppose, there was the natural embarrassment of a man who has revealed more of himself than would normally be considered wise. Yes, embarrassment; and perhaps a little resentment too. So – no Banks; but I have the pleasure of your good company and' – he raised his glass – 'I'll gladly drink to that.'

We drank to quite a number of things during the course of the meal, Redbourne considerably more deeply than I, so that by the time the coffee was brought in, he had already passed through the stages of relaxation and affability and was leaning heavily forward across the table, his face flushed and a little sullen.

'What you haven't told me,' he said, reaching for the coffee-pot, 'is what brings you here. Yes, I know you've been engaged to work on the church, but that's not quite what I mean. Why this job rather than another? – particularly since it must put you to so much inconvenience.'

'Every commission is attended by difficulties of one kind or another.'

'Let me put it more specifically. You have a practice, and you have a home. You've left both to spend – what? – three months? – six? – in this benighted place when you might easily have put the job in the hands of a contractor and overseen it from a comfortable distance. Why? Forgive me, Stannard, but I can't help feeling there must be more to this than meets the eye.'

'Not much more. My home is a set of rooms rather larger and better furnished than my present accommodation, but scarcely more inspiring. I have to contend with Mrs Haskell's inane chatter, of course, but otherwise I'm almost as comfortably placed here as there.'

'And your practice?'

'In good hands. It's a small firm, just the two of us. Aaron will deal with all routine matters in my absence and keep me informed of any significant developments.'

'I take it you're the senior partner?'

'Technically, yes, though in fact we're more or less of an age. The capital was mine or, more precisely, my father's. But Aaron has a way with him – an energy, an outwardness – which clients find attractive, and he's always managed to give the impression – not of seniority exactly, but of his own relative importance.'

'Relative to yours? That must create certain tensions in your professional life.'

Redbourne seemed to me to be pushing very close indeed to the line separating legitimate curiosity from unwarrantable intrusion, but I judged it politic to reply.

'There have been differences of opinion,' I said. 'We haven't always seen eye to eye, particularly in discussions concerning the future of the firm. But there's a sense in which we need one another, and we both know it.'

'Maybe so; but isn't there any connection at all between those tensions and your presence here?'

'If you're suggesting that I'm seeking refuge from professional difficulties—'

'It's a plausible reading.'

'A misreading, Redbourne. Take my word for it.' I rather disliked the turn the conversation had taken and I was anxious to move to more hospitable ground. 'Your own life,' I said quickly, 'seems enviably well appointed.'

He sat back in his chair, frowning as though I had offended him in some way. The logs shifted in the fireplace, sparked and flared. 'You really consider my life enviable?' he asked at last.

'Of course.' I gestured around me. 'All this . . .'

'Oh, this.' He shrugged. 'I can take very little pleasure in what I persist in regarding as the property of others.'

'That is, if I may say so, a sentiment more appropriate to a social revolutionary than to a man in your position.'

'I meant nothing so interesting. Simply that what I have was amassed in the past by men I never knew, and that I recognize myself as little more than the inept custodian of their leavings. Don't misunderstand me: I'm not suggesting that I could give it away tomorrow without a second thought. On the contrary, I lean heavily on these privileges and should be utterly lost without them. But I should be a fool to imagine that, in any but the most superficial sense, they were mine. What you see when you look around you is the dubious façade of a life; you must be careful not to mistake it for the life itself.'

He reached for the wine and refilled our glasses before continuing.

'Let me tell you how I see myself. I'm a social maladroit, without any particular moral or intellectual gifts, presiding in solitude over the decline of an insignificant country estate. I have neither wife nor child and take no interest in the management of lands which, at my death, will pass to relatives too distant to mean anything to me. You've read your Darwin, Stannard. Do I look to you like one of nature's survivors?'

'We're not beasts, Redbourne, and we don't live our lives in blind submission to the pressure of natural forces. Take your life into your own hands. Five years hence you might well be walking your grounds in the company of a young wife and a brace of sons.'

He gave a wry smile. 'I rather think not. That troubles me now – the question of succession, I mean – though at one time I was able to delude myself that I had a different and higher vocation; that I was sacrificing my hopes of domestic fulfilment, such as they were, on the altar of science. I saw myself as another Darwin, pressing further and further into the uncharted regions of the earth, probing more and more deeply into the complex processes of life; perhaps even ultimately establishing the existence and nature of some force or pattern not entirely inconsistent with conventional notions of the divine. I travelled a little; I added substantially to my collection; I wrote a number of papers. But as I quickly realized, I'm no philosopher; not even a scientist. I'm just a collector, Stannard, an undisciplined hoarder of whatever bright fragments happen to fall into my hands. And I eventually came to see that the whole project was fundamentally flawed – not, in fact, a disinterested prospecting of new territories, but a desperate attempt to reconstitute something of my own past.'

He paused for a moment, then rose clumsily to his feet.

'Come with me,' he said. 'I'd like to show you something.'

He took the lamp from the sideboard and led the way across the hall and up two flights of stairs to the door of an attic room. He entered, motioning me to follow, and set the

lamp down on a grimy side-table. I had a general impression
of clutter: a collapsed stack of books in one corner, papers
scattered across the floor, dusty boxes of seashells and fossils
occupying the entire surface of a vast mahogany desk. At
the centre of the room was a marble statue, a little less than
life-size but dominating its surroundings both by its position
and by what I can only call its presence. The figure was that
of a young man stepping forward almost to the point of
imbalance, his left arm slightly extended, his right held firmly
by his side. He wore a light cloak, pinned at the shoulder by a
brooch and lifted clear of the back by the extended arm, over
which it hung in stiff folds; the body was otherwise entirely
naked. The face, framed by a mass of intricately worked curls,
seemed oddly ambiguous: around the lips an almost feminine
sweetness, but the eyes stern and resolutely fixed on a point
in the middle or far distance.

Redbourne glanced at me.

'You're admiring the marble?'

'It's certainly a striking piece.'

'Yes, though like many things in this house, not quite what
it appears to be. It's a modern copy; not worth a great deal,
but self-evidently the work of a genuine craftsman. Whoever
made it had an intimate understanding not simply of the
form itself but of the Greek feeling for that form – I mean,
specifically, the male form.'

He stepped forward and ran his hand down the hollow
curve of the back, then he looked up at me with uncharacteristic directness.

'Are you a connoisseur of such things, Stannard?'

'I'm an architect. Naturally I know a certain amount about
sculpture, but I'd hardly describe myself as a connoisseur.'

He lowered his gaze and withdrew his hand.

'Of course not. In any case, this isn't what I wanted to show
you. Come over here.'

He crossed the room, opened the doors of a large rosewood cabinet and pulled out one of the drawers. 'Look at this. All around us the work goes on: men constructing railways, composing symphonies, building empires. And I hide myself away in a corner with my collection of insects.'

'It's a respectable hobby.'

'Exactly.'

There was a long silence. A whiff of camphor rose from the cork-lined tray. I leaned awkwardly over the pinned specimens, uncertain how to respond.

'*Sphingidae*,' he said at last. 'A remarkable family. Almost every member found in this country has a claim to be ranked among the most beautiful of our moths. This elephant hawk-moth, for example. You see the combination of pink and ochre? Aesthetically almost unthinkable, but blended here with such extraordinary delicacy. And this lime hawk: a common enough insect, yet each time I take a new specimen I feel its beauty as a kind of shock.'

'You still collect these things, then?'

'It's my only permissible passion. But you're right: it's an activity I should have outgrown years ago.'

'I didn't say so.'

He passed his hand across his face as though suddenly fatigued. Then he pushed back the drawer, closed the doors and straightened up.

'I could show you more,' he said, 'but it would make no difference. You'd still be as far as ever from grasping the essence of the thing. I'm not blaming you. What you see is a drawerful of faded husks. What I experience, though with increasing difficulty these days, is the excitement of discovery – no, not the excitement itself, perhaps, but a faint, thrilling aftertaste. I've tried to explain it to others, always with the feeling that I'm missing the point or, at least, failing to convey it. But let me try you. Listen. I'm about ten years old. I'm on my knees in the shrubbery. Perhaps someone is looking for me; certainly I have a sense of having deliberately concealed myself. I'm gazing at a moth, a brown triangle on the glossy surface of a laurel leaf. The sunlight falls in small flecks and lozenges around me, shifting as the twigs stir. The leaf-mould disturbed by my feet sends up a smell so dark and potent that I enter what a man of Banks's persuasion might describe as a state of ecstasy. As I lean forward the moth begins to vibrate, gently at first but with increasing vigour, half revealing the brilliant crimson of its underwings; and it's with a shudder or start that I return to myself, reach into my jacket pocket for one of my pill-boxes and clap it over the insect before it can take flight.'

He paused, breathing heavily.

'Does this mean anything to you?' he asked.

'Very little, though I sense something of what it might mean to you. Each to his own: my buildings, your bugs.'

'Quite so. An admirably uncomplicated response.'

I thought I detected the faintest hint of mockery in his voice, but his face gave nothing away. He leaned over and laid his hand gently on my shoulder.

'It's late,' he said, 'and you no doubt have a great deal to do tomorrow. I shouldn't detain you.'

I had wondered earlier whether I might be invited to stay on as an overnight guest, but he gave no sign of having even entertained the idea. I should not have minded except for the sudden drenching shower which swept the hillside as I descended towards the lane, so that I reached my lodgings wet, cold and as thoroughly miserable as I had been at any time since my arrival in the village.

8

Jefford's return to work was hardly a cause for celebration. Banks, who had been visiting him regularly, had hinted in broad terms that he was by no means fully recovered, but I was nevertheless disconcerted to see with what evident difficulty he was moving as he made his way up the path at Harris's side, limping a little, slightly stooped, his face taut with anxiety or pain. I realized at once that our progress was not going to be significantly accelerated by his return, though I was naturally careful not to betray my disappointment and the warmth of my greeting must, I think, have appeared entirely genuine.

'Welcome back, Jefford. I'm glad to see you on your feet again. How are you feeling?'

'Much better, thank you, sir. A bit stiff, and not as strong as I'd like, but a few days will see me right.'

'And Mrs Jefford?'

'Not as bad as she was, but this is a difficult time of year for her. She spends the whole winter longing for spring. She wanted me to give you her apologies for having been out of sorts when you visited us. We can't offer much in the way of entertainment at the best of times, but she wanted you to know—'

'There's no need to apologize. Now listen, we're about to begin the final section of the underpinning. Harris knows what needs to be done. I suggest you work alongside him, perhaps clearing up the loose as he undercuts the footings. I don't mind how you organize it. What's important is that we speed up the process and get ourselves back on course again.'

Jefford limped to the edge of the trench and peered in. 'It's like a prison down there,' he said. 'All those bars and struts. A man would be hard put to it to get out in a hurry if he needed to.' And then, turning with an odd shudder, a catching of the breath: 'I don't suppose you'd have anything else for me to do, would you, sir? I'm sorry to ask, knowing how good you've been to me, but I feel I'm not ready for—'

'I don't think you'll find the work too strenuous, Jefford. Go at it reasonably easily, resting when you like. But this is undoubtedly where you'll be most useful at present. If we can complete the underpinning by the end of the afternoon, we shall be able to backfill the trench tomorrow; then we can start work on the interior. Just stick at this for today. It's not too much to ask, is it?'

He looked away and turned up the collar of his thin jacket, shivering miserably, his shoulders hunched against the wind. I suppose I might have relented at that point. The idea certainly crossed my mind; but it seemed to me that it would be unwise, particularly in Harris's presence, to say or do anything that might be interpreted as a sign of weakness.

'I'll leave you to explain matters, Harris. I shall be in the church if you need me.'

It was a relief to be out of the worst of the wind, though there was no escaping the draughts which crept beneath the door and shrilled through the holes in the inexpertly patched windows. It was difficult to believe that a church could have been allowed to decline to such a point. The state of the pews in particular was atrocious, a fact I had emphasized in my preliminary report. Two of those in the north aisle had collapsed sideways, clearly unusable; a third had been barred with a rough lath, evidently to ensure that nobody made the mistake of sitting there. I got down on my knees and put my hand into the damp space between the rearmost pew and the wall, feeling again the sponginess of the wood, smelling rot on the boards, in the air, on my wet fingers as I withdrew them. And as I knelt there on the flags, my head bent over my stinking hand in what I suddenly recognized as a disquieting parody of prayer, I felt disgust mounting in me like a tide; a wave of loathing or nausea which had me on my feet and making for the door before I was able to regain control of myself. Indeed, I think I should have continued my irrational flight if Harris had not entered when he did, stamping his boots on the door-sill, plucking his cap clumsily from his head.

'What is it, Harris?'

It occurred to me that my discomposure must be apparent, but he gave no sign of having noticed anything out of the ordinary.

'It's about Jefford, sir. Could I have a word?'

'Go on.'

'He shouldn't be down that trench. He's shaking all the time – I mean shaking so he can hardly hold his shovel. And he can't concentrate on anything: I tell him things, but it all goes by him. You've only to look at him to see the state he's in. With respect, sir, it would be better for him to start on the indoor work now before his nerve goes completely.'

'I'll be the judge of that, Harris. Let me speak with him.'

Harris stood aside to let me pass, and then followed me out. Jefford had abandoned his task and was walking aimlessly around the top of the trench, his hands thrust deep in his pockets, his head bowed. He looked up as I approached and started towards me, stumbling on the upcast, speaking with the nervy urgency of a troubled child.

'I'm sorry, sir. Truly I am. But I can't stay down there on my own. To be honest with you, I don't know if I can stay

95

down there at all. I was thinking about it before I set out this morning. I shall be all right when I get there, I said to myself. And I believed I should be, only somehow I can't seem to . . .'

He tailed off, staring miserably into the distance, evidently on the verge of tears. I was struck by the uncomfortable thought that his return in this abject state might actually hinder our progress.

'Are you sure,' I asked, 'that you're well enough to rejoin us?'

'Well enough? Oh yes, sir. No question of it. If I can only work above ground, I shall be fit for anything.'

This was so plainly untrue that I almost challenged it, but there seemed little point either in doing so or in holding out any longer against his request.

'Very well, Jefford. Harris will finish off out here. You can start dismantling the pews.'

He gave me a puzzled look.

'When you say dismantling—'

'I mean cut them up. Break them up. It's immaterial how you go about it. I'll show you where to start.'

I picked up a sledgehammer and a saw from the porch as we entered; then I led Jefford across the nave to the most severely damaged of the pews.

'This should be easy enough,' I said. I put down the tools, gripped the backrest and rocked the pew towards me – quite gently, but there was a sharp crack and a splintering of wood as the rickety structure lurched backwards. Jefford looked nervously about him.

'Do we have to do this, sir?'

'Of course. We're replacing them with new ones. One of the effects of that will be to brighten the nave a little: I'm having them made in Canadian pine, an altogether lighter wood. But the most obvious benefit will be the improved safety and comfort of the congregation. Those have naturally been my prime considerations.'

'It seems wrong, though. Breaking things up inside a church.'

'Believe me, Jefford, I regret it as much as you do. But look at the condition of the wood. How could we possibly preserve this?'

I picked up a fragment from the floor and tapped it smartly on the back of the pew. It cracked along the grain, releasing a cloud of buff powder into the air. I held out the splintered rectangle. 'Feel this,' I said. 'Go on. The weight, I mean.'

He took it gingerly on the palm of his hand.

'It's very light. But—'

'Riddled. Absolutely riddled. Look at the inside; it's like a honeycomb.'

'It can't all be as bad as that, sir. After all, most of the pews are still in use.'

'In a number of cases that seems little short of miraculous. And if there's one thing we can be sure of, it's that they will continue to deteriorate. Not only that, but the infestation will spread – perhaps not rapidly, but inexorably.'

He frowned as though he were having difficulty with the idea, though on what grounds I couldn't imagine.

'Let me show you something.' I retrieved the fragment from his outstretched hand and indicated with my thumbnail the small larva still lodged in its broken chamber. 'Take a close look at this: this is your true agent of destruction, not the luckless architect called in to deal with the problem.'

He seemed reluctant to concede the point.

'That's natural, sir. But what we'll be doing—'

'Listen, Jefford, I don't expect you to understand all the implications of this, but an architect's work is, more or less by definition, one long battle against nature. It's a losing battle, inevitably so; but one of the measures of our success is the length of time we can hold back the inevitable. The buildings we construct, the monuments whose upkeep we undertake on behalf of our predecessors, are under permanent siege. Frost and rain, these beetles, the fungus eating away at the base here, mosses, lichens, stonecrop, the force of gravity itself – they're all in league against us. The architect's work is, in a quite literal sense, man's bulwark against nature's encroaching forces; and if what we do appears at times a little drastic, that's simply because we see, more clearly and less sentimentally than most, both the necessity and the enormity of the task that faces us.'

As I had anticipated, this was rather over Jefford's head; at least, he gave every appearance of having failed to grasp my argument.

'What if we just mended the worst parts, sir? A good carpenter could fix these so you'd hardly know it had been done. And at a quarter the cost of the new pews, I shouldn't wonder.'

Reflecting on the moment, I find it difficult to account for the violence of my response. I can see that my patience must have been wearing thin, but there was really nothing in Jefford's words to justify my actions. I tugged off my jacket and flung it to the floor; then I seized the hammer and drove it hard at the back of the pew, sending the dusty splinters flying. Jefford stepped back a pace, visibly startled.

'It's all to go,' I shouted. 'This' – I swung the hammer again – 'and this; and this. The whole filthy lot's to be cleared and burned. The sooner the better. Is that understood?'

I threw down the hammer and looked away in momentary confusion, the blood throbbing at my temples, congesting my throat and chest. I realized almost immediately, of course, that I had behaved foolishly: I remember hoping fervently as I stood there that Jefford would not report my outburst to Harris, and recognizing with sudden sobering clarity that he almost certainly would. I turned to him.

'I owe you an apology, Jefford. It's just that the question of the pews has already been discussed and my proposals given approval by the Dean. It's no longer a subject for debate, either between you and me or at any higher level.'

'No, sir. I meant no harm.'

'I accept that. But you must remember that these are matters which are properly the concern of others. Your role is simply to carry out the tasks I assign to you.'

'Yes, sir.'

I watched him for a moment as he gathered together the splintered fragments, down on his knees among them, every movement so careful, so absurdly decorous, that I could have cried out with frustration.

'The wood's to be burned, Jefford. Just clear the scraps to one side and get on with the job. I'll have Harris take them away as soon as he's free.'

I turned and walked slowly down the aisle towards the chancel, breathing deeply in an attempt to regain my composure; but before I had gone a dozen paces I heard the south door grind open. I swung round to see Harris approaching, briskly at first but slowing to a standstill as he drew level with the wreckage of the pew. I saw him flash an interrogative glance at Jefford, but as he lifted his eyes to mine his face was stonily impassive.

'It's a necessary part of the work, Harris. I shall want to involve you as soon as you've finished out there. I hope you're maintaining a good pace.'

'Good enough, sir. I've only broken off to let you know Arthur Webster's outside, wanting to see you. He won't tell me what it's about. Says he has instructions.'

'What kind of instructions?'

'You'll have to ask him that. He wants me to tell you it's important.'

'Very well, Harris. I'll attend to it.'

'You'll want your jacket, sir. It's blowing a gale out there.'

Later on I would examine and re-examine that moment: Harris stooping to pick up the jacket, his broad back turned to me; then swinging round so that I saw his meaty hand moving clumsily over the fabric.

'Dust all over this, sir. You'll need to take a brush to it.'

He held the jacket out to me at arm's length, his stance peculiarly stiff and awkward.

'You'll find him waiting in the porch. Said he wouldn't come in.'

I don't know what I was expecting – certainly not the small tow-headed boy who stood huddled in the porch doorway, hands jammed in the pockets of his stained breeches, grinning as if at some private joke.

'Was it you who wanted to see me?'

His grin broadened and he peered up at me through his ragged fringe.

'I've got something for you.'

He drew a folded square of paper from his pocket and held it towards me. I reached out, but before my fingers could close on it he snatched it back, his eyes narrowing suddenly.

'You are Mr Stannard, aren't you? Only I've got instructions. This is to be given to Mr Stannard personally. I'm not to put it into anybody else's hands.'

'I'm Stannard. Give me the paper.'

As he still hesitated, I leaned forward and twitched it from his grasp. His mouth gaped and his eyes filled with tears.

'You shouldn't have done that,' he whined. 'I had instructions.'

'Indeed you did, and you've carried them out admirably.

You were asked to deliver this to me, and you've done so.'

He seemed to consider for a moment before changing tack.

'She gave me money,' he said.

'Who gave you money?'

'Annie Rosewell. Are you going to give me money too?'

What was it that lifted me then, sending, if I might put it that way, my spirit soaring, so that I found myself laughing out loud at the sheer effrontery of the horrible child? I felt in my pocket for my purse.

'Yes,' I said, 'I'll give you money.'

I seldom carry a great deal with me, but there is a peculiar unpleasantness about losing even a small amount. Standing there under the boy's expectant gaze, hunting feverishly through my pockets, I felt absurdly compromised, as if I had been caught out in some petty deceit.

'I'm sorry,' I said at last, 'but I seem to have mislaid my purse. Come and see me tomorrow morning.'

'You'll pay me then?'

'Of course I will.'

'How much?'

'You'll find out tomorrow. Now go away or you'll get nothing.'

He flicked his hair back from his eyes and stared into my face with a faintly disturbing insolence. Then he turned and made his way obliquely across the churchyard, vaulted the wall and was gone.

I returned to find Jefford leaning against the aisle wall, eyes closed, his pale face tilted to the light from the clerestory windows.

'What's the matter?'

His eyes flickered open, dull and expressionless.

'Nothing, sir. Just this weakness. It comes and goes. I'll be right as rain if I can rest for a moment or two.'

'Very well, Jefford. Lay off for a while. Have you seen my purse? Rough green leather with a black drawstring. It must have fallen from my pocket sometime this morning.'

He passed the flat of his hand across his forehead, pushed himself clear of the wall and stood more or less upright, swaying slightly on his thin legs. His jaw worked spasmodically and I thought he was about to speak, but his body suddenly sagged and all his attention seemed to be directed to manoeuvring himself into the nearest of the undamaged pews. His breathing, I noticed as he sat down, was unhealthily rapid and shallow.

'Where's Harris?'

He looked up at me with the disquieting helplessness of an injured animal and gestured feebly towards the chancel. I called out sharply and Harris emerged from the shadows and came towards us, a patched blanket over his arm.

'This is all I could find,' he said. 'It's a bit damp, but better than nothing.'

He leaned over Jefford and draped it across his shoulders. Jefford's hand came up and clutched the fabric at his throat, but he gave no other acknowledgement.

'He's cold,' said Harris, turning to me.

'Cold? The man's sweating.'

'True enough, sir, but he says he can't get warm. I found the blanket on the vestry floor.' He leaned towards me and lowered his voice. 'I can't think it'll make much difference in itself, but it helps a man to know he's being looked after.'

I began to walk up the aisle towards the door, motioning Harris to follow.

'How long do you suppose this is likely to go on?'

'His illness? I wouldn't know, sir. I'm not a medical man. But I can tell you he's in a poor way at the moment.'

'Do you think he's too sick to work?'

He avoided my eyes.

'I didn't say so.'

'But do you think so?'

He glanced back to where Jefford sat hunched in his pew.

'I shall need to get on if I'm to finish by nightfall,' he said. 'Call me in if he needs me.'

He was at the door, fumbling with the latch.

'I hope that won't be necessary,' I said.

He looked hard at me as though meditating a reply; but he let himself out without a word.

I realize with the benefit of hindsight that it would have been more sensible to postpone my examination of the note until I was alone in my lodgings, but the tower appeared to offer a degree of privacy and Jefford seemed in any case too deeply absorbed in his own misery to be likely to pay much attention to my activities. I tucked myself into the corner behind the arch, unfolded the square of paper and began to read.

What was the source of my disappointment? Not, I think, Ann's childishly unformed handwriting or her unsophisticated phraseology but something rather less predictable. I was disappointed, quite simply, by the propriety of the note. It enquired after my health; it hoped that my recent fall had not affected my work; and it wished me well. Just that. I read it over several times and was still scanning it, searching, as I was subsequently obliged to recognize, for some deeper resonance in the lines, when Jefford poked his head through the archway and peered in. I started and stuffed the note hurriedly into my pocket.

'I thought it was you, sir, but I wasn't sure. All these noises in the building. And then I fell to wondering if you'd gone out and left me. Most of the dead here will be at peace, I know, but with so many around there's bound to be a few still walking. I don't mind telling you, sir, I shouldn't like to be in the place on my own.'

'Don't be foolish. There's nothing to be afraid of here.'

'With respect, sir, it's no folly to be mindful of the dead.'

He was trembling with weakness or fear, almost tearful, and I realized that this was not the moment to give him the benefit of my rather uncompromising views on the supposedly supernatural; but there was, I admit, a certain asperity in my response.

'If you've enough energy to debate such matters, Jefford, you've enough to get back to work. Might I ask you to do so?'

'Yes, sir. I think I'll be all right now.'

He moved slowly back down the aisle, picked up the hammer and set to, grimacing with each blow. While he worked I searched the nave thoroughly, even lifting the scattered fragments of the pews to look beneath them. There was no sign of my purse.

9

Nor was the purse to be found in my lodgings, though I ransacked the cupboards and drawers and went through my belongings one by one. Mrs Haskell, entering with my tray next morning, remarked on the state of the room.

'All your clothes lying about anyhow, Mr Stannard; and I left everything so neat yesterday.'

'You were in here yesterday?'

'Just tidying up.'

'I don't suppose you came across my purse? Green leather, tied with a drawstring.'

'Have you lost it?'

'Of course I've lost it. That's why I'm asking.'

She bridled, her plump cheeks flushing slightly.

'If I were to find a gentleman's purse in my rooms, Mr Stannard, I'd leave it exactly where it was.'

'I didn't suggest that you'd moved it. I simply asked whether you'd seen it.'

'Well, the answer's no.' She banged the tray down on the desk and began to fumble in her apron pocket.

'This came for you.' She pulled out a small folded paper, clumsily sealed with a shapeless lump of wax. 'Slipped under the door this morning before most of us were stirring.'

My name on the front; the childish script instantly recognizable. I took the paper from her, but she showed no inclination to leave.

'That'll be from someone in the neighbourhood,' she said.

'So it would appear. That will be all, thank you, Mrs

Haskell. If you should come across my purse I'd be grateful if you'd bring it over to the church.'

'It'll turn up. Things don't just disappear, do they? Lost, borrowed or stolen, everything comes to light in the end.'

Like many of Mrs Haskell's observations this seemed highly questionable, but I knew better than to engage in debate with her. As soon as she had gone I cracked open the seal and began to read.

> *I wrote yesterday but it was not what I wanted to say and so I am writing to you again. I have been thinking about you. And because I see in your face that you are a good man I know you will not take it amiss that I say I want to know you better. And how is a woman like me to bring that about? I have been asking myself that question, lying in my bed, not able to sleep. And now I have decided. I shall be open with you. Honesty is the best policy my mother always says, and I am being honest. Am I breaking the rules? I know some people would say so but I do not care what they say. Perhaps the rules stop us from being honest.*
>
> *Sometimes I walk at dusk along the footpath above the village. The path to the Hall. I am asking nothing of you. But I hope.*
>
> *Ann*

I must have read the letter a dozen times before I eventually put it in my pocket and left for work. By the time I reached the churchyard Harris had removed the shoring from the trench and was stacking the spars and planks against the wall. As I approached, he straightened up and gestured towards the adjacent heap of bones.

'These will need to go back,' he said.

'Of course. But I'd like to deal with the coffin first. The bones can go in later, along with the backfill.'

'I shouldn't want to tumble them in just anyhow, sir.'

'Do as you see fit, Harris. But I want the job completed by the end of the day.'

'Backfilling too, sir?'

'Why not? I'll work alongside you to speed things up.'

He shook his head doubtfully.

'We'd do well to let the mortar harden off a bit more. Monday morning would be soon enough, I'd say.'

I climbed into the trench and ran my fingernail down one of the joints.

'It's reasonably firm, Harris. I don't want to leave the body in the spoil-heap any longer than necessary; and once it's back in the ground we may as well press on and get the job finished.'

He shrugged. 'Whatever you say, sir. Shall I fetch George over to help me with the coffin? It'll be more than Will can manage, the way he is at the moment.'

'Let's leave George out of it,' I said brusquely. 'I'll give you any assistance you need.'

A fleeting glance, a flicker of the eyes; but he made no objection.

It might, I suppose, have been more decorously accomplished – the clumsy struggle to the trench-edge, the pole shuddering between the pegs, the ropes lengthening suddenly as the coffin dropped like a bucket into a well – but the thing landed on its base, not far from its original position; and that was good enough for me. I left Harris untying the ropes and walked over to the porch to fetch the other shovel.

It was perhaps unwise to look in on Jefford. It was a good ten minutes before I was able to rejoin Harris, and by that time Banks was at his side, staring gloomily into the trench. Harris had patched up the lid before sinking the coffin in the spoil-heap, and its occupant was quite invisible; but Banks's gaze was fixed on the buckled lead as though he could still see the brown face looking back at him from its stained pillow.

'She can rest now,' he said softly.

'No reason why not,' I replied. 'We're just about to backfill the trench. Once that's done, she might well lie there undisturbed until judgement day.'

He ignored the remark, apparently lost in thought. I turned to Harris.

'Let's get started,' I said.

Banks looked up sharply. 'If you don't mind,' he said, 'I'd like to mark the reinterment in an appropriate fashion.'

'We've simply returned the body to its original position. I didn't think there'd be need of any ceremony.'

'Scarcely that, Stannard. I'm not a man for ceremony. A few simple words, that's all.'

He took a pace back from the edge and bowed his head. Harris removed his cap and stood twisting it between his grimy fingers. There was a long silence.

'Wherever we walk,' Banks began at last, 'we walk on the buried past. May we, O Lord, step lightly; and where, as here, we cannot help but disturb, may thy mercy fall upon us, disturbed and disturbers, the living and the dead, that all may know the blessing of thy peace.'

There was a further pause before he pronounced the amen. 'Amen,' echoed Harris loudly, replacing his cap. Banks glanced into the trench again before turning away.

He was clearly in no mood for conversation, but my own concerns were pressing. I fell into step beside him as he brushed past.

'Just a brief word,' I said. 'I lost my purse yesterday. Possibly in the church. I don't suppose you've seen it?'

He shook his head. 'I've not been in since our last discussion. I felt the need to distance myself from your work. The whole business has affected me far more deeply than I would have imagined possible.'

We were on familiar ground. I let him run on for a moment, but once I was sure we were well out of Harris's hearing, I came straight to the point.

'I'll be blunt with you, Banks. I believe the purse has been stolen, and I suspect Harris of the theft.'

He came to a dead stop and stared searchingly into my face.

'Harris? It seems most unlikely.'

'Why? You're surely not going to tell me the man's the pattern of moral integrity?'

He permitted himself a tight-lipped smile. 'No,' he said, 'I wouldn't describe him in those terms, but I very much doubt that he'd sink to theft. He sometimes drinks more than he should, and there have been occasional incidents – disorderly behaviour, minor brawls, that kind of thing – but nothing that would lead me to suspect him of dishonesty.'

'Yet the purse has gone.'

'No doubt; but it's not clear to me why you should assume that Harris is responsible for its disappearance.'

'I should have explained. He handled my jacket just before I discovered the theft.'

'Handled it?'

'Picked it up from the floor and handed it to me. He might easily have removed the purse as he did so.'

'In full view? Wouldn't you have noticed?'

I tried to picture again Harris's unbalanced stance and the movement of his calloused hand across the fabric.

'We don't always know what we've seen.'

'Quite so.' He paused reflectively. 'How much have you lost?'

'A sovereign and a little silver. Nothing to speak of.'

'Then let it go. Forget about it.'

'I'm surprised that you of all people should be so little concerned about matters of principle. Theft is theft, whatever the sum involved; and if we turn a blind eye to crime – to sin, as you might say – it will flourish unchecked.'

'I like to think,' said Banks primly, 'that sin is held in check by a power which operates quite independently of our own rather questionable impulses and actions. And let me just add this: the evidence is at best inconclusive, but whether you're right or wrong, you can't bring your suspicions into the open without losing a first-class labourer.'

The argument seemed vaguely unrespectable, and I might have said as much; but Banks, evidently considering the discussion at an end, broke away and struck off across the churchyard towards the rectory.

I am stronger than I look and I think I rather surprised Harris, standing alongside him and matching him shovelful for shovelful, maintaining a brisk pace until lunch-time. By that stage it was apparent to me that I should be able to complete the job alone well before the end of the day, and after Harris had eaten his bread and dripping, I sent him off to clear the debris from the aisles.

'And where's it all to go?'

'Burn it. On the waste ground opposite.'

'That's church land. Have we got the rector's permission?'

'I'm answerable to Mr Banks's superiors. I've no need to ask his permission.'

'No need, maybe, but my advice—'

'Keep your advice to yourself, Harris. I'll take full responsibility.'

It seemed that I was beginning to wear down Harris's resistance to my authority. At all events, he withdrew immediately and sloped off towards the church, leaving me to continue the backfilling at a more leisurely pace. The wind had veered round now, bringing with it a mildness which made me think of spring; and whether for that or some other reason – and my hand strayed repeatedly to the pocket which held Ann's letter – I found myself working with an unusual degree of satisfaction, so deeply absorbed in my own actions that I was unaware of Banks's return until he was almost upon me.

'What's the fire over there?'

His voice was shaking, his body rigid. I followed his gaze across the lane to where a plume of grey smoke rose above the hedge.

'Harris is burning the pews,' I said.

'All of them?'

'There's nothing reusable there. But you'll be pleased to know that I've salvaged one item. Come and see.'

He followed me reluctantly into the church.

'There you are,' I said. 'I've had Jefford put your chorus-girl aside for you.'

I gestured towards the wall and the pew-end which leaned against it. Jefford had managed to detach the piece without significant damage, and I was rather taken aback by Banks's ungracious response.

'She's not mine. She belongs to the church.'

'It was agreed long ago that the pews were to be replaced. No one will object to your taking the thing.'

'I don't think you've quite grasped my point. Her place was here, and it would be quite inappropriate for me to set her up as a curiosity in the rectory drawing-room.'

'Set her up here, then. You might display the piece on the wall, just below that plaque perhaps. Or wherever you like. I could find you a couple of stout brackets and get Harris to do the job for you.'

He walked over to the pew-end and pulled it away from the wall. He examined the figure closely for a moment, craning around it, running his hand with a faintly repellent tenderness over its smooth contours.

'No,' he said at last. 'It wouldn't do. Let her go. Let her go up in smoke with the rest.' He gave the pew-end a savage thrust so that it fell back against the wall with a dull jarring sound.

'Come now, Banks, this is absurd.'

'Absurd?' He straightened up and turned to face me. 'Listen to me, Stannard. Throughout the years of my curacy here this figure has been a potent emblem for me; of continuity, of the illimitable joy of worship. Now – place her where you will, view her from any angle – she's violation, she's loss. I don't want to see her again. Go ahead: take the thing out and burn it.' And he stormed down the aisle and out of the door before I had time to frame a suitable reply.

And why, I thought with a spasm of irritation, should I say anything? If Banks wanted to sulk – and he was, I felt, behaving like a thwarted child – then let him do so. And if, urged on by what I could only construe as pique, he had made a decision he might later come to regret, was that my fault? I manoeuvred the pew-end out of the church and down the path, leaving it by the gate for Harris to collect on his return.

10

I should have liked to leave earlier but Jefford detained me with an interminable catalogue of miseries – his wife's cough, his own aches, his children's uncertain future – and the sky was darkening by the time I set off down the lane. I was not aware of having thought my way through to any decision, yet the matter had, it seemed to me, been brought to some kind of resolution while I worked.

I walk at dusk . . . I imagined her stepping towards me out of the shadows, one hand outstretched in a gesture at once respectful and tender, her eyes half lifted to mine. And her voice gentle, a little hesitant, as she murmured – what? My own name, perhaps; or *love, dear love* – the words breathed out like perfume from a summer garden. Sheer folly, I told myself; but as I struggled up the hillside, sweating like a man in the grip of a fever, I could think of nothing else.

I came upon her, as I had obscurely known I should, half-way between the village and the Hall, standing a little aside from the path, still and stiff against the dark mass of the beechwood. Not the slightest pretence on her part that this was an accidental encounter: she was waiting for me, and plainly thought nothing of my knowing it. I began to frame a greeting appropriate to the delicacy of the situation, but it was she who spoke first, impulsive and direct.

'My letter reached you, then?'

It would have been foolish to pretend otherwise, though the thought not unnaturally crossed my mind. I tapped my breast pocket.

'I have it here.'

'Next to your heart?'

I peered through the gloom, scanning her face for confirmation of the faint hint of mockery I thought I might have detected in her tone. As I did so, she stepped up to me, her body confronting mine so closely and so squarely that I found myself obliged, in the interests of propriety, to turn aside.

'Perhaps we might walk a little,' I said.

We continued towards the Hall. The evening was still, and for a while I could hear nothing but my own breathing and the whisper of her heavy skirts trailing across the wet grass. When she spoke again her voice was hushed, though not without a certain vibrant intensity.

'I knew you'd come,' she said.

I was on the point of retorting that she could have known nothing of the kind when it struck me how poorly placed I was to challenge her presumption. I should have to find firmer ground.

'I was a little uncertain,' I said, 'how to interpret your communication.'

'I didn't know whether I should set such things down. I wondered what you'd think.'

She looked up at me, her face suddenly lit by a smile of such challenging intimacy that for a moment I found myself almost unable to meet her gaze.

'About your letter? If you want my frank opinion, I thought you might have taken greater pains in the writing of it.'

Her eyes widened slightly. The smile flickered and faded.

'I meant, I wondered whether you'd think me too forward.'

'It was a letter,' I said carefully, 'of a kind I should not have expected to receive from a lady.'

'But might have expected from someone like me?'

'I didn't say that.'

'But perhaps you meant it.'

There was a long silence.

'I have my reputation to consider,' I said at last.

'And I have mine. But sometimes we have to let go of small things if we want to lay hold of greater ones.'

'You think a gentleman's reputation's a small matter?'

She stopped and turned slowly to face me.

'I think it's a smaller matter than the love that might grow up between a man and a woman,' she said. She placed her hand on my sleeve and leaned her body lightly against mine. Then she reached up and, with a movement at once awkward and inexpressibly gentle, drew my face downward, touching my cheek with hers.

My instinctual recoil seemed to startle her, but she moved with me and, as I half turned, slipped her arm through mine. And at that moment I became aware of some deep shift in the ground of things, or in my understanding of their nature. It was still the same path, of course, the same hillside, the same broken skyline; but now irradiated – and as we resumed our walk the moon actually emerged from behind the clouds – in such a way as to appear at once alien and familiar, like a childhood landscape revisited after a long absence.

I am not sure how long our silence lasted, but I know that it was she who broke it, her voice at my shoulder sweeter and more musical than seemed humanly possible.

'Do you mind that I did that?' she asked.

I remember her having to repeat the question before I could respond.

'Mind? What should I mind?'

'I thought you might have been offended.'

'No. Not offended. Surprised, perhaps. And . . .'

I felt her arm tighten its hold on mine as I faltered.

'And what?'

'I don't know.'

'Tell me,' she insisted.

What should I have told her? That a life might be shaken to its dusty core by a look, by a touch, by the peculiar inflections of a woman's voice? It made no sense; and it was, at the same time, self-evidently and incontrovertibly true.

'Not now,' I said. 'Not just now.'

She seemed to withdraw slightly. Not, I think, physically; but I sensed what I thought of at the time, perhaps rather fancifully, as a contraction of the spirit. And when she spoke again her voice was cooler and a little strained, as though it were reaching me from some more distant or difficult place.

'May I ask you something?'

Just then I would have given her anything. I spread my hands in a gesture intended to convey as much.

'What did you mean when you said I might have taken greater pains with my writing?'

'It was a thoughtless and unreasonable remark. How should a girl like you, born and raised in a village like this, aspire to greater fluency or sophistication?'

Perhaps she failed to recognize my apology for what it was. At all events, her face clouded and she took a pace backwards.

'Shall you want to see me again?' she asked.

My hesitation, though momentary and quite unintentional, appeared to heighten her discomfiture. She began to edge away, her head slightly averted but her eyes fixed sullenly on mine.

'Of course I shall.' I reached out with a decisiveness which I think took us both by surprise, gripping her arm and drawing her firmly towards me. For the barest instant she resisted; then I felt her body sway forward, half crumpling, half nestling against my own.

I should like to be able to anatomize that moment, to find some way of accounting for the wave of pure exhilaration which, as she pressed close, her head bowed and her hair partially unpinned and tumbling loose about her cheek and forehead, swept over or through me. I can grasp the elements of it – the strange sweetness of her breath, the warmth coming off her skin, the childlike sigh as I smoothed back her hair and bent to brush with my lips the soft hollow just behind the angle of her jaw. But each time I come at it I seem to miss something, something not present in the details: some ambience or essence which, I have reluctantly concluded, may be inherently insusceptible to analysis.

And even the details – or some of them at least – seem questionable. That kiss, for example. Not, I mean, the chaste brushing of the skin beneath her ear, but what followed as she raised her face to mine, her eyes wide with – astonishment, was it? or exultation? – and then, reaching up with her right hand, drew my head down, not gently this time but with a terrible abruptness, her fingers catching in the tangles of – but that's where it all begins to break down. Because it has occurred to me on subsequent reflection that the tugged hank of hair might have been hers, the entangled fingers mine; and if that was indeed the case and if, as I have also come to suspect, her sudden stagger and near-collapse were caused by my own impulsive movements, then I shall have to acknowledge that I conducted myself, at that particular juncture, with quite uncharacteristic indelicacy.

Yet that was by no means the way the matter presented itself to me at the time. Emphatically not. The rasp of her breath at my ear, the chafing of her mantle against the inner surface of my wrist, the soft working of her mouth on mine – there was no shame there, no distaste or guilt; only a sense of things drawing together, of a world come right at last. And when she attempted to pull away, with a stifled cry which might have indicated either pleasure or distress, it seemed the most natural thing imaginable to try to hold her there, where she belonged, in that warm, still place which we ourselves had created.

'No,' she whispered. 'Not that.'

She broke my hold and stepped backward; and as I reached out for her she turned and began to make her way back down the hill, stumbling on the uneven ground. I hung back for a moment and then hurried in pursuit, clutching at her mantle as I drew abreast of her. She twisted to face me, breathing heavily.

'I have to get home,' she said.

'I'll walk with you.' I took her arm and we moved on, more slowly now. She was trembling, I noticed, like a trapped bird.

'You know I'd do nothing to harm you,' I said.

She stared hard at me for a moment but did not speak until we reached the open ground beyond the line of the beechwood. There, where the path forked, she stopped.

'That's your way down to the village,' she said.

'And you?'

'My home's out there.' She gestured vaguely into the darkness ahead.

'Will you be safe?'

'There's no danger. I've been walking this path for years.'

'Alone? In the dark?'

'Darkness and daylight, sunshine and storm. What should I fear?

'This is hardly the most civilized corner of the country. A young woman alone . . .'

'Oh, that.' She gave a faint snort of laughter. 'There's not a man in the parish would so much as steal a kiss of me without my say-so.'

'Without your say-so? Then—'

'Never,' she said emphatically. And she passed her hand lightly across mine where it lay in the crook of her arm.

The barest touch of her fingertips against my knuckles before she broke away and was lost in the night, yet as

I walked down the hill towards the village it struck me that some tacit compact had been made between us at that moment. I experienced a fleeting tremor of anxiety; and then my heart, as the old ballad has it, took wing and soared.

The end of my day is governed by certain rituals, habits formed in childhood and essential, I have always felt, to a good night's sleep. First I fold back the bedclothes, smoothing the exposed area of the undersheet with the flat of my hand. Then I remove all items from my pockets and place them on a convenient surface. My clothes must be neatly folded, my face splashed with water – forehead, cheeks and chin, in that order – and patted dry. I no longer kneel, but I still address a word or two to my Maker before slipping carefully between the sheets and extinguishing my lamp.

But on this occasion I flung my clothes in disarray across the back of the chair and got into bed without washing. Sleep was out of the question, but sleep was not, in any case, what I wanted. I lay on my back in the yellow lamplight, staring at the ceiling and reviewing, in a state of extraordinary excitement, the events of the past few hours.

It was a state, I suppose, of trance or rapture. No, not quite that, since my mind ranged restlessly, revisiting this phrase, that look or gesture, unable to settle; but so intense was my absorption that I was for several hours insensible of my surroundings or of the passage of time, and it was with real astonishment that I heard the clock in the hallway chime four.

A little before five I rose, put on my greatcoat and, taking the lamp from my bedside, went down to the sitting-room. I seated myself at the table, drew a sheet of paper from my writing-case and took up my pen. This, I remember thinking as I stared at the lamplight reflected in the rippled glass of the window, is the sweetness I've waited all my life for; and as I framed the words, I began to write, without restraint, perhaps even a little carelessly, yet knowing it all made perfect sense. It was a letter of a kind I should once have dismissed as unacceptably extravagant, both in its substance and its expression. Not any longer. These were the things I had to say, and this was the only way of saying them. I was discovering a new language – or so I phrased it to myself – for a new mode of living.

I I

How could I possibly have fallen asleep, fired up as I was?
At one moment I was writing like a man inspired, and then,
without apparent transition, I was raising my head from the
table as Mrs Haskell rapped on the door and stepped into
the room with my breakfast-tray. How could that passionate
flow of interfused thought and feeling have been so suddenly
and decisively interrupted?

I could see Mrs Haskell eyeing the letter as she approached.
I shifted position, covering the sheet with the sleeve of my
greatcoat.

'You've been at your work all night, haven't you, Mr
Stannard?'

'Leave the tray there, thank you. I'll attend to it myself.'

'You'll make yourself ill. All that brainwork when you ought
to be asleep in bed. You can't do that and stay healthy. Mr
Lashley – he was rector before Mr Banks – he was a man for the
midnight oil. Midnight and beyond: sometimes the lamp would
still be burning in his study at dawn. And then you'd see him in
the pulpit – my heart went out to him, Mr Stannard – so weary
he could hardly hold his head up, and his eyes so dark and sad.
I'd think to myself, that man's not likely to be among us very
long; and of course he wasn't. Dead before he was thirty, and
tucked up snug enough in the churchyard these ten years and
more. But he might have been with us now if he'd only taken
more care of himself. You heed my advice, Mr Stannard; there's
a time for work and a time for sleeping, and when people act as
if they don't know the difference—'

I suppose I might have checked her a little less sharply but I dislike unsolicited advice at the best of times, and at that particular moment my desire for solitude and silence outweighed all other considerations. I waited until I heard the kitchen door slam below, then took up my pen again.

Walk with me, I had written just before I fell asleep, *walk with me, sweet angel, beloved guide, dear guardian of—* Of what? If you had asked me an hour or so earlier, I should have said the torrent was inexhaustible. Now I sat there in the cold half-light staring at a text I barely recognized, groping for whatever phrases might allow me to bring the letter to a not completely inharmonious conclusion. *My soul*, I wrote at last, and hesitated. In what sense might such a woman be appointed guardian of a man's soul? To what extent was my integrity compromised by the very notion? I flexed my stiffened fingers and began a new paragraph.

I am aware, I wrote carefully, *that the above might appear excessive to you as, indeed, in certain respects it does to me. The language of love is not, after all, the language of everyday use. But I send you these words as evidence of the passion stirred in me by your presence in my life and I trust that you will accept them in the spirit in which they are offered.*

I signed off with an awkward flourish. Then I folded the letter neatly in four, secreted it in my writing-case and turned the key.

Harris appeared to share none of his colleague's distaste for demolition work. All morning the church echoed to his hammer-blows and the sound of splintering wood, and by late afternoon all pews had been cleared from the north aisle and a start made on those in the nave. Jefford was predictably reluctant to dismantle the latter, pointing out that most of them were still, as he quaintly phrased it, right as ninepence.

'True enough, Jefford, but my intention is to give some kind of coherence to the interior. I can hardly do that if I piece and patch as you seem to be suggesting.'

'You're leaving Mr Redbourne's pew in place.'

'Yes, but very much against my will. Mr Redbourne was apparently insistent that the improvements shouldn't rob him of the privacy provided by his box, and my instructions are to let it stand.'

He mumbled something I couldn't quite hear.

'What was that, Jefford?'

Harris raised his head from his work.

'He said it's a shame some can insist while others can't get themselves any kind of a hearing at all.'

'You stay out of this, Harris.' I turned back to Jefford. 'Is that true? Was that the gist of your remark?'

He shook his head. 'Not exactly, but . . . Don't misunderstand me, sir. I'm not one for oversetting the order of things. Only I can't bear to see waste and damage. This pew' – he ran his hand along the smooth grain of the backrest – 'might last another five hundred years, properly cared for.'

I could see he was set to begin all over again and Banks's arrival at that moment seemed providential, though it quickly became apparent that the tiresome business of the pews was inescapable. Even as I approached him he stopped in his tracks and gazed across at the north aisle, shaking his head slowly from side to side.

'I can hardly believe this is going ahead,' he said, ignoring my greeting. 'One tries to prepare oneself for certain events, but there's still a sense of shock when they materialize.'

'I appreciate that. I can't share your views on this matter, of course, but I recognize the strength of your feelings.'

He smiled wanly. 'I know my behaviour yesterday must have seemed a little irrational, but you have to consider my role here. I've always understood curacy – and the term's a significant one for me, Stannard – as implying not simply the care of my parishioners' souls but also, by extension, an enlightened guardianship of whatever nurtures those souls. The church – I mean the building itself as well as the faith it represents – is just such a nurturing presence, and I'm naturally upset by what's been going on here over the past couple of weeks. Once the job's done I shall no doubt be suitably grateful; but I'm deeply troubled by all this' – he gestured miserably around the nave – 'and I can't help letting it show.'

'There's no need to apologize.'

'I suppose this is less an apology than an explanation, but thinking about the matter this morning, I was obliged to admit that my judgement had been warped by what you rightly characterize as strength of feeling. Your suggestion that we might preserve the carving was a good one, and it was both foolish and discourteous of me to reject it. I've come to tell you that I'd like the piece to be displayed on the south wall as you suggested, and that I'd be very grateful if you could make the necessary arrangements.'

'I'm afraid that won't be possible now.'

'Why not?'

'The carving's gone.'

It says much about Banks's view of the world that he should have imagined that the thing would still be sitting there more than twenty-four hours after our earlier discussion. I had been aware, of course, of certain underlying complications, perhaps even a degree of confusion on his part; but his instructions had been quite explicit and I had naturally not hesitated to act upon them.

'When you say gone—?'

'Burned. I left it by the gate for Harris to pick up. I assume he did so.'

Banks's distress was clearly genuine, but there was a characteristic touch of extravagance in his performance. He stared at me fixedly for a moment before burying his face in his hands, his bent shoulders quivering; then he threw back his head and strode up the aisle and out of the church, crashing the door shut behind him. I called Harris over.

'Yes, sir?'

'I take it you burned the pew-end I left out there yesterday? The one with the figure of a woman on it.'

He hesitated, just long enough for me to entertain the fleeting notion that the carving might have been set aside and saved.

'I did, sir. I thought that was why you'd put it there.'

'I suppose you actually saw it burn?'

'Of course.' His gaze flickered uneasily. 'Hadn't you meant it for burning?'

'Don't worry about it, Harris. I'll deal with the matter. I shall be at the rectory if you need me.'

Banks had not in fact returned home but was loitering disconsolately in the lane just outside the gate. He looked up as I approached, and I saw that his cheeks were flushed and his eyes rimmed with red.

'I've been ferreting around,' he said. 'I thought it was just possible—'

'I'm afraid it isn't. Harris has confirmed that the piece has been destroyed. I naturally regret that but, as you'll remember, I took the trouble to consult you and in fairness I can hardly be blamed for having taken you at your word.'

He was silent, staring at the ground, rigid with suppressed misery. I felt like a schoolmaster called upon to console an unhappy child.

'This won't last,' I said. 'A year or two from now you'll

look around the church and wonder why you ever attached
so much importance to these things.'

He shook his head. 'We see the world differently, Stannard,
you and I; we come at it from different angles. I'm not saying
I've got it right myself, or that you've got it all wrong, but
– let me be blunt – I find myself perturbed by the way you
go about your affairs. There's a clumsiness, even perhaps a
degree of callousness—'

'I don't accept that. The situation is really quite simple:
I've been charged with making certain improvements to the
church, and the removal of the existing pews is a necessary
part of the work. That's all there is to it.'

'Well, there's actually a good deal more to it than that,
though I can see why you might be reluctant to acknowledge
the fact. It's my belief that most lives reveal, on inspection,
a certain coherence or consistency, and that those who live
misguidedly in relation to one aspect of the world are apt to
find themselves replicating their errors in other relationships.
Let me tell you something. There's a church not fifteen miles
from here in which every sculpted figure – every saint, every
angel – has been literally defaced. Someone has simply taken
a chisel and obliterated the features of each one. Looking at
the liveliness of the flowing hair and pleated garments, you
know at once that these would have been faces of remarkable
beauty. All gone, quite irreplaceably. Sometimes I imagine
those puritan inconoclasts at home with their families; try as I
will, I'm unable to convince myself that the hands which dealt
so brutally with those faces are likely to have touched a wife's
forehead or a child's cheek with warmth or compassion.'

The implied comparison was outrageous, and I should have
said as much if Banks had given me the opportunity, but he
scarcely paused for breath before continuing.

'Why does it happen so often, Stannard? What impels
people to destroy the loveliest and most delicate creations of

God and man? I've sometimes wondered whether it might not be a kind of thwarted love, an unfulfilled yearning manifesting itself as rage. And if that's the case, might we not find ways of purifying the impulse, of restoring it to its elemental form?'

The questions were plainly rhetorical and I made no attempt to reply. Another sermon, I might have said; but there was a febrile emotionalism about this effusion which differentiated it from his professional discourse and which, I have to add, rather disgusted me. I excused myself and walked away, half expecting him to follow; but looking back from the porch I saw that he was still in the same place, his head bowed and his arms folded across his chest.

I should not, perhaps, have left so abruptly; but standing in the nave, turning the matter over in my mind, I was obliged to recognize that nothing I could do or say would be likely to console the man. Indeed, I reasoned with myself, my presence might well be inflammatory, and the best thing I could do would be to stay out of his way until he had come to terms with his loss.

And besides, I had my own preoccupations. Ann had been in my thoughts all day, a vague but insistent presence; and now, as the light began to fade, I found myself unable to concentrate on anything else. At just this time, I thought, glancing up at the windows, she would be setting off on her walk – opening the door, stepping out into the damp air, pulling her mantle about her shoulders. I suddenly saw or felt her fingers on the braided fastening, one knuckle denting the soft flesh of her throat, the apprehension so acute that, just for an instant, I lost all sense of my actual surroundings. And when I came to myself again it was with an overwhelming awareness of my own need to be out there with her.

I should have liked to leave at once but I had no wish to encounter Banks again, and it was a good ten minutes before I felt it safe to set out. Once in the lane I stepped out briskly, anxious to reach the footpath before the light failed.

I heard the voices first, indistinct but audibly charged with emotion, and then, rounding the bend in the lane, saw Ann approaching slowly in the company of a young man – the same, I think, who had greeted her outside the church on the first Sunday of my stay; though since that particular brand of vacant handsomeness seems to be shared, perhaps as a result of inbreeding, by a fair proportion of the young men of the village, it was difficult to be certain. The two were deeply engrossed in what appeared to be some kind of altercation, the young fellow insistently laying his hand on Ann's arm, while she repeatedly attempted to step out of range. Their words became clearer as I advanced.

'. . . and in any case I deserve better from you. What are you up to with him? I've a right to know what's going on.'

'A right? What right can you claim? I don't belong to you.'

'You gave me reason to think so last summer. The things you said when—'

'Those weren't solemn promises. They were words wrung from me by you, against my will.'

'Against your will? Listen to me, Annie—'

'Take your hands off me.' She shrugged him violently away and staggered backwards, snagging her skirts on the hedgerow brambles so that she was obliged to stoop to disengage them.

It would perhaps have been prudent to have retraced my steps at that stage, and had I been certain of remaining undetected I should probably have done so. But a sense of dignity – or, rather, of the indignity of retreat – kept me moving forward until, raising her head suddenly and tossing back her hair, she caught sight of me.

Even at a distance of twenty yards her confusion was

apparent. The young man bent to help her, tugging at the bramble stems while she pulled furiously at the snagged fabric, her breathing heavy and punctuated by little childlike sobs. My own composure was, I remember thinking as I stepped forward, unassailable.

'Allow me.'

She stiffened a little but said nothing. Her companion stood aside while I carefully unhooked each of the thorns in turn, bending the stem back on itself as I did so, working with a cold, indefatigable concentration. She was watching my movements, I knew, looking down at me as I knelt there; but I worked on without haste, without emotion.

'There you are,' I said at last, rising to my feet and brushing the roadside dirt from my trousers. 'You're free now.' And, I should have added had I not felt the subtlety of the observation to be beyond her, so am I. I took a step backward, bowed courteously and continued on my way.

So complete had been my mastery of myself and the situation that, waking a little before dawn the next day from a fragmentary dream of loss or betrayal, I was for several minutes disinclined to acknowledge any connection at all between this apparently conclusive encounter and the wave of irrational sorrow which swept over me as I lay there on my back waiting for the light.

12

Jefford's work-rate had, if anything, declined since Harris had joined him on the job. He would lean against one of the piers, occasionally wiping his sleeve across his brow as though he were the one doing the work, and watch as Harris attacked the pews with a savage, undisciplined energy. Every so often the two would huddle together, Harris stooping over his companion and speaking into his ear, too softly for me to be able to make out his words. Then Jefford might pick up his tools and set to for a few moments before resuming his position against the pier. I decided to separate them, putting Jefford to work on stripping the blown plaster from around the chancel arch while Harris completed the demolition of the pews.

Jefford's inertia notwithstanding, we had the scaffolding up by mid-afternoon. Not the most professional of structures, as I made the mistake of observing to Harris, but good enough for the job.

'I don't know about professional,' he said, 'but it would have done no harm to have gone at it with a bit more care. We want no more accidents.'

'And we'll have none,' I said sharply. 'I meant simply that the structure looks rather crude; there's no question of its failing to serve its purpose. If you've finished securing the ladder you can get back to the pews.'

Jefford had withdrawn again and was sitting on a pile of smashed wood, his head bowed and his hands resting limply on his knees. I called him over.

'Come with me,' I said. 'I'll show you what's to be done.'
I led the way to the platform. Jefford climbed slowly, the
trembling of his body transmitting itself through the ladder
to my own feet and hands. His face, I noticed, as he reached
out for the handrail and pulled himself on to the planking,
was shining with perspiration.

'This won't tax your strength unduly,' I said. 'Essentially,
the whole lot needs to come off from here' – I described a
sweeping arc with my right arm – 'to here. It's obvious enough
where it's parted company with the wall.' I rapped the plaster
smartly with my knuckles. 'You hear that?'

He nodded blankly.

'You'll find a hammer and a bolster in the tool-chest in the
porch. Let the debris lie where it falls – Harris can clear it up
later. If you need me you'll find me outside.'

There was an unaccustomed brightness in the air and it
seemed an opportune moment to investigate what I had
latterly come to recognize as a potentially serious problem.
Where the rainwater pooled at the base of the north wall, the
fabric had rotted and crumbled, at one point to an alarming
degree. The drainage could be improved easily enough but
the erosion of the stonework might, I thought, prove both
costly and time-consuming to rectify. I was by no means
eager for additional work, but once the matter had come
to my attention I naturally felt a professional obligation to
follow it up.

I took a pointing-trowel from the tool-chest and went
round to the far side of the building. I was relieved to be
out of doors, away from the noise of splintering wood, and
I settled to my task with something approaching pleasure,
squatting on the puddled ground like a small child.

It may be that I heard her approach, but I have no reason
to believe so. I was probing the loose mortar at the base of one
of the buttresses, utterly absorbed in the task, thinking, so far

as I am aware, of nothing in particular. Certainly not of her. And yet it seems to me that I knew, in the half-second before I straightened up and swung round, that she was there. And it was in the instant of my turning and of her stepping towards me from the deep shade of the yew that the sunlight burst through the ragged clouds so that her face, pale above the grey stuff of her mantle, appeared to glow with the concentrated radiance one sometimes finds in Renaissance portraiture. She stopped a few paces from me and stood still for a second or two, one hand lifted to the fastening at her throat, her head tilted a little to one side and her eyes fixed on mine. An icon, I remember thinking, of almost preternatural composure; but her voice, when she spoke, was tremulous and uncertain.

'Are you busy?'

'Always busy.' I indicated the buttress and the scatter of rotten mortar at its base. 'There's no end to the work on a building like this. Ideally one would rake out and repoint the north and west walls in their entirety, as well as—'

'I wanted to talk to you about something closer to my heart. Closer, I think, to yours too. Could you spare a few minutes?'

'A few, maybe.'

'Perhaps we could walk?'

'I've no time for walking, I'm afraid. You asked for a few minutes. If you want more than that, you'll have to wait for a more opportune occasion.'

'When might that be?'

'Next week, perhaps. I don't know.'

She seemed to consider this for a moment.

'You're angry with me,' she said. 'I can tell you are. But you've no cause. If you'll give me time to explain—'

'Explain what?'

'The boy I was walking with yesterday. It's not what you think. He's my cousin.'

'Really? The little I witnessed suggested a more intimate relationship.'

'Intimate? In what way?'

'I imagine you understand my meaning. The fellow seemed to think he had some claim on you.'

'We've known each other all our lives, and we were in each other's company a good deal when we were younger. Perhaps he still feels some of the old childish attachment to me. But we all have to grow up sometime, don't we?'

She looked up at me with a slight frown, as though perplexed by something in or behind her own words.

'We can't stay in the old places,' she continued. 'Our lives change and we find the things we wanted before don't satisfy us any more. There's a sense of space, glimpses of other ways and faces. And then fortune, or whatever you want to call it, throws us something new, gives us a chance to move on; and if we don't take that chance . . .' She tailed off, staring into the distance.

'If we don't take it?'

There was a moment's pause. Then she rounded on me with a flash of something like anger.

'We have to take it,' she said. 'We've no right to refuse. You know that as well as I do.' And then, still with the same odd intensity: 'Listen, I've written to you again.'

'I've received nothing.'

'I haven't sent the letter. I wanted to give it to you myself.'

She slid her hand beneath her mantle and drew out a folded sheet. I caught a faint warmth, a breath of perfume on the damp air.

'Why don't you simply tell me what you have to say?' I asked.

An obvious question, I should have thought, but she seemed momentarily taken aback. The letter slipped from her fingers and fell to the ground.

'I don't always get things right when I say them. This' – she stooped to retrieve the letter – 'is what I'd like to be able to tell you to your face but can't manage. I'm nervous when I speak to you. I forget words, or if I remember them I can't put them together in the ways I want. In the ways you'd want me to.'

'Let me see it.' I held out my hand.

'You're not to open it now. I'd like you to read it later, when you're back in your lodgings. Promise me you won't look at it till then? I want you to have time to think, to imagine—'

She blushed, faltered.

'Imagine what?'

'Imagine me sitting there writing it. For you. Finding words to tell you of my love.'

How easily we may be caught off balance: a look, a phrase, fingers brushed lightly across a sleeve. And the heart springs suddenly wide, the lips part. *Love*, I might almost have breathed, *is the only word: we need no others*. And I suspect that my residual sense of the notion's absurdity would not of itself have prevented me from articulating it, but I retained enough self-possession to see how unwise it would have been, at that particular juncture, to say more than the situation actually demanded.

'Give me the letter,' I said. 'I'll read it tonight.'

Jefford was perched on the scaffold a little to the right of the chancel arch, prising the plaster from the wall in thick flakes. He was evidently too close to see what I, entering by the north door, spotted at once.

'Lay off for a moment, will you, Jefford? Step aside.'

He scrambled clumsily across the planks, dislodging a shower of whitish dust.

'What is it, sir?'

His voice shook a little. I realized that he had imagined himself to be in danger.

'It's all right, Jefford. I just want to see the wall you've been working on.'

The images were by no means entirely clear, but from where I stood it was possible to make out a naked female figure, arms raised high above her head, emerging from, or sinking thigh-deep into, a gloomy waste of rippled water. The artist had highlighted the woman's protuberant belly and breasts, as well as the sinews of her long neck. Her head was tilted to the right, and just above her left shoulder hung a reddish whiskered face whose goggling eyes leered sideways and upward as though seeking her attention. Her own eyes were averted and seemed, I thought as I approached more closely, expressive of unmitigated horror. Her mouth was wide open in what I could only interpret as a scream. Beside her, still partially concealed by the plaster and severely abraded around the head and shoulders, a second figure, apparently male, grappled with what I took to be a beaked serpent. The left arm held back the reptile's head, but the scaled coils looped tightly around the lower part of the torso chillingly suggested the inequality of the struggle.

There was a spurt of light from the scaffolding above. I took a pace or two backwards and looked up to see Jefford holding a flickering match to a candle stump.

'We don't need that,' I said.

'It's strange, sir, but I've been working on this wall all afternoon without seeing—'

'The less we see of such things the better.'

Even as I spoke, I became aware that the dark patch running diagonally across the woman's left hip and into her groin was not, as I had previously thought, an area of damage or discoloration but a clawed hand, red-brown against the pale tints of her flesh; and following back the line of the wrist, I was just able to distinguish the outline of another body, shadowing hers, in the darkness at her back. Despite the guttering of the flame and the relative dullness of the pigments, I saw immediately how this body connected with the leering face above her shoulder, and I was seized by the certainty that what I was witnessing – what the painter had depicted – was the bestial coupling of the woman and her grotesque consort.

'He's got her in his clutches all right.'

I started. Harris had come up behind me and stood gawping at the wall.

'Get back to your work.'

He ignored the command.

'The rector will be interested in that,' he said.

'I sincerely hope not. And in any case I don't want Banks, or anyone else, to be told of this. Do you understand?'

'You can't stop him finding out.'

'I'm not going to discuss the matter with you, Harris.'

'No, sir. In any case, that wasn't what I came to speak to you about.'

'What is it, then?'

'I've been worrying about Will. Do you think he should be working up there?'

'I can't see why not. It's a dusty job, but relatively undemanding.'

'Maybe so. But I was thinking, if he has one of his turns, he might easily lose his footing.'

'I appreciate your concern, but if he's to receive his wages he'll have to do something to earn them. I'm doing what I can to accommodate him, but the plain truth is that he shouldn't be here at all. If you want to take it upon yourself to explain that to him, I shan't object. I'm sure there are others in the village who would be only too happy to take his place.'

Jefford stopped work and looked towards us. I lowered my voice.

'I've been more than generous in this matter, Harris. From a strictly practical viewpoint my retention of Jefford's inadequate services is sheer folly. I've made very considerable allowances for him, and shall no doubt have to make more. But you must realize that I can't pay him to stand around doing nothing at all. Now get back to your own work and stop worrying about other people's.'

I had known, of course, that Harris was right about the impossibility of keeping Banks in the dark, but I was not prepared for his arrival at that particular juncture. I think it was the scaffolding that drew his attention at first, but he was quick to spot what lay behind it. He strode down the aisle and stood a couple of paces behind me, his head tilted upward.

'It's a doom painting,' he said.

'I know that.'

'And quite a remarkable one by the look of it.' He fished a small *pince-nez* from an inner pocket and perched it on the bridge of his nose. 'I've seen quite a number in my time, but nothing directly comparable to this.'

He began to move backwards and forwards experimentally, ducking and weaving where his sightline was impeded by the scaffolding. Jefford had stopped work and now moved to the edge of the structure to offer a clearer view. Banks's face was flushed, his voice thick with suppressed excitement.

'Do you mind if I go up, Stannard? I'd like to take a look at some of the details.'

I hesitated, but I could hardly refuse the man in his own church. 'Do as you wish,' I said, 'though I can't imagine you'll find the thing much improved by closer acquaintance.'

He scrambled up the ladder and squatted on the platform

in front of the painting. There was a long silence before he rose to his feet again.

'Have you a soft brush?' he asked, leaning over the hand-rail. 'A paintbrush or something of the sort?'

I knew exactly what he had in mind, and I was having none of it.

'I'm afraid not. And we need to press on with the job.'

'Of course. But I'd like you to see this. Would you mind . . .'

I climbed the ladder in a state of considerable irritation and joined him on the platform. As I had anticipated, the painting was even less impressive at close quarters than it had appeared from ground-level, and I saw no reason to keep my opinions to myself.

'But look at this, Stannard. This face. These hands. There's real delicacy here.'

'Delicacy? The term seems singularly inappropriate.'

'And at the same time, a quite extraordinary vigour in the execution of some of the larger masses. Here, for example.'

He ran his fingers lightly across a patch of flesh-coloured pigment. The action struck me as unnecessary and faintly distasteful.

'Primitive cultures always display a certain vigour,' I said. 'What they lack is restraint. And now, if you don't mind, I'd like Jefford to get back to work.'

'Of course. But make sure he goes carefully. You see this, Jefford?' He indicated a deep scratch across the scaly tail of the serpent. 'No more gouging. Keep the blade flat. Any plaster which doesn't come away cleanly should be left for the moment.'

I could see the business taking a highly undesirable turn, and I stepped in quickly.

'Jefford's in my pay, Banks, not yours.'

'I'm sorry. I'm simply concerned to avoid further damage.'

'We'll do our best. But in the end we shall have to score the whole surface for re-rendering, and a little damage at this stage is really neither here nor there.'

Banks stared at me as though I had been guilty of some gross impropriety. 'We can't do that,' he said. 'It's out of the question.'

'On the contrary, it's absolutely essential. If the job had been done properly last time we shouldn't have this problem now. No plasterer worth his salt would dream of applying rendering to a surface as poorly prepared as this.'

'What I mean,' said Banks slowly, 'is that we shouldn't even be considering re-rendering. The doom must be conserved and displayed.'

I should have responded rather more sharply if Jefford had not been present.

'My task here is difficult enough as it is,' I said. 'I should prefer to avoid unnecessary complications.'

There was a long, uncomfortable pause.

Jefford shuffled forward.

'Shall I get on now, sir?'

Banks held up his hand. 'Just one moment, please. Listen, Stannard, I realize that this isn't quite in your usual line of business, but as an architect you must be aware that there's been considerable public and professional concern lately about the over-zealous restoration of our churches. A great deal has been lost in recent years.'

'Most of it not worth keeping. We've come a long way, both technically and morally, since this was painted. What purpose do you imagine might be served by lumbering ourselves with daubs like this? Why should we cling to the nightmares of a graceless age, or sanctify its follies?'

Jefford shifted uneasily from one foot to the other. Down below, Harris had stopped work and was staring up at us. Banks reached out and touched me lightly on the arm.

'Perhaps we should save this discussion for another day,' he said. 'I should like the Dean's opinion on the matter. I hope you won't object if I invite him to pay us a visit.'

It was a shrewd move. I nodded to Jefford.

'Carry on,' I said. 'Carefully.'

I was still seething when I got back to my lodgings. By involving Vernon, Banks was issuing an oblique challenge to my own authority. He had not struck me as a man skilled in the ways of the world, but he had certainly identified a point of leverage and would not, I imagined, hesitate to make full use of it.

I might well have spent the evening brooding on the matter if I had not been reminded, removing my jacket, of Ann's letter. I took it from my pocket and carefully unfolded it; and as I began to read the world and its irritations seemed to recede, as though I had come home to some shared space and found her waiting for me.

It was a surprising letter, strikingly irreticent and, indeed, decidedly presumptuous in its implicit claims; yet I was obliged to recognize that its very audacity constituted a significant part of its appeal.

Dearest,

I am writing this letter late at night; and you must picture me sitting in the firelight with my hair loose about my shoulders, glad of this respite from the business of the day. It is at moments such as this that I feel most keenly the need to communicate with you, to send my thoughts out to you across the dark space that lies between us.

It will not always be like this. I imagine another world, a world shining under the bright light of the sun; a world in which love and order hold sway and in which we walk as one, your hand in mine, towards a deeper fulfilment than our

*present lives allow. The details are unclear, and perhaps it is
better so; yet the vision itself has transformed my innermost
being and given focus to the inexpressible longings of my
thirsting soul.*

*The clock ticks in the shadows, beating out time. And
who registers the passage of time more acutely than those
who love? Yet in loving truly we may also come to know
those moments of timeless wonder that bring us close to the
very source and centre of life. In your dear company I have
indeed known such moments; moments which now, relived
in your absence, give me at once the strength to continue
and joy in continuance.*

*I have been dreaming, drifting in and out of sleep. And
now the first birds are beginning to stir and sing. The fire
is almost out, a heap of grey ash in the grate. But the
love in my heart, my darling, is unquenchable and will
blaze out through this present gloom, a beacon guiding
you safely to the haven of my arms. I await, eagerly but
without impatience, the realization of my vision.*

The letter's astonishing intimacy was, if anything, enhanced
by the absence of any signature. It was as though the writer
had broken off to gather her thoughts and might at any
moment resume her discourse; or, I imagined with a sharp
thrill of pleasure, as though she could not bear to bring the
communication to a close.

And I was taken, too, by the letter's style: florid certainly,
more than a little overwrought, but suggestive of an appreciably higher level of sophistication and accomplishment than
I had previously given its author credit for. Yes, I thought,
suddenly flushed with excitement, I could make something of
the girl; and though I suppose I should not at that or at any
other time have felt entirely comfortable about articulating
the word, it was undoubtedly marriage that I had in mind.

I3

Taking his cue from Banks, Jefford worked with infuriating delicacy, spinning out the job until the end of the week. I had resolved not to intervene in advance of the Dean's visit, but found my patience tested to the limit.

His pride on completing the task was almost as irksome to me as the pointless meticulousness with which he had carried it out. I arrived a little late that morning, tired and irritable after a third successive evening spent in fruitless vigil on the hillside, to find him in the middle of the nave, contemplating what he had clearly come to think of as his own handiwork.

'That's a job well done,' he said, glancing my way as I approached. 'Though I say so myself.'

His demeanour had lightened noticeably while he had been occupied with the painting, and my suspicions had not unnaturally resurfaced. I was not inclined to humour him.

'Faster done would have been better done,' I said brusquely.

'I was mindful of the rector's words, sir. Go carefully he said, and that's what I did. There was a fair bit lost before they covered it up but there's been no damage in the uncovering, barring a scratch or two. Even at that edge there, where the plaster had bonded—'

'It's immaterial to me, Jefford, though I've no doubt Mr Banks will be delighted.'

'Yes, sir. He was good enough to say as much.'

Banks had spent more than an hour up the scaffold on the afternoon of the previous day, examining Jefford's fresh discoveries in minute detail. I had resisted his invitation to join him there, having seen enough from below to convince me that I should be wasting my time.

The painter had evidently possessed only the most rudimentary sense of perspective. A ladder footed in the grey water a little above the right shoulder of the screaming woman ascended without diminution to the top of a towering cliff from which a gang of blood-coloured demons were pitching the small white bodies of their victims, while at the base of the cliff, and in indeterminate spatial relationship to the four larger figures below them, a man and a woman stood naked on an island of ochre stone or sand.

There was, it was true, something about the handling of this couple which hinted at a slightly greater degree of sophistication. There was a compelling tension in the attitude of the two figures, their bodies leaning towards one another, their long fingers almost touching, while at the same time their averted faces stared out over the desolate waters as though even that prospect were preferable to the meeting of eyes. And I was struck, too, by the uncharacteristically fluent treatment of the flames which flickered around the couple's loins – suggestive, it seemed to me, not so much of ambient hellfire as of an inward conflagration erupting uncontainably from its hidden centre. I was, I must confess, faintly intrigued, but these discoveries could hardly be said to compensate for the general crudeness of design and execution which had been apparent from the first. Vernon might conceivably find Banks's enthusiasm engaging, but surely, I thought, the facts would speak for themselves.

The Dean's arrival was felicitously timed. I had just set Jefford to work on the area of cracked tiling around the base of the font and was having a quiet word with Harris about the removal of the remaining pews when the door swung open and Banks ushered his visitor into the church. First impressions are important, and Vernon would have seen nothing at that crucial moment to suggest either slackness or disharmony. I strode forward to greet him, and as I did so, the sick fatigue which had oppressed me all morning seemed to lift like a summer mist.

He met me half-way down the aisle, clasping my hand with extravagant warmth. He was very much as I had remembered him – the thick mane of hair a little greyer perhaps, the face a little fuller; but the years had obviously dealt leniently with him.

'It's good to see you here,' he said. 'Very good indeed. And what a splendid figure now. Let me have a look at you.' He grasped my shoulder and thrust me back a pace, holding me from him at arm's length, scanning my face with unabashed curiosity.

'Well,' he said at last, relaxing his grip, 'I believe you have more of your mother than your father about you. No bad thing: she was a fine-looking lady. And a lady, I might add, of considerable character.'

He paused just long enough to suggest appropriate respect for my mother's memory, but not so long as to let the shadow of her death chill the atmosphere.

'And your father? Well, I trust.'

'Tolerably well for a man in his seventieth year.'

Vernon gave a deep chuckle. 'I'm not far short of that myself. You're still a young man and can hardly be expected to understand, but these can be – I speak from my own experience – years of great fulfilment.'

'Of course. But my father seems to have aged a good deal recently, whereas you seem to be—'

'In excellent health and spirits, thank the Lord. But I've always held that it's essentially a question of attitude – the state of mind in which one tackles life's demands. As any cricketer will tell you, the player who steps forward with confidence to meet the ball is the player who makes the runs. No use ducking or bobbing at the crease – foot firmly forward and a bit of power in the elbow. The analogy can be sustained and amplified – I've given more than one sermon on the subject – but you'll appreciate the fundamental point. Foot firmly forward: simple advice but no less valuable for that. Take it to heart, young Stannard, and you'll live to thank me for it. Am I not right, Mr Banks?'

Banks averted his eyes. 'Perhaps we should examine the doom,' he said. 'I don't want to rush you, but I know how busy you are.'

'Ah, yes, this – what did you call it in your letter, Mr Banks? – remarkable example of mediaeval English church art. I take it' – he gestured towards the chancel wall – 'that this is the work in question. Rather unprepossessing from our present vantage-point, I have to say, though perhaps its charms will become apparent upon closer inspection.' He stepped forward, squinting up between the scaffolding-boards and the guard-rail. There was a long silence, then he turned to Banks.

'Is this the full extent of the thing?'

'A certain amount is concealed by the scaffolding.'

'Yes, yes, I realize that. But you're not expecting to discover any more of it, are you?'

'There's no reason to suppose that we shall. The painting would originally have extended across the top of the archway, of course, but nothing of the other half seems to have survived.'

Vernon nodded reflectively and returned to his examination of the wall, his face impassive. Banks seemed to hesitate for a moment before speaking again.

'We might get closer. If, that is, you don't object to the climb . . .'

'No, I don't object, though I find it difficult to see how my appreciation of the work could possibly be enhanced by such intimate scrutiny. Surely it was designed to be viewed from ground level?'

'That's undoubtedly true, but there are one or two details I should like to point out to you. I can do so more easily at closer range.'

'As you wish. Will you lead the way, Stannard?'

He was hard at my heels as I climbed the ladder, moving, despite the unsuitability of his attire, with the agility of a far younger man. He swung himself round the upright and squatted down on the boards a yard or so from the painted surface. He looked up as Banks stepped on to the platform.

'Well, Mr Banks,' he said, 'I'm afraid I shall have to ask you to enlighten me. Which particular details should I be looking at?'

'You might start with the brushwork: as you can see, it's by no means delicate, but there's a sureness of touch which suggests an artist of more than common ability. The highlighting of the body's contours here, for example; or here. And these faces' – he indicated the features of the screaming woman and her demonic companion – 'are, it seems to me, unusually expressive. Then there's the artist's rendering of perspective: rather primitive, I admit, to the modern eye, but not entirely unremarkable by the standards of its own time. Don't misunderstand me: I'm not suggesting that we're looking at a work of genius. But there's evidence here of something more than routine workmanship, and I very much hope you'll take account of that in your deliberations.'

That our behaviour alters according to our circumstances is a truth so obvious as hardly to need stating, but I was sharply and forcefully struck by the difference between the Banks I had seen shortly after my arrival in the village – master of his flock, master of his own compelling discourse

– and the figure who now squatted awkwardly beside the Dean, waiting for the word of approval or support which, I could see, was unlikely to be forthcoming. I think Banks was aware, too, that he was, as Vernon himself might have put it, batting on a losing wicket: when he resumed it was with the anxious and brittle enthusiasm of a man who feels his audience slipping from his grasp.

'And there's something else that might interest you. By rights, as Mr Stannard will tell you, the whole surface should have been rough-tooled before the new rendering was applied. But look at this: a bare minimum of tooling, and what there is has been placed so as to cause the least possible damage to the figures. That's why the plaster has lifted, of course; that's why it peeled away so easily. A source of irritation to you, Stannard, I know, but I must confess that I like the thought of that workman, at some time in the distant or not-so-distant past, compromising his own craft out of respect for that of one of his predecessors.'

Vernon glanced in my direction, clearly expecting me to respond. It was the moment I had been waiting for.

'It's an interesting hypothesis, Banks, and I understand the appeal it must hold for you. But I know Dr Vernon will agree with me when I observe that sentimentality and professional-ism make uneasy bedfellows, and I think I know where his sympathies would lie if he were obliged to adjudicate between the two. I have a job to do here, a job which I naturally wish to complete in good time and to the highest professional standards. I am, of course, sensitive to the context of the enterprise – any Christian edifice, however humble, rightly commands our respect – but I don't believe that I should allow my work to be hindered – or, to take up your own term, compromised – by every residual scrap inadvertently exposed as I go about my necessary business. I'm prepared to accept that this particular fragment is, of its kind, unusually good; but the modern observer is far more likely to register its deficiencies than its virtues. And then there's its subject: how many of your parishioners do you think would wish to be confronted by these images as they sit in their pews? More to the point, would you yourself wish your congregation to be confronted by them?'

It was, I flatter myself, a well-judged intervention: I was aware, as I spoke, of Vernon nodding at my side in what I took to be agreement. Banks was silent, registering, no doubt, the disabling force of my final thrust.

Vernon reached out for the guard-rail and pulled himself to his feet.

'I think I've seen enough,' he said quietly. 'Perhaps we should return to firmer ground.'

Banks led the way, pausing at the foot of the ladder to steady it as Vernon descended.

'Thank you, Mr Banks. And thank you for your helpful advice. I very much value your views and your willingness to share them with us.'

'Then you agree that the painting should be preserved?'

'I neither said nor meant to imply anything quite so definite. It's a complex question, and one to which I shall have to devote some thought. And now, if you don't mind, I should like a word in private with Mr Stannard.'

Banks opened his mouth as if to speak, but seemed to decide against it. He inclined his head slightly and withdrew. Vernon watched him out of the door before turning back to me.

'Let me make my position plain, Stannard. I'm speaking confidentially, you understand, but I'm with you entirely on this matter. As you suggest, the mural itself is fragmentary and, to put it at best, unedifying. Then we have to consider the question of delay – and preservation always, in my experience, involves delay – and the inescapable financial implications of that. Banks is in many respects a good curate – a good man – but he has, shall we say, a rather limited perspective on these issues. You and I understand, far more clearly than he does, the practicalities which – the term seems apposite in the circumstances – underpin his faith. Even so . . .'

He paused ruminatively, fingering his collar.

'Even so?'

'There are difficulties. The truth is that Banks hasn't dealt entirely straightforwardly with us. He seems to have communicated his concerns – without any consultation with me, mark you – to a society of architectural enthusiasts, one of whose representatives has just dashed off a letter to the Bishop arguing for what he terms a stay of execution. Briefly, this fellow wants us to stop work on the chancel wall pending evaluation of the mural's merits. And the fact that I now know those merits to be negligible doesn't, unfortunately, release me from the obligation to meet him when he turns up here to give us the dubious benefit of his scholarly opinion.'

'When might that be?'

'Not before the end of next week, I'm afraid. I'm sorry, Stannard. It's such a waste of everybody's time. To be frank, I've no patience at all with these people: they impede progress, offering by way of compensation only a hazy retrospect on a world we've long outgrown. But the problem is that we can't readily dismiss them. Many are learned men – ostensibly so, at least. Some have a certain social standing. Collectively, they exercise a surprising degree of influence. The Bishop himself seems disposed to – well, perhaps it's simply that he's a more charitable man than I am.'

Suddenly, surprisingly, he threw back his head and laughed, setting the nave ringing. And at the same moment Ann peered round the edge of the door.

If I was pleased to see her – and I suppose I must have been – I was also acutely embarrassed. For one panicky instant I imagined her walking down the aisle to stand at my side, obliging me to introduce her; then, with a faint, disquieting smile, she withdrew, closing the door softly behind her.

Vernon could not have seen her, and seemed not to have noticed my own discomfiture. He drew a heavy silver watch from beneath the folds of his cloak and held it at arm's length, scrutinizing the dial through half-closed eyes.

'Time,' he said, tapping the glass with a blunt forefinger. 'Never enough of it. You must forgive me: I have other duties to attend to. I hope this unfortunate business won't hinder your progress unduly.'

'There's plenty to keep me occupied. The fabric of the north wall—'

'We can talk about that at my next visit. I shall let you know when I have further news. In the meantime' – he draped his arm across my shoulder and walked me firmly towards the door – 'let me just reassure you that your work here is very much appreciated. I like a man who recognizes nonsense when he comes across it – and between you and me, Stannard, the world is full of nonsense of one kind and another – and I'm even fonder of the man who knows how to deal with it. You have a way about you, no doubt of it, and I'd like to see you get on in the world. Perhaps we can do something about that. And now,' he concluded, hauling open the door, 'I really must be on my way. Please convey my regards to your father when you next see him. I've promised to visit him myself when circumstances permit, but such opportunities are rarer than one would like.'

Ann was waiting for me. Not, fortunately, in full view; but I had barely seen Vernon out of the churchyard before she emerged from the far side of the tower, hurrying across the drenched grass to head me off as I walked back up the path. This was, I suppose, the moment I had anticipated or imagined so keenly through four restless nights; but there was an unbecoming audacity about her approach – a certain presumptuousness perhaps – that kept me on my guard. She laid hold of my sleeve and might well, I thought, have embraced me had I not stepped smartly out of range. Her face clouded momentarily, but she kept her eyes on mine.

'We must talk,' she said.

'Here?'

'Wherever you like. We might take a turn down the lane.'

'Now? In broad daylight?'

'Why not?'

'I should have thought that was obvious. Besides, I have work to do.'

'This evening, then. Meet me on the hillside.'

'At what time?'

She broke away abruptly and walked down the path, not pausing until she reached the gate. Then she looked back over her shoulder, her face set, her voice suddenly hard.

'When it's dark enough for you,' she said.

14

I am conscious now of the absurdity of my actions – sprucing myself up for an evening on a windswept hillside with all the care of a man preparing for a visit to the opera – but that was not the way the matter struck me at the time. I washed, shaved, pared and cleaned my fingernails and brushed back my hair, sprinkling it with oil until it shone. And though I knew perfectly well that most of my clothing would be concealed beneath my greatcoat, I changed my shirt and trousers and put on my dark jacket.

The truth is that I had begun to play the lover in earnest. I remember casting about for a gift, a token – for something that might convey to Ann my sense of the evening's significance; and it was at that point that I recollected my letter. I went down to the sitting-room and retrieved it from my writing-case; then I slipped it into my coat pocket and hurried out.

If I were of a more superstitious turn of mind, I might be tempted to imagine that what I experienced over the next few minutes was a form of premonition. Just a vague unease at first, depressing my spirits and slowing me in my stride as I made my way up the lane; but climbing the hillside in the gathering dusk, I found myself gripped by a kind of terror, shivering violently, my strength gone. I worked my way round to the lee of a stunted thornbush and stood there waiting for the tremors to subside. And as I waited she came into view, a small dark stain moving steadily across the hillside above me. The thought crossed my mind that if I were to remain absolutely still, I might escape her notice, slipping quietly away when she had passed. Then she began to move obliquely down the slope towards me, and I knew it was too late to change anything.

I was still trembling when she reached me, and she too, I noticed, scanning her face in the dying light, showed signs of agitation. She held out her hand in a gesture so ambiguously poised between the familiar and the formal that I was uncertain how to respond.

'Shall we walk?' she asked.

I am not sure that I made any answer, but she took my arm and we walked together towards the black bulk of the beechwood. It seemed to me that I was not moving entirely of my own volition, yet there was nothing obviously coercive about the light pressure of her hand on my sleeve.

'You're shivering,' she said.

'I'm cold.'

She stopped and turned to face me; then she reached up and fastened the collar of my greatcoat, her small knuckles grazing my throat as the button slipped through the stiff cloth. It was a gesture of extreme simplicity, yet charged, I felt, with unfathomable meaning.

'I have something for you,' I said. I fumbled in my pocket and drew out the letter.

She took it from me and unfolded it, peering at it as though she might have been able to read it.

'It's too dark,' she said. 'Tell me what it says.'

'It says,' I began, and faltered, wondering how I might translate the letter's florid excesses into an idiom more appropriate to my immediate situation.

'Tell me,' she insisted.

'It's a message of love. You must read it when you get home.'

'Thank you.' She tucked the letter away beneath her mantle and latched on to my arm again.

By the time we reached the wood it had begun to rain, a fine pervasive drizzle driven by a light wind. We stood under the sighing boughs with the darkness deepening around us, her face close to mine but inscrutable now, a shadow among shadows. It might, it occurred to me, have been any one of the faces upon which, over the years, in tram-cars, drawing-rooms or crowded streets, my imagination had played so hungrily, creating for itself the illusion of a moment such as this.

'Kiss me,' she whispered with sudden breathless intensity, her body stiffening as she strained upwards, one hand pulling at the lapel of my coat. I was like a bather on an unfamiliar shoreline feeling the sands shelve unexpectedly beneath his feet, struggling for balance.

'At the churchyard the other day,' I said, 'seeing you standing there in the sunlight, I'd have said you were—'

'Sssh,' she said, and pressed her mouth against mine, stifling the words on my lips. And as she did so, it all receded – the remembered face, the apt phrases, the daylight world itself, all lost in the breathing dark. I slipped both hands beneath her mantle, feeling through the harsh stuff of her dress the movement of her shoulder-blades as she locked her fingers behind my neck; and then, sliding my left hand round beneath her raised arm, I let it come to rest – though not, I am certain, with any dishonourable intention – against the warm curve of her breast.

She gave a muted cry and writhed sideways, bringing her arm between us.

'What is it? What's the matter?'

She placed her open palm gently against my chest, half cautionary, half caressing.

'You do mean well by me, don't you, Mr Stannard?'

It was the first time I had heard her speak my name. The form of address seemed, in the circumstances, faintly absurd, yet I found myself peculiarly resistant to the idea that she might address me with greater familiarity.

'Mean well?'

'I need to know you'll make it right for me.'

There was a long silence. I felt her breath come and go against the chilled skin of my cheek.

'I don't want to lose you,' she said, her voice quavering and breaking suddenly like a tearful child's. 'If I lost you—'

'Why should you lose me?'

It did not, I have since reflected, speak particularly well for the girl's character that she should have proceeded as she did on the basis of such ambiguous reassurance. She pressed close again, drawing me down, searching my face with her fingertips, with her damp mouth. Then she grasped my wrist and, with a movement at once delicate and deliberate, returned my hand to its place against her breast.

I find it difficult to account for what followed. It would be unreasonable, of course, to deny my own complicity in the act but I was, I feel justified in saying, an unwilling accomplice, caught up in a whirl of events I was barely able to comprehend, let alone control. I might, and indeed to some extent must, blame the girl – her soft hand questing, coaxing, guiding, her lips moving against my cheek, framing with a brutal, unfeminine directness ideas so unthinkable, so irre-sistible, that I could scarcely believe I was not dreaming. But a moment later she herself was stretched out helpless in the grip of the thing, her head thrown back among the dead leaves, one arm flung up and outwards, her long throat vulnerably exposed; and through it all, those tender obscenities, punc-tuated by sighs, by childlike sobs and whimpers, until her whole body suddenly hardened and arched backward like an epileptic's and I was lost – we were lost – in a storm of illimitable sensation, our voices crying out, torn from us, it seemed to me, and hurled into the surrounding darkness.

The wind had risen, and now the rain began to fall more heavily, slanting in from the north-west. I tried to disengage myself, but she held me to her, bearing down with her right hand on the small of my back. She was shuddering violently, her breathing hoarse and irregular. I lay still, listening to the hush of the rain, my hands braced against the wet earth.

Little by little her hold slackened, allowing me to draw away. I raised myself slowly. And kneeling there in the dark between her splayed legs, I conceived the scene as I could not possibly have seen it, as if from a little distance, a sorry tableau illustrating man's subjection to the flesh: the woman supine on her own hoisted skirts, her white skin smirched with woodland muck; and myself before her, head bowed in an attitude simultaneously suggestive of ungodly worship and insupportable shame. I scrambled up, tugging feverishly at my disordered clothing, and backed away from her.

'Where are you going?' Her voice was raw, touched with panic.

'We can't stay here.'

'Please—'

I could just make her out, sitting now and leaning forward between her own bent knees. I think one hand was extended towards me but I made no answering movement, and she struggled to her feet unaided. I began to pick my way across the rough ground, making for the footpath.

'Wait for me.'

She stumbled to my side and laid hold of my arm. It was, I can see now, neither tactful nor gentlemanly to disengage myself, however delicately, from her grasp, but I find justification in the reflection that a more welcoming response would have been a less honest one. We walked on in silence, Ann limping slightly, until we reached the junction of the two footpaths. I made some show of willingness to accompany her further on her way but I was, to tell the truth, relieved by her refusal.

'No,' she said. 'You go on down. There's no point getting wetter than you need to.'

I turned to go, but as I did so she stepped hurriedly forward and clutched at my sleeve, drawing me back to her.

'A kiss,' she whispered. 'You might give me that.'

Her face was cold but there was a subtle warmth on her lips which, just for an instant, raised a corresponding warmth somewhere far down in my own chilled body. I pulled away.

'I want to see you again,' she said. 'Soon. There's so much to talk about.'

I could think of nothing I wanted to discuss with her. Nothing whatsoever.

'Soon,' I said, turning away again.

Mrs Haskell emerged from her parlour as I entered the house. The encounter was not, I think, as purely accidental as she would have liked it to appear.

'It's no night for walking out, Mr Stannard. Look at the state of you.'

I must indeed have presented an abject picture, my hair plastered to my forehead, my face rigid with cold, my clothes soaked and filthy. I stood stupidly in the middle of the hallway, rainwater pooling at my feet while she fussed around me.

'Let me have that. And your jacket. And just look at these – mud all over. Whatever have you been up to?'

'I slipped and fell. Coming down the hill.'

'I can't imagine why you should have been out there in the first place on a night like this. You'll be lucky if you haven't caught your death.'

'I shall be fine, thank you, Mrs Haskell.' I took off my

shoes and moved stiffly to the stairs. 'Would you be good enough to bring me up a hot drink in a moment or two?'

Once in my room, I stoked up the fire and changed my clothes, but I had been so thoroughly chilled that, even after gulping down the steaming toddy provided by Mrs Haskell, I was still shivering. My body ached and my mind worked restlessly, alternately circling and veering away from the disquieting events of the evening; and finding it impossible to settle, I retired early to my bedroom.

I undressed and poured a little water from the ewer into the basin. Forehead, cheeks, chin; and as I ran my hand down my face I became aware of the smell of her – not on my hand alone, but rising from my body like a subtler version of the smoke I had observed emanating from the loins of the stranded lovers in the doom. I poured more water and began to scrub at myself with the wetted corner of the towel, lightly at first, and then with a frenetic energy, chafing and reddening the soft skin of my belly and the insides of my thighs, desperate to be clean.

Yet I could still smell her as I slipped into bed, fainter now but unmistakably present; and though I fell asleep almost at once, I awoke repeatedly during the course of that long, confusing night imagining, with the strangest commingling of shame and pleasure, that she was there in the bed beside me.

15

I rose early the following morning, hoping that a brisk start might help me to throw off the morbid clutter of the night. But my throat was tight and dry and my head throbbed painfully, and by the time Mrs Haskell came in with my breakfast-tray I had exhausted what little energy I had woken with and was sitting limply in my chair, staring out of the window.

'See if I wasn't right,' she said, scanning my face narrowly, not without a trace of satisfaction. 'You go running about the countryside at all hours in the wind and rain and you're bound to come a cropper, one way or another. You're sickening for something, I can tell just looking at you.'

'I'm well enough, Mrs Haskell. A little under the weather, that's all.'

'A good deal under, I'd say. If you value my advice you'll stay home today and let me take care of you.'

An unappealing prospect, I thought, imagining the incessant intrusions, the hours of inescapable chatter.

'Thank you,' I said, 'but that won't be necessary. I'm tougher than I look. It would take more than a slight chill to put me out of action.'

'And you'll have more than a slight chill, I can tell you, if you don't look after yourself. It's a holy place you're working in, but not a healthy one – musty as an old henhouse, and all those draughts whistling around you.'

'I'm needed there, Mrs Haskell. In half an hour's time, in fact. So if you don't mind . . .'

She did mind, of course, and her expression said as much;

but she withdrew without further debate, leaving me to my breakfast and my sombre reflections on the unfortunate events of the previous evening.

I struggled on in the church for as long as I could, but it became increasingly apparent that I should have to admit defeat. My limbs were heavy and unresponsive and my body had begun to shiver again, deeply, as though the icy rain to which it had been exposed on the hillside had penetrated skin and flesh and pooled at its dark centre. I was able, by and large, to attend to the modest tasks I had set myself, but I seemed at times to be moving in a cloud or shadow, and at some point, I think early in the afternoon, I found myself seated on a pile of discarded floor-tiles with Harris leaning above me from what appeared to be a considerable height, one hand extended towards me, his heavy features creased with concern.

'I'm all right,' I remember saying, waving him away. 'It's nothing serious.'

He withdrew his hand and stepped back a little. 'Maybe not,' he said, 'but you look sick as a dog, if you don't mind me saying so.'

'I've taken a chill. I need to rest.'

'No sense resting here, sir. I'll see you back to your lodgings.'

I drew myself together and rose unsteadily to my feet. 'There's no need,' I said. 'I can see myself back. I'd like you to work on as usual in my absence. Keep Jefford at it too: he's still inclined to take it easy when he thinks he can get away with it.'

'Sometimes,' said Harris quietly, 'sickness gives a man a sharper understanding of other people's sufferings.'

The observation was so oblique, and my mind so clouded, that I failed at first to see the mischief in the words. When

I realized what he was driving at, I began to explain the difference between Jefford's case and my own, but in so confused and elaborate a fashion that I eventually lost the thread of my argument and ended up talking stark nonsense. Harris might well have pressed home his advantage, but he turned away and took up his tools again; and I, with the disquieting impression of having been dismissed, gathered up my belongings and left.

Mrs Haskell was all too obviously delighted to find herself vindicated. I had barely eased myself into my chair before she came hurrying in, eager to remind me that she had told me so, tiresomely anxious to be of service.

'If you'd be good enough to draw up the fire, Mrs Haskell, and see that I'm well provided with coals, I shall want nothing else.'

'But you'll need to eat. I'll bring you a bowl of broth.'

'Thank you, but I'm not hungry.'

'A pot of tea, then? A hot toddy?'

I shook my head, and the room seemed to blur and swim.

'Nothing, thank you, Mrs Haskell. Nothing but peace and quiet.'

'You should be in bed. Shall I warm the sheets for you?'

'No,' I said, leaning back and closing my eyes against the sick sway of my surroundings. 'No, I shall be comfortable where I am.'

Nothing could have been further from the truth. As the afternoon wore on, my headache and giddiness worsened, while the constriction which had begun in my throat spread down to my chest, making a painful chore of the simple act of breathing. By nightfall, restless and feverish, I was more than ready to retire to my bed.

I lit the lamp and managed to reach the door without undue difficulty. But as I stepped out on to the landing and looked up, the stairway seemed to tilt and recede and I lurched sideways, striking my shoulder violently against the wall. My cry brought Mrs Haskell running into the hallway below.

'Did you call, Mr Stannard?'

I am not sure that she caught my feeble reply, but she was at my side within seconds, visibly flustered, peering anxiously into my face.

'Do you want me to send for Dr Barratt?' she asked.

'No doctors, thank you. I just need sleep.'

'Give me that,' she said, easing the lamp from my grasp. 'Hold tight to the stair-rail as you go. I'll follow you up.'

At the top of the stairs she took my arm and I let her guide me into my room. I sat on the edge of the bed, watching in a kind of stupor as she bustled about – drawing the curtains, raking up the fire, shaking out my crumpled nightshirt and draping it across the back of the chair to warm in the glow of the turned embers. And then she was in and out with this and that – an extra blanket, a warming-pan, a cup of hot milk – until, presumably recognizing that she had done all she could, she wished me goodnight and left me to myself.

I was relieved, undoubtedly, when she finally withdrew; but a few moments later, curled on my side in a darkness that seemed, to my fevered mind, even more intense than usual, I came close to wishing her back. At one point, indeed, I even imagined her sitting there at my bedside, not as herself but, most implausibly, as an upright pillar of unperturbed white light. I tried to fix my attention on her – on this manifestation, I mean – but she faded under my gaze, and the dreams came flooding in.

I can see the folly of attempting to impose a spurious order on an experience marked by nothing so strongly as its incoherence, but I find it possible to isolate from that terrible welter of dream-nonsense one or two passages which lend themselves – though not, I admit, very readily – to some form of articulation. This, for example. I was standing on the scaffold high above the nave, hacking the plaster from the wall as Jefford had done. The surface crumbled away like pie-crust, the shameful images proliferating beneath the chisel blade as though I myself were their author. I worked frenziedly, choking on dust, oppressed by the stench that rose inexplicably from the painted surface. All about me (and it is only as I relive this that I realize that at some unspecifiable point I ceased to be a spectator and became a participant in their sufferings) the pale bodies squirmed and sighed in what I remember as a shallow wash of warm salt water; and I writhed among them, aching for contact but knowing that if I were so much as to brush against their tormented flesh I should be marked for ever. And all the time I seemed to burn inwardly, so that when one of the figures leaned forward, holding a flask in her slender hands, offering it with a gesture so disturbing, so darkly enigmatic that I tremble now even as I think of it, I seized it and drank.

And then the hands took over, soft hands slipping me, by some bewildering sleight, out of my clothes and laying me down in the salt wash, working my body as a modeller might work his clay. I remember trying to interpose my own hands between the kneading palms and my nakedness, feeling my flesh loosen and melt beneath their blind ministrations. Sssh, they whispered, moving easily to and fro over the slackening surfaces, sweeping aside my resistance. And perhaps it was then, perhaps a little later – for I know that far more was compressed into that indeterminate span than I can now lay hold of – that I felt them beginning to peel the skin back from my chest, carefully at first, the fingertips sliding cleanly under the raw, parted edges; and then more savagely, tugging and tearing until, looking down, I saw my entire rib-cage laid bare, its contents glistening in the attenuated light. I watched helplessly as the hands reached in and fastened on what looked like a small black coal, easing it gently out between the ribs; and knowing that this was my heart, I lunged forward to snatch it back. But hands and heart withdrew or, more accurately, effaced themselves; and as they faded, I heard a grieving voice ring out through the darkening waste. Lost, it cried, or gone, or perhaps some other word; monosyllabic certainly, but deeply resonant, setting my stripped frame vibrating in mournful response.

And thinking about it now, it occurs to me that the voice might well have been my own, echoing through the house as I started up with my drenched nightshirt tight as a winding-sheet around my body. What else would have brought Mrs Haskell hurrying to my door? I can see her there, framed in the doorway, one hand clutching a frayed woollen shawl about her shoulders and the other holding up a flickering candle, her eyes wide in her round face.

Nothing of what followed is as distinct as that luminous image. I suppose, since I remember sitting slumped in the chair while something went on around me, that Mrs Haskell changed my sheets; and I am tolerably certain that a conversation of some kind took place between us, though I am unable to recall a single word of it. More vaguely still, I have the impression of having sensed, as I sank back into sleep and the fever took hold again, that whatever I was dealing with had only just begun its work on me.

16

When I try to reconstruct the events of the succeeding days and nights, I find myself at something of a loss. Many of my memories have proved, in the light of subsequent knowledge or sober examination, to be imaginary constructs or, in some cases, misinterpretations of actual occurrences, while others were apparently authentic; the problem has been to distinguish between the two. Talking at length with Banks during my convalescence, discreetly questioning Mrs Haskell, I was able eventually to make some kind of sense of it all; but engaging once again with that welter of fragmented and equivocal impressions, I can hardly avoid registering something of my original confusion or acknowledging areas of continuing uncertainty.

The exercise of reason may give us some grip on our illusions but it cannot entirely dispel them. I know now, for example, that my father was never at my bedside and that our argument could not have taken place; but I can still recall with disquieting clarity my own frenzy of impotent rage as he hauled me head foremost from the bed, his looming face expressing anger and disappointment by turns, his stick raised as though to beat me. 'I'm not a child,' I cried over and over again, 'I'm not a child.' But for much of the period in question that is precisely what I was; and I still flush with shame at the thought of Mrs Haskell's breast pressed to my mouth, the nipple swelling against my teeth and tongue. For days afterwards I retained the most acute apprehension of that moment – the expansive pressure, the sweetness at the back of my throat, my own greedy nuzzling – so that I was obliged to remind myself, as Mrs Haskell herself entered the room with my tray or stooped over me to rearrange the blankets, that our perverse intimacy had been nothing more than the invention of a fevered mind.

And what of Banks, sitting quietly beside my bed night after night, often still in his chair at dawn, jotting down at my dictation in a fat leather-bound notebook the startling insights which, it seemed to me, needed only to be properly ordered for the meaning and purpose of human existence to be revealed? Yes, he told me later, he had visited on a number of occasions, sometimes for an hour or more at a time, and I might well have seen him there as I gabbled and moaned, thrusting back the sheets, sporadically attempting to rise; but the notebook, I learned with a pang of unreasonable sadness, did not exist.

And then there are the areas of total blankness, gaps in my knowledge of real events. I remember nothing of the storms which, I gather, battered the region for three days on end shortly after the onset of my illness, nothing of Redbourne's visit; and though I was able, with Banks's assistance, to retrieve and reconstruct much of what he referred to as my midnight excursion, a number of crucial details remain tantalizingly obscure.

To begin with, I simply do not know how I got to the church. I mean, I assume that I must have taken my usual route, cutting through the meadow and diagonally across the churchyard; but I have no recollection of that particular journey. Was I not cold, stepping out barefoot across the frosted grass, my coat, as I now understand, thrown over my nightshirt but apparently unbuttoned, my bedside lamp in my hand? What was in my mind as I pushed back the door and made my way, as I must have done, down the aisle towards the chancel arch?

This extraordinary blankness is the more surprising to me in that many details of my involuntary visitation are remarkably clear or, if not exactly clear, powerfully present in my memory. I remember, for example, standing beneath the scaffold, holding the lamp above my head, disconcerted and I think frustrated by the feebleness of its glow in that hushed space. Yes, and the piers immediately to left and right of me glimmering faintly against a ground of shifting and indeterminate shadow; the deeper shades beyond that; and the sudden dizziness I experienced as I lifted my eyes to the impenetrable obscurity above me.

I remember, too, that my legs trembled as I climbed the ladder, so that I was obliged to stop as I reached the top, my free hand gripping the guard-rail, before heaving myself clumsily and with rather greater difficulty than I had antici-pated on to the platform. I stumbled forward and fell heavily to my knees, jarring the boards, the sound echoing through the nave like thunder.

But here I find another gap. I can see myself there on my knees, the lamp beside and a little behind me so that my own shadow bobs and flutters across the painted figures. I can see the woman's agonized stare, her chalky lips framing their soundless cry; the pale expanse of swelling flesh and the dark insinuation of the body at her back. But where did I get the – chisel, is it, or gouge? – with which, with savage, sweeping strokes, I am scoring the decorated surface, slashing at breasts and belly, at the long throat and the tilted face? Did I bring the implement with me, in my coat pocket perhaps, or did it come accidentally to hand as I knelt there on the dusty boards? And what did I think I was about as I dragged the blade backwards and forwards across the disintegrating mortar, my hands and wrists aching and showered with dust? I surmise now that, feverishly confused and with my mind running obsessively on the work, I was misguidedly attempting to prepare the surface for re-rendering; but this doesn't seem to me to explain either the ferocity of my actions – I remember grunting and sobbing like a madman, breathless with effort, the sweat stinging my eyes – or the peculiar sense of anxiety that accompanied them. There is something here which eludes me; and this part of the episode seems in any case to be overshadowed by what happened after I upset the lamp.

Perhaps I struck it with my foot, or with the skirts of my coat. I have, in fact, very little sense of how it might have happened, but I retain the most vivid impression of its leisurely, uneven roll to the edge of the boards and its long fall into the shadows below. It hit the floor with a metallic chime; then the globe splintered and flew in all directions while what was left of the oil flared and sputtered at the base of the scaffold.

My fear at that stage was straightforward and essentially rational: I imagined the flames licking upward, the crackle and roar as they took hold of the timbers, my own body caught in the conflagration. I grasped one of the uprights and leaned out over the guard-rail, the blood rushing to my head as I craned forward and down; but as I did so the flames subsided and went out.

I find it difficult to analyse the terror of that moment. I have never had any particular anxiety about heights and in normal circumstances the twenty or so feet above which I hung, my right hand gripping the rough wood of the upright, would have caused me no concern. But in that blank intensity of darkness I seemed to float above – no, not above, since that suggests precisely the grasp of spatial relationship which, at that moment, utterly deserted me. I mean that there was, quite simply, nothing out there, nothing at all; and, more terrifying still, that my own presence, extending interminably into the blackness or irresistibly infiltrated by it, was itself in doubt. I can still feel the convulsive effort with which I jerked myself back from the edge. I groped my way over to the wall where, with my shoulders pressed hard against the plaster and one elbow on the side-rail, I spent what seemed an extraordinary length of time fumbling for my matches before realizing that I had none.

That was the point at which I began to shake. More terrible than anything I had experienced out on the hillside, this was a shuddering which gripped my entire body, forcing itself up and through me from some unfathomable centre, transmitting itself to the rocking boards so that I felt, or seemed to feel, the whole structure in motion beneath me. I eased myself down the wall, whimpering, moaning, crying upon a Maker whose very existence was called into question by the formless darkness around me, and began to crawl forward, groping my way towards the ladder.

What checked me was the notion that I might fall – fall, I thought with a spasm of redoubled terror, and go on falling. Or that the ladder might descend, like that in the mural, to the depths of – but again, that misses the point. For the world I envisaged as I lay huddled on the boards, knees drawn up to my belly, hands locked together at the nape of my neck, was not illuminated by hellfire or inhabited by demons; nor was it home to any suffering spirit but my own. No, the ladder, if it existed at all, would descend for ever, through undifferentiated darkness, and whatever vestigial scrap of consciousness or selfhood clung there would, of necessity, be obliterated. I recognize now, of course, the sheer absurdity of all this, the blind irrationality into which my illness had plunged me; but the illusion presented itself to me at the time with such compelling force that I could do nothing but lie where I was. I was not waiting for anything: I am fairly certain that the idea of the eventual approach of daylight never so much as entered my head. I was simply incapable of movement.

How long did I lie there before the light returned? Not daylight, for the clerestory windows were still dark, but a yellow glow stealing up from below, making me think at first, quite illogically, that the fire had, after all, taken hold. I lifted my head. Footsteps. A crunching of broken glass. Banks's voice.

'Who's there?'

I wanted to answer but was unable to do so. My mouth worked, but soundlessly, my own name dissolving off my tongue. I rolled over and peered down into the nave. Banks lifted his lantern and looked up, his angular face lit like a saint's.

'Is that you, Stannard? What are you doing here?'

I shook my head helplessly. I remember his expression darkening suddenly, his abrupt movement to the foot of the scaffold.

'Are you hurt? Can you get down?'

I raised myself to my hands and knees and shuffled forward. I have a particularly strong recollection of manoeuvring myself into position above the ladder, my left knee on the platform supporting my weight, my right leg extended and feeling for the rungs. I am thinking or muttering to myself: it's all right, it's all right. But it is patently not all right because my body is heavy and unresponsive and, although my right foot finds what it is looking for, my left leg refuses to move. I cannot look down, but I feel Banks clambering up the ladder below me, feel his hand gripping my right heel.

'Now bring your other leg down. I'm supporting you.'

I bowed my head, pressing my cheek against the upright. I am not sure whether, from where he stood, Banks was able to see, let alone interpret, the gesture, but he must have realized very quickly that he would need to do more for me. A moment later he was at my back, coaxing, bullying, one hand grasping the top of the ladder, the other tapping and tugging at my left foot until, quite unexpectedly, I found myself able to move it. He positioned himself more securely behind me, still talking, encircling me protectively with his arms and body as I recall my father doing on the first occasion he allowed me to help with the apple-picking. After that it was easier. Even now I did not look down; but I kept going, hand and foot, hand and foot, determinedly focused on the grain of the rungs before my eyes, on their pressure against my instep, until I stood at last on solid ground.

I say solid, but that wasn't the impression I had as I hesitated there at the foot of the ladder, unsteady as a man newly disembarked from a rough crossing, feeling the floor shift and slide beneath me. I was acutely aware of Banks's gaze, though I avoided meeting it.

'What's going on, Stannard?'

'Nothing.' My voice rose unrecognizably thin and childish from my lips and was lost in the dim space above us. I felt like a small boy apprehended in an act of mischief which had got out of hand. 'Nothing,' I repeated stupidly, 'nothing.' I closed my eyes and leaned heavily against the scaffolding.

He was running his hand across my forehead, touching my cheeks with his knuckles. Opening my eyes again, I saw his face disconcertingly close to mine, his brows puckered with anxiety.

'You're still sick,' he said. 'Very sick. I must get you back to your lodgings. Do you think you can walk?'

He appeared to consider my silence carefully, as though it were an answer. Then he picked up his lantern, moved round to my side, drew me gently away from the scaffold and, half guiding, half supporting, walked me up the aisle and out of the church.

Was Mrs Haskell there as we mounted the stairs to my bedroom? I have a faint sense of her presence at the stairhead – holding a lamp, perhaps, opening a door – though I imagine she must have left it to Banks to attend to me. My feet, I seem to remember, were bleeding, cut, it may have been, by fragments of the shattered globe. I have a memory of Banks stooping over the end of my bed, dabbing at my soles with a wet cloth. His face is tense and, brightly lit from the side, appears vaguely distorted. But the images come and go; and this particular manifestation is, I realize as I struggle to call it up again in all its hallucinatory brilliance, neither more nor less real to me than the stunted figure which, after the lamp had been extinguished, lunged towards me out of the darkness screaming a single, terrible word; a word which, though it eludes me now, seemed at the time to encapsulate all I had ever experienced of emptiness and loss.

17

Banks was later to intimate that Mrs Haskell's care of me during my illness had been exemplary, and I am certainly not ungrateful; but I am not sure that my convalescence was assisted by her continued presence at my bedside. She would sit there hour after hour in the wicker chair, her embroidery draped over her knees, stitching and talking. One anecdote after another, while I drifted between sleep and waking, catching at whatever fragments presented themselves during my more lucid intervals.

'. . . but every night she'd shriek and howl, beating on the door with her fists, keeping the whole neighbourhood awake with her din. In the end they hit upon the idea of burying the body in a new grave somewhere beyond the village—'

'You've already told me this story, Mrs Haskell.'

'Maybe I have. When they got to the place they'd fixed on, they laid the thing down on the ground, still in its sailcloth shroud, and began to dig. And as they lifted the turf they heard a wailing from the marshes, a queer mournful sound coming and going on the wind. And Cassie's great-grandpa looked at the rector and saw his face as pale as death in the light of the lantern—'

'The rector wasn't there, Mrs Haskell.'

'How do you know?'

'You told me it was the sexton who went out with the girl's father.'

'What if I did? They tell this more ways than one.'

'But you must realize that only one version can be true.'

She paused in her stitching and gave me a sly sidelong glance.

'I'm surprised you should think either of them's true, Mr Stannard, but if you want the sexton you shall have him. White with fear he was, and shaking like a leaf; but he picked up the bundle and the two of them followed the sound, stepping from tussock to tussock, working their way slowly down to the estuary. And when they came to the water's edge they saw them gathered there, swimming a little way out, lifting their faces to the moon and crying, with their mouths wide open – and their mouths are like fishes' mouths, Mr Stannard, with hard bony lips – and their faces shining with tears and brine. When they saw the two men most of them scattered and dived; but one swam steadily towards them, completely silent now, until it touched land. Then it hauled itself up on to the mud and lay there, with its arm stretched out like this' – she extended her left hand towards me, palm upward – 'and with its head thrown back so that its cold eyes stared straight up at them. It wants the body, said Cassie's great-grandpa. So the sexton stepped forward and squatted down, holding out the bundle at arm's length, not liking to get too close but not wanting to show disrespect by dropping or throwing the thing. And as he did so, the creature lunged out and snatched it from him – and as long as he lived he never forgot the touch of its hand – and then turned and wriggled back into the water, slick as an eel.'

She tilted her embroidery towards the window and screwed up her eyes. 'I used to be able to see every stitch,' she said. 'Even by lamplight. Nowadays I can't really be sure of the details. Does this look all right to you?'

She leaned over, holding out her work. I made a show of examining it.

'It's excellent, Mrs Haskell. I wonder if I might ask you to draw the curtains when you leave.'

'Are you tired?'

'Very tired.'

'Don't you want to hear the rest of the story?'

'I thought you'd finished.'

'Not quite. As it swam back, the others rose to the surface and clustered around it. There was a terrible stillness, as if they were waiting for something. Then the creature lifted the bundle high above its head and they all began to sing, their voices softer than before and the sound so sweet and sad that the men couldn't keep from crying. At last the whole group drew off, heading for the open sea; and as the singing died away the men stumbled back across the marshland, still crying like children. And that was really the end of the business, except that—'

'I'm sorry, Mrs Haskell. I must sleep now.'

'Lift your head a moment.' She placed her embroidery on the blanket-chest and bent over me to rearrange the pillows. Soap and camphor, the crisp rustle of starched cloth; her wrist, plump and lightly downed, closer to my face than I cared for.

'There's no need,' I said.

'Did your mother never do this for you when you were a child?'

'Possibly. But my childhood's long past.'

'Or tell you stories?'

'I don't believe so.'

'She should have done.'

I think the light touch of her hand on my cheek was accidental, but I jerked back my head involuntarily. She straightened up and retrieved her embroidery.

'Mr Banks visited this morning,' she said. 'While you were asleep. He said he'd call again later.'

'I've no wish for company.'

'He's been a good friend to you in your illness, Mr Stannard, and I hope you'll keep that in mind.'

I pressed my head back into the pillows and closed my eyes.

'The curtains, if you don't mind, Mrs Haskell.'

She pulled them to and left me to myself in the darkness.

I had reckoned without the sheer boredom of a protracted convalescence. By the beginning of the following week, tired both of my own thoughts and of Mrs Haskell's mindless prattle, I had come to anticipate Banks's regular visits with something approaching pleasure. Never, in my view, an entirely engaging conversationalist, he nevertheless brought with him a welcome sense of life going on somewhere beyond the confines of my sickroom, and I was able to use our talks as a means of re-establishing contact with a world which had, I felt, almost slipped from my grasp.

'What about the work?' I asked him one evening.

'At a standstill until you return. Harris finished hacking out the rotted plaster from the north wall, but said he'd do nothing more without your instructions.'

'And Jefford?'

'Jefford's condition seems to have worsened again. He hasn't been out of the house for more than a week.'

'Have they said anything about their wages?'

'Not to me. Do you want me to convey any message to them?'

I shook my head. 'I'll speak to them myself,' I said.

Banks looked searchingly into my face.

'You know it will be quite some time before you'll be well enough to start work again? Dr Barratt was very clear on that point.'

'How long?'

'Another fortnight. Maybe more.'

'Nonsense,' I said. 'I shall be back by the end of the week.'

Brave words; but the following afternoon, making my way down to the living-room for the first time since the onset of my illness, I knew I had overestimated myself. Even with Banks's support, the descent took several minutes, and by the time I slumped into my armchair I was dizzy and breathless, fit for nothing. Banks fussed busily around me, plumping cushions, adjusting the position of my footstool.

'Do you want me to fetch down a blanket?' he asked.

I was on the point of protesting that he was treating me like an invalid when it struck me that that was precisely what I was.

'No,' I said. 'No blanket.'

'A drink?'

'No. I shall be comfortable as I am for the moment. In any case, I can hardly expect you to go on ministering to my needs for the next fortnight.'

'Oh,' he said quickly, 'don't worry about that. But I've been wondering whether you might want to return home for a week or two once you're well enough to travel. These rooms are perfectly adequate in normal circumstances, of course, but while you're convalescing . . .'

'I should be no better off in my own rooms. Perhaps worse.'

'But you must have family?'

'My father. I don't visit very often.'

'It's often salutary in times of difficulty to remind ourselves of our parents' love for us. The family home – the place in which we were most fully aware of that love – can be a tremendous source of sustenance. Go back for a few days at least. Your father's care may be exactly what you need.'

The distorted face, the rough hands dragging me from the

bed, the stick raised above me. Only a fever-dream, I reminded myself.

'I'll consider it,' I said. 'Listen, I've been meaning to ask you about the doom. When I try to remember what happened, I find that I'm not entirely sure – I mean, the dreams seemed so real, and other things so questionable. Did I—?'

'Don't trouble yourself about it now, Stannard. You were sick.'

'Very sick, I know. And lucky not to have harmed myself.'

'Lucky? Well, perhaps. I've given a great deal of thought to the incident, and I've come to feel that I was witness to the workings of a force far more powerful and mysterious than anything implied by your formulation.'

'I was speaking loosely. Let's say, if you prefer, that your arrival on the scene was providential.'

He drew up a chair and sat down opposite me, his brow furrowed as though he had been confronted with some intractable problem.

'You have to remember the hour, Stannard – nearly two in the morning. I should normally have been asleep – indeed, I had been asleep for some time, but something – a dream, a sensation, I don't know – woke me with a start so violent that I was out of bed before I knew clearly what I was doing. I remember lighting a candle; and as I watched the flame brighten, I felt – really, it was quite extraordinary: such an overpowering sense of danger, with not the slightest clue as to the nature of the threat. Intruders? The house was silent, but the notion seemed as plausible as any. I took the candlestick from the table and made my way downstairs; and as I rounded the turn above the hallway, I caught sight of your lamp through the fanlight over the door. And what haunts me is the delicate precision of the patterning. Think about it, Stannard: a little sphere of light, framed in that small, clear space for – what? – five seconds at most, as you made your way across the field; and me at the only point in my descent from which I could possibly have glimpsed it. That's something more than luck, wouldn't you say?'

Banks seemed, as so often, to be making a metaphysical mountain out of a rather insignificant molehill but it would have been churlish, in the circumstances, to have pointed this out to him. I felt it best to say nothing.

'Not that I realized at the time, of course, what was afoot. I checked the doors and windows and searched the downstairs rooms; and it wasn't until I was back in my bedroom that I began to think carefully about what I'd seen. Not the gleam of a lantern, but the softer incandescence of an oil-lamp. That was odd, and the more I thought about it, the more apparent it became that I should have to investigate. I dressed and went down again –'

I was momentarily distracted by a series of sharp knocks from below. I heard Mrs Haskell shuffle through the hall and open the front door.

'– prints plainly visible in the frost. When I reached the church, I saw at once that the door was ajar, and I naturally – are you expecting visitors, Stannard?'

Footsteps on the stairs; a man's voice. And then Mrs Haskell peering round the door.

'Mr Redbourne to see you.'

I glanced at Banks. Just a faint tightening of the muscles around the mouth, a narrowing of the eyes; but rising to greet Redbourne, he was already clearly preparing to leave. Redbourne, for his part, barely acknowledged the rector before addressing himself to me. 'How are you feeling now, Stannard?'

'Not as strong as I'd like. But the fever's gone.'

Banks reached the door before Mrs Haskell had finished closing it.

'I must go,' he said. 'I've work to do. I'll call by again at the same time tomorrow.'

He gave a brusque nod and followed Mrs Haskell downstairs. Redbourne settled himself in the chair and stretched his hands to the fire.

'It's good of you to call,' I said.

'I visited earlier, when I first learned of your illness.'

'So Mrs Haskell told me. I've no recollection of the occasion myself.'

'You were delirious. We spoke at some length but I couldn't help feeling,' – he permitted himself a tight-lipped smile – 'that you'd mistaken me for someone else. I tried to reassure you that I had no designs whatsoever on your soul, but you seemed unconvinced.'

'There were dreams . . . Did I say anything else?'

'A great deal, none of it either coherent or memorable. As you probably realize, I've none of Banks's patience with the sick, and it seemed sensible to leave you to his tender mercies until you'd recovered your capacity for rational discourse. Now, it strikes me, you may need other company: a man can take only so much solicitude, only so much high-minded forgiveness.'

'Forgiveness?'

'The doom. You presumably know—'

'Seriously damaged?'

'Ruined. Apparently Banks took it very badly at first, moping around the church or walking up and down the lane outside, latching on to passers-by like some latter-day ancient mariner with his mournful tale of damage and desecration. And there's no doubt that he blamed you for the business.'

'It was the fever. I didn't know what I was doing.'

'He realized that, I'm sure. But sick or sound, he said at one point, it makes no difference: the man's actions – yours, he meant – are all of a piece. Even at that time he was visiting you regularly, of course, but with a look on his face which suggested that the milk of human kindness had turned decidedly sour. And then, quite suddenly according to Mrs Haskell, he let the whole lot go – tiles, pews, stained glass, doom – as if none of it mattered any more. The power of prayer, Mrs Haskell says; and who are we to doubt it?'

The question, unemphatic, faintly ironic, hung in the air between us for a moment, and then he was off on a new tack – some personal preoccupation with estate boundaries – leaving me to follow as best I could. I tried to maintain my side of the conversation, but my eyelids were heavy and I found it difficult to concentrate.

'You're tired, Stannard.'

'A little, yes.'

'More than a little, by the look of you. Let me help you back to your bed.'

'Thank you, but I'll stay down here for a while. Mrs Haskell will give me any help I need.'

'As you wish,' he said, 'but don't overtax your strength. Take good care of yourself now and you'll be back on your feet all the sooner. And when you are' – he rose abruptly from his chair – 'you must come and visit me again. Any time you like. I shall look forward to seeing you.'

I nodded my thanks as he left; but at that particular moment I could no more envisage myself walking out to the Hall than flying there.

18

If Banks had not been so persistent in his argument and so eager to make the necessary arrangements, I should no doubt have completed my convalescence in Mrs Haskell's house; but he seemed unable to relinquish the idea that a period spent with my father would speed my recovery and, after a few days of rather feeble resistance, I let him talk me round.

I had, in fact, reason of my own for falling in with his proposal. I wanted to see a reputable physician. Not Barratt, who had struck me, on the single occasion I had attempted to discuss my progress with him, as the worst kind of country quack, at once ignorant and opinionated; but a practitioner with whom I could talk on terms of equality, man to man.

A reputable physician? Yes, of course; but what I wanted above all else was one who had no connection with the life of the village. It was not – or not primarily – my recent fever that I wished to discuss, but a matter of greater delicacy. I had not anticipated any danger from a girl barely entering womanhood and reared, as I knew her to have been, in rural seclusion; yet symptoms that had developed in the fever's aftermath had forced me to entertain a possibility which, whenever it presented itself, made me sick with anxiety and shame.

By the morning of my departure my strength had increased significantly, and it was perhaps a mark of my improvement that I now found myself faintly irritated by Banks's ministrations. He helped me to pack my valise, hovered attentively at my side as I made my way down to the front door, settled me into the glorified farm wagon he had hired to convey me to the station; and I should not have been entirely surprised if he had offered to accompany me there.

'Make sure you keep warm,' he said, taking a filthy travelling-rug from the seat beside me and spreading it across my knees.

'Thank you, Banks. I shall be comfortable enough.'

'If you need help at the station, Wardle' – he indicated the driver – 'will look after you.' Wardle turned and gave me what he must have imagined to be an encouraging smile. Banks reached out and grasped my hand.

'Have a safe journey,' he said. 'And don't return until you're ready.'

'I shall be back next week.'

Wardle clicked his tongue softly against his palate and the wagon began to move.

My father refrained from commenting on my condition until the third evening of my stay. We were seated at the table and the maid had just ladled a thin fish soup from the tureen. As she leaned over to place my bowl in front of me, the smell rose to my nostrils with such overpowering intensity that I gagged and averted my face, clapping the linen napkin to my mouth and nose. The maid started back. My father looked at me with a mixture of disgust and concern.

'Just how sick – that will be all for the moment, thank you, Muriel – just how sick are you?'

I shook my head and pushed away the bowl, careful to avoid looking too closely at its contents.

'Have you seen a doctor?'

'Not yet.'

'You should let someone examine you. Shall I send for Holcombe?'

'No.' I leaned back in my chair and folded my napkin. 'No thank you. I'll see my own doctor.'

'But that will mean a journey into town.'

'I've already arranged it. In any case, I need to call in at my office to see how matters stand there. I shall go tomorrow.'

'Very well.' He picked a bone from his soup and placed it on the rim of his bowl. 'Are you sure you won't have any of this? It's not one of Mrs Ford's better efforts, I admit, but you need to eat if you're to recover your strength. I've not seen you like this since you had scarlet fever as a child.'

'Thank you, but I'm more in need of rest than food. Will you excuse me?'

His deafness had evidently worsened since my previous visit. He made no reply, but looked up irritably as I rose and left the room.

I slept fitfully and woke unrefreshed. The walk to the station chilled me through, and I was still shivering as I stepped off the train and made my way through the back-streets towards the office. Aaron, seizing me by the hand as he opened the door to me, commented at once on my coldness and pallor. 'And you've lost weight,' he added, leading me through to the back room. 'You've not been looking after yourself, John. Finish the job and get back to civilization as soon as you can.'

'I may well have to stay out there for a couple of months yet. You were right, of course; I should have turned down the work.'

'You had your reasons, I know. And it was a slack time for us. Since you've been gone, though . . .' He hesitated, as though searching for an appropriate form of words.

'Since I've been gone?'

'Well, things seem to have taken a turn for the better. Look, I've got something to show you.'

He strode over to his desk and with a triumphant flourish swung the drawing-board round to face me. I stared at the plan for a moment, slowly absorbing its detail.

'Have we actually secured this?' I asked at last.

'More or less. They've asked for a few modifications – that's what I'm doing now – but they've left me in no doubt that the contract will be ours.'

'How long have you been working on this?'

'Three weeks on and off. Maybe a month.'

'But this is a major undertaking. We agreed that you'd keep me informed of any significant developments. I've not heard from you since the beginning of November.'

'I've been busy. Not only with this project – there are several others in the offing. I've scarcely had a minute—'

I pushed past him and stood by the hearth, spreading my hands to the fire.

'Not even to write a letter?'

'I'd planned to give you a full account of this and other recent developments in a week or so, when I forwarded the new contract for your signature.' He flashed me one of his dazzling smiles. 'I'd intended it as a surprise.'

'A surprise? This is a business enterprise, Aaron, not a schoolboy game. I've no time for such silliness.'

He flushed deeply, half turning to the window, the smile fading from his face; then he swung round again and slammed his open hand down on the drawing-board.

'Is this silliness?' he demanded. 'Or this?' He reached across the desk and dragged a bulky file towards him, scattering papers. 'This correspondence – no, I want you to look at it – this correspondence represents a new phase in our development. Negotiations are at an early stage, but if even half of these proposals are taken up – and I have reason to suppose that the proportion will actually be rather higher than that – we'll have enough work to keep us busy for the next three years. And before those three years are up, my reputation – I mean ours, of course – will be sufficiently well established to ensure continuity. I believe we shall be in a position to expand the firm significantly within five years. You're right in one respect: I should have communicated all this to you earlier, and I'm willing to apologize for not having done so. But I'll not allow you to accuse me of silliness. I've never been more serious about anything in my life, or more confident of achieving my aims.'

For as long as I have known him Aaron has been prone to bouts of febrile and frankly unjustifiable enthusiasm, and my role in the partnership has generally been to hold in check what I have tended to regard as the excesses of a brilliant but undisciplined mind. Leafing through the correspondence as he paced excitedly about the room, I realized that he had, in my absence, seriously compromised the restrained professionalism that has always seemed to me to be the mainstay of any respectable business enterprise. I twitched a letter from the file and held it out to him.

'Did you actually send this?'

He peered short-sightedly at it, his neck twisted at an angle.

'Of course. I may have refined one or two of the phrases in my final draft but it's essentially—'

'Listen to me, Aaron. I've spent years – literally years – cultivating Oliver Drewett's acquaintance and, latterly, interest, and you send him this. Drewett is not merely a figure of considerable distinction but a sensitive and discerning man. Can you imagine the kind of impression such a letter would be likely to make on him?'

Aaron was lapsing into the defensive surliness with which he so often responds to my advice and guidance.

'A very favourable impression, I should think. Have you looked at his reply?'

'We can't go around touting for custom like common tradesmen.'

'So you've always said. But it's becoming increasingly clear to me that we can't sit about for ever in the hope that our discreet integrity will one day have clients beating a path to our door. The world doesn't work like that, John, and we can't make any headway until we acknowledge the fact.'

'Once a firm descends to an unseemly scrabbling for custom, it loses the respect not only of potential clients but also of existing ones.'

'I asked whether you'd looked at Drewett's reply. It might dispel some of your anxieties.'

'I don't wish to read his reply, nor would it help me to do so. My point is a general one concerning the conduct and reputation of this firm. In future I want to see all significant correspondence before you send it out. Is that understood?'

He said nothing. My whole body, I realized, was trembling with rage or weakness, my mind faintly hazed by the dizziness that had afflicted me periodically since my illness. Thinking for a moment that I might fall, I stepped over to my desk and pulled back the chair, only to find it piled high with papers.

'What are these?' My voice was thick with anger.

'More correspondence. Sketches. Notes. I've been meaning to put it all away but I haven't had the time. Since you were away there seemed no harm—'

'And these plans on my desk?'

'I wasn't expecting you. I could clear the whole lot in twenty minutes if you want. It's such a small matter. Why are you so upset?' He seemed genuinely perplexed, frowning at me like a troubled child.

'Not upset, Aaron. Simply aware – as you yourself have never been – of the need for a degree of discipline in life. The world has a natural tendency to disorder; the mark of a man of character is his resistance to that tendency. Look at this' –

I picked a wad of unopened letters from the floor and flung it on to his desk – 'and this. This is my chair, Aaron, my working space. Learning to respect the boundaries of other people's territory might prove a useful starting-point when you eventually decide to impose order on your own.'

He reached out and gently patted my arm, a gesture more patronizing, I felt, than placatory.

'Let's not quarrel about this,' he said. 'Will you sit down for a moment?'

I glanced at my chair.

'Please.' He pulled his own chair forward and offered it to me. 'There's more to tell you. Look at this.'

He pulled another letter from the file on his desk and handed it to me. More of the same, I thought, suddenly afflicted by a wave of nausea and quite unable to concentrate either on the letter itself or on Aaron's exposition of its details. He showed no sign of having noticed my indisposition. I sat back and let him jabber on for twenty minutes or so, excitable, self-engrossed, his eyes blazing in his flushed face as he talked; then, with a careful formality which I hoped might function in some subtle way as a warning, I took my leave of him and let myself out into the street.

The surgery was less than ten minutes' brisk walk from the office, but I had made insufficient allowance for the debilitating effects of my illness and I arrived breathless and a little late, to find Dr Freeman waiting for me.

He helped me out of my coat and hung it on a stand behind the door.

'Still the same problem with your shoulders, I see.'

'Is it so obvious?'

'To anyone used to observing the human body, yes.' He motioned me to sit down. 'A doctor – a good doctor, I mean – becomes acutely sensitive to nuances of posture and movement. I've only to see you easing your shoulders out of your coat to know that the stiffness is still there and, I should imagine, increasing.'

'Yes, it's been particularly bad recently. But that's not what I came to see you about. I've been away for a while, working in conditions which – well, the reasons don't matter, but a few weeks ago I contracted an illness. A high fever – sweats, delirium, my whole body invaded. I was lost for days.'

'Lost?' He took my wrist and placed a finger on my pulse.

'I didn't know where I was. On one occasion—'

'You're not feverish now.'

'No, but my appetite's poor, and the slightest exertion—'

'The natural effects of a natural process. I could give you a full examination if you wish, but it's apparent to me that the illness itself has passed. You're in a weakened state, certainly, but I've no reason to doubt that your appetite and energies will be restored in time. You might take this tonic' – he sat down and scribbled briefly on a small scrap of paper – 'but don't regard it as a substitute for the period of rest your body really needs. Will your work allow that?'

'I'm staying with my father at present. I plan to spend a further week there.'

'Ideally I'd recommend longer, but a week should set you on the right track.'

He reached across the desk and handed me the prescription. I folded it carefully and leaned back in my chair.

'And what else would you like to discuss with me, Mr Stannard?'

'Nothing else. Whatever makes you think—?' I stopped, conscious of the rush of blood to my neck and cheeks. He narrowed his eyes and scanned my face thoughtfully before resuming.

'You're surprised; but think about it for a moment. Just as

a certain physiological imbalance can be inferred from the set
of your shoulders, so your behaviour provides clues to other
forms of unease. You can have no idea how often a patient
will come to what appears to be the end of a consultation yet
remain seated, exactly as you are now, displaying the most
remarkable reluctance to leave. It's not difficult to deduce in
such cases that something has been left unsaid, and I usually
find that the unarticulated problem is – from the patient's
point of view at least – the truly significant one. So let me
press you on the matter: what aspect of your health do you
most – or least – wish to discuss with me?'

He placed the tips of his fingers together and smiled, his
gaunt face softening, and it suddenly occurred to me that I
might tell him everything. It was not simply a discussion of
my symptoms that I envisaged at that moment – the vague
discomfort on making water, the perpetual sense of heat and
fullness in the affected area – but a laying bare of the whole
shameful affair; and for a second or two I entertained the
absurd notion that I might feel those long fingers laid on my
forehead in a priestly gesture of healing and absolution.

'There's nothing,' I said, rising abruptly from my chair.
'Nothing at all.'

He removed his spectacles and placed them gently on the
desk. I thought he might question me further, half hoped that
he would; but he walked over to the stand and, without
another word, reached down my coat.

The rain was falling heavily as I stepped into the street,
great stinging drops driven by a vicious wind. I walked
quickly, head down, making directly for the station, but
as I turned the corner into Wheeler Street, I found my way
blocked. I pushed forward impatiently, shouldering a passage
through the crowd, and it was only when I reached the space
at its centre that I realized what was going on.

The dray's wheels still spinning; barrels scattered over the gleaming cobbles; the horse lying across the broken shaft, its neck and head in the running gutter. I remember the lips drawn back from the yellow teeth, the wild rolling of the eyes as it tried desperately to lift its head clear of the water. But it is, above all, the woman who stands out for me. I can see her now, squatting beside the creature, one hand on its straining neck as the drayman cuts away the harness, her skirts spread around her, soaking up the roadside filth. Her companion hovers over her, a well-dressed and distinguished figure, clearly embarrassed, urging her to leave. They will be late, he is saying, look at the state of her clothes, she can do nothing for the animal. But she stays put, her face shining with tears and rain; and only when the huge body is finally still does she allow herself to be led away.

What was it about that scene – about the woman – which held me there, which holds me now? She was not obviously beautiful: a woman of rather conventional appearance, perhaps in her mid-forties, inclining to plumpness; her features too round and soft to be considered striking. But there was something about her face and her attitude as she squatted there, not exactly oblivious to the agitation around her but untouched by it, a spot of clear, uncompromised intensity focused like light through a convex lens. The drayman grunts and curses, the knife-blade squeaks against the taut leather of the harness, men shout advice or press forward, gripping the spokes, the sides, the unbroken shaft; the dray rocks and crashes back on to its wheels. But all that stir and bustle is an irrelevance. What matters is the quiet face, bowed a little as though in prayer or meditation, the extended arm, the firm white hand – and I felt the pressure of the palm as though I myself were the recipient of that incomprehensible grace – laid on the beast's shuddering neck. I remember starting towards her as she rose to leave, thinking I might – that I might speak with her perhaps – I don't quite know what I had in mind. But even in my susceptible and no doubt slightly irrational state I was able to recognize the absurdity of the impulse, and I simply watched as she took her companion's arm, stepped into the crowd and was lost to sight.

19

In the event, I stayed at my father's house for almost a fortnight. Not that I was entirely comfortable there – far from it – but once ensconced in my old room and caught up in the familiar domestic routines, I found it peculiarly difficult to contemplate leaving.

My physical condition continued to improve, but I was in a delicate state of mind, edgy, restless and easily roused to extremes of emotion by the most banal objects or events. I would stop repeatedly in my tracks as I walked around the garden or through the meadows behind the house, drawn to the shine on the wet box leaves perhaps, or the reflection of the sedges on the agitated surface of the dew pond. I was obsessed by the intricate detail of things: the whorls of a snail shell, the dark seeds in the split laburnum pods, the lichens crusting the garden wall. I remember standing beneath a tree contemplating a shrivelled apple as though it were a work of art, before peeling the bark from one of the twigs with my thumbnail and sniffing the moist white wood. It was a kind of hunger I experienced then, a profound longing which, however long I stared, however deeply I inhaled, I was unable to satisfy; and I would pass on at last with a faint sense of disappointment, a troubled awareness of something simultaneously intimated and withheld.

I might have stayed on even longer if my father had not taken a stand on the matter, confronting me one evening after dinner in a manner which made it clear I had outstayed such welcome as he had felt able to extend to me. Throughout the meal he had barely acknowledged my presence, but as Muriel withdrew with the dishes he leaned towards me, fixing me with the challenging stare I had associated in childhood with the gaze of God himself.

'I take it you have plans to return to your work in the near future, John?'

'As soon as I'm well, yes.'

'You look well enough to me. Still a little peaky, perhaps, but I can't imagine that it would do you any harm to set your shoulder to the wheel again. On the contrary, I suspect that nothing would do you more good at this stage.'

'I'm strong enough, I suppose. But I can't summon up any enthusiasm for the work.'

'Can't summon up enthusiasm? What kind of talk is that? Enthusiasm is for poets and schoolgirls, John, not for responsible members of a civilized society. We have our duties to attend to; we attend to them. That's all there is to it.'

'Possibly. But it seemed to me at one time that there was something more. I had a vision—'

'That's one of the prerogatives of youth; and it's one of the marks of maturity to know when to relinquish our visions and get on with the business of living. You've indulged yourself for far too long, and I, to my shame, have been an accomplice in your folly. Without my money you'd never have got started as an architect.'

'I've always been grateful for your support, Father.'

'I don't want your courtesies, John. You know very well what I'm driving at. My support enabled you to embark on a career for which you were patently unsuited. You'd have had reason for genuine gratitude if I'd insisted on your following the obvious path. We'd have made a perfectly competent solicitor of you.'

'But I had no interest in the profession.'

He made an impatient gesture with his left hand, striking

the sugar-shaker and sending it rolling across the table. I rose to retrieve it, glad of the diversion.

'Oh, for goodness' sake. Leave it for Muriel to attend to. Listen: the Stannards have been comfortably bedded into the legal profession for five generations. And there's a reason for that. As a family we're thoroughly dependable – meticulous in our attention to detail, careful in our dealings with others, temperamentally resistant to unnecessary change. People trust us precisely because they know that we won't sacrifice their interests to grandiose schemes or theories; in short, that we've no time for visions. I suspect that you've inherited something a little more wayward from your mother's side, but you're a Stannard at heart, John, make no mistake about it. And you've taken a wrong turn.'

I could feel the blood rising to my face; my hands had begun to shake.

'That's rather a sweeping dismissal of my achievements,' I said, as coolly as I could. 'I may not have accomplished much yet, but I can hardly be accounted a failure. What about my present commission?'

'Small-scale renovations in an obscure parish church. The best I could do for you in the circumstances.'

'The best you could do for me? What do you mean by that?'

'Commissions don't simply drop from the sky, John. You must have realized that Vernon's initial approach to you wasn't fortuitous.'

'Well, I assumed that your long friendship—'

'Friendship be damned. Vernon has never been particularly interested in me or my doings. Once your mother was gone, his visits simply stopped. No, I had nothing so substantial as friendship to build on.'

'Then what was your part in the business?'

'To put it bluntly, I made a nuisance of myself. On your

behalf, of course. I reminded him that he had frequently commented on what he saw as evidence of early promise in you. I even hinted that you were on the brink of fulfilling that promise – a pardonable exaggeration I thought at the time, though on reflection I have come to feel that a more rigorously honest approach would have been preferable. In a nutshell, John, I suggested that he might find work for you.'

'I didn't ask for your help.'

'Not exactly, no. But you need it. Somebody has to take action on your behalf. Somebody has to help you make the best of a fundamentally bad job.'

'I don't accept your assessment of the situation, Father.'

'Really?' His eyes glittered, with malice perhaps, or triumph. 'You wander aimlessly around the place for days on end as though you had nothing better to do, and when I question you on the matter you admit that you lack the necessary motivation to return to work. What am I to make of that, John? More importantly, what do you make of it? No, don't answer now – but I suggest you give the matter serious thought over the next day or two.'

He hauled himself out of his chair and stood over me for a moment, breathing heavily. And then, without another word, he turned and stalked out of the room.

My father's logic is by no means impeccable, but his command of the high ground in such exchanges has always been absolute. Undressing for bed, I found myself, as so often in the past, pointlessly framing the defence I had been unable to offer in his presence. And later, huddled sleepless in the dark, I felt it all flooding back – all the hurt and humiliation of those unequal contests: the stinging words, the slaps and cuffs, the irrepressible tears of a helpless and bewildered child.

And something else. A memory of my mother, perhaps called up by my father's words. She is sitting in one of the high-backed chairs in the living-room. The sunlight pours through the open window, heightening the lustre of her smooth skin, irradiating the mass of auburn hair about her face and neck. Someone – and it may indeed be Vernon – sits opposite her, and she leans towards him, animated, voluble, her hands uplifted as though they held some extraordinary gift, her garnet necklace flashing at her throat. I am perched on a low stool in the corner of the room, basking in the sunlight, in the glow of her unaccustomed vivacity, listening not to the words but to the lilt and ripple of her voice. And then the door opens, and my father enters.

He says nothing. Absolutely nothing. But my mother is silenced. She shrinks back into her chair, her hands dropping to her lap like a pair of wounded birds. And the clouds, if my memory is to be trusted, sweep in from nowhere and blot out the sun.

I lay in bed until I heard the clock in the hallway chime six. Then I packed my valise, scribbled a brief note to my father and left the house.

Banks must have been waiting for my return. I was barely reinstalled in my rooms when I heard his voice rising from the hallway, his light step on the stair. He knocked gently and pushed back the door.

'May I come in?'

I was tired and irritable, my neck and shoulders still aching with the strain of my journey, and I had no wish for company. Given the opportunity, I might have said as much, but before I could speak he stepped briskly forward and grasped my hand.

'It's good to see you,' he said. 'And on the mend, by the look of you.'

'Yes. It's been a miserably slow process, but I'm more or less fit now. We'll start work again tomorrow.'

'Harris will be more than ready, but I'm afraid Jefford won't be joining you.'

'Still ailing?'

'He's very sick, Stannard. Sick and troubled. I wonder if you'd be willing to call on him tomorrow?'

'I should have thought your company would be more of a comfort to him than mine.'

'I visit regularly. But he has something on his mind – something he wants to discuss with you.'

'I'm unlikely to have a great deal of time to spare tomorrow. Can he not wait a day or two?'

'I think you should see him as soon as possible. May I tell him you'll call round on Thursday morning?'

I hesitated, but I could see that nothing short of a firm commitment would satisfy him and I was unwilling to debate the issue.

'As you wish,' I said, 'though you might want to warn him that I shall be unable to stay for more than a few minutes. Have there been any other developments in my absence?'

'The new pews have arrived. The joiner says he'll be back to assemble them when you give the word. And I've had a brief correspondence with the Dean.'

'I've a few matters to discuss with him myself. Has he set a date for his next visit?'

'He has no plans to return; not in the near future, at least. I understand that the destruction of the doom has caused him a certain amount of political embarrassment, but it has also freed him from what he clearly saw as an onerous duty. He asked me to convey his best wishes for a speedy recovery.'

'Any other message?'

'No. Were you expecting one?'

'Not really.' I leaned back in my chair, suddenly overcome with fatigue. 'I'm sorry, Banks, but I need to rest now. I had an early start and a rather tiring journey.'

'Forgive me. I should have given you time to settle in, but I couldn't rest until I'd spoken with you about Jefford. I'll leave you in peace now.'

I must have dozed off within minutes of his departure; certainly I was soundly asleep when Mrs Haskell knocked and entered. I started forward and stared into the gathering dusk, panicky and bewildered, momentarily unable to recognize her or to remember where I was.

'It's only me, Mr Stannard. I'm sorry to disturb you, but I thought this might be urgent.'

She held out a small, creased envelope. No postage-stamp; just my name on the front. In the grey half-light I could barely make out the handwriting, but I knew at once whose it was.

'It can't have been lying there more than a moment or two,' she said. 'I'd have seen it when I went through the hall to the kitchen.'

'Thank you, Mrs Haskell.' I leaned forward and took the letter from her outstretched hand. 'Would you mind lighting the lamp before you go?'

'Word gets round so fast in this village. You've not been back three hours and already—'

'The lamp, Mrs Haskell.'

She did as I had asked – though not, it seemed to me, with the best of grace – and left the room. I waited until I heard the click of the kitchen door-latch; then I opened the letter and began to read.

Dearest,
I wanted to see you when you were ill but would you have wanted to see me then? Would it have been right for me to come to the door? Would I have been allowed in? I asked myself those questions many times but I did not know the answers so did not come. And then when you went away I thought you had gone for good but the rector said no, only to recover your health which I hope you have done. And shall

*we meet now that you have come back? Mr Banks says you
have been very ill and I know you should not walk out in
this weather. But if you come to my house we could talk. It
is quiet here and my mother will be away so we shall not be
disturbed. At two o'clock tomorrow afternoon. Follow the
footpath – our footpath I call it now – for half a mile in
the opposite direction to the Hall, there is only one house
there. And I shall be waiting. Ever your loving*

Ann

The letter gave off a delicate fragrance, so faint as to be
scarcely discernible, so potent in its associations as to set
my whole body quaking. Terror, of course, the terror of
that unforgettable intimation on the bleak hillside as we
moved inexorably towards one another in the failing light;
but something besides, I thought, holding the folded paper to
my face, breathing its subtle exhalations as one of the blessed
might breathe the airs of paradise; something besides.

20

Not, it should be emphasized, that my decision to take up Ann's invitation was based on any but the most rational considerations. It had become increasingly clear to me during my convalescence that our liaison could not possibly be perpetuated; what was less clear was whether it had been satisfactorily terminated. It was, you might say, a question of honour. I needed to meet the girl face to face and explain to her, firmly and without equivocation, how matters stood, and a few moments in the privacy of her home would, I felt, afford me the best possible opportunity for such an interview. If other considerations presented themselves – as, in the natural course of my deliberations, they might conceivably have done – I knew better than to give them house-room.

The interior of the church seemed even colder and danker than I had remembered, Harris's company even less appealing. I spent much of the morning avoiding both, out in the churchyard, notebook in hand; and I was in such haste to get away that afternoon that I found myself at Ann's house a good ten minutes before the appointed time.

What had I expected? Certainly not this – the broken wicket, the untended garden, the scatter of cinders forming a path to the door. Or the house itself, evidently neglected for many years, its walls partially obscured by ivy, its window-frames split and rotting, their lower edges black with moss. As I raised my hand to the iron knocker I saw that it hung askew, loosely attached by a single nail. I remember thinking in that instant that there was still time to turn and leave; and then the door swung open.

I had expected this to be a difficult moment and had spent some time mentally preparing myself for it, polishing phrases at once cool and courteous, anticipating with a mixture of anxiety and pleasure the light reciprocal pressure of hand on hand as we greeted one another in the doorway. What I had not been prepared for was the possibility that the door might be opened by anyone but Ann herself.

Face to face with Enid Rosewell, I was obliged to recognize the deceptiveness of my earlier impression of her. She was statuesque, certainly, only an inch or so below my own height, and her eyes looked into mine with the directness and assurance one usually associates with women of breeding; but the skin of her face was coarser than I had remembered and her complexion, rather more highly coloured than her daughter's, had an appearance of ingrained dirtiness. Her dark hair was threaded with grey and gathered loosely at the nape with a grubby ribbon of blue satin which, even as she welcomed me, she reached up to adjust.

The shock I experienced at finding her there must have been apparent. I stood stupidly on the doorstep, glancing from her face to the shadows behind her, looking for some explanation for her presence, uncertain how far I should explain my own.

'I thought Ann . . .'

'Ann's here and waiting for you.'

She stood aside to let me enter. I hesitated. 'I feel I'm intruding,' I said. 'Perhaps some other day would suit you better.'

'But we're expecting you. Isn't that so, Ann?'

There was no reply, but I became aware of movement in the room behind her, away to the right of the doorway, just out of sight. I heard the rustle of stiff fabric, the dull chime of china against some hard surface.

'Annie! Come here, girl, and greet your visitor.'

The woman took a couple of paces backward, beckoning me after her with a gesture rather more intimate than the circumstances warranted. I might have resisted, but her gaze was fixed on me, unwavering, inexplicably authoritative, and I stepped over the threshold and into the warm fug of the room.

Ann was standing in front of the window, half supporting herself on the sill. She looked pale and ill. Her eyes were dull, rimmed with red, and I noticed a large purplish bruise on her left cheekbone, spreading back almost to the ear beneath the tumbled mass of her hair. She smiled weakly as I stepped towards her, but said nothing.

'Take the gentleman's coat, Ann. Whatever are you thinking of?'

'It's all right, Mrs Rosewell. I shan't be staying.'

'Not staying? But I thought . . . You'll take a cup of tea with us, at least?'

It was becoming clear to me that the matter required delicate handling. I took off my gloves and allowed her to help me off with my coat.

'Thank you, Mrs Rosewell. Just for a few moments, if I may.'

As she turned to hang the coat on the back of the door, I glanced at Ann. I think I wanted a clue, a signal of some kind; but her haunted eyes gave back nothing I could make sense of.

The table was set with pink sprigged china and a good fire blazed in the grate, but the room was otherwise cheerless. The furnishings were rudimentary and in remarkably poor condition – one leaf of the table propped with a rough batten and one of the four chairs clearly unusable. To the left of the fireplace stood a low dresser, perhaps originally possessed of a certain rustic charm but now coated with a dull green paint;

to the right, a rickety bookcase packed with cheap novels. The whitewashed walls were heavily discoloured with mildew and bare apart from a single picture: in a plain ebony frame, a crude oil-portrait of a thin-faced young man sitting stiffly in front of an open window which, in turn, framed a distant view of the sea.

Mrs Rosewell motioned me to sit down.

'I'm sorry we have to receive you in the kitchen, Mr Stannard. We've had to make over the parlour to my mother. After her fall we brought the bed down and' – she lowered her voice – 'I doubt we shall be carrying it upstairs again while she's in this world.'

There was an awkward silence. She moved over to the hearth and inspected the kettle while Ann busied herself unnecessarily with the teacups on the table. I nodded towards the portrait.

'Is that a relative?'

'My husband, rest his soul. Lost at sea.'

I was suddenly and forcefully struck by how little I knew of Ann's world.

'I'm sorry. I hadn't realized—'

'Almost ten years ago. For the first few years I used to think he might turn up on the doorstep at any moment – perhaps as I was rinsing the clothes, or in the evening as I got the children ready for bed. You read of such things. You know how they tell it: the man flinging down his bag and throwing back the door, his wife and children rushing to his arms. Tears of joy, tales of past hardships, a new start for everyone. All that and I don't know what else.'

She tugged a dirty handkerchief from her sleeve and blew her nose loudly. I naturally hoped that this might signal a change of subject, but she resumed almost immediately.

'And, of course, his body was never found. What do you do with a man's belongings when you don't know for certain whether he's dead or living? I'll tell you: you do nothing. His Sunday suit hangs in the wardrobe upstairs as neat as the day he put it there. And so many bits and pieces. A pair of dice, a muffler, his leather tobacco-pouch. The thing that makes me cry, even now, is a little pot on the sill, half full of macassar. I should have thrown it out long ago; but at first you don't do so because you think he might come back, and then you don't because you know he's never coming back and these scraps are all you have of him, all you'll ever—'

She was interrupted by a series of sharp knocks. She turned abruptly to the closed door behind her and called out in a harsher tone.

'All right, Mother, I'm coming.'

She gave me an apologetic smile. 'Will you excuse me, Mr Stannard, while I attend to my mother? She needs a great deal of attention at the moment. It's her thigh: the bone won't knit. And then there's her heart—'

The knocking began again, louder and more urgent. She turned away with an awkward gesture of helplessness or resignation, and pushed open the door.

I could see nothing at first but the flicker of firelight on the walls; then she crossed to the far side of the room and drew back the curtain. In a bed to the right of the window an old woman leaned forward from a disorderly heap of pillows, brandishing a stout stick. Her thin face, framed by a nimbus of unruly white hair, worked convulsively as though with pain or rage.

'I've been knocking,' she said, raising the stick aggressively.

'I know that, Mother. I came at once.'

The old woman glared at her.

'For hours.'

'No, Mother, you've been asleep. Perhaps you've been dreaming again.'

'Perhaps I have.' She lowered her arm and lay back wearily among the pillows.

'I heard a man's voice,' she said. 'Have we got visitors?'

Mrs Rosewell glanced in my direction. 'It's Mr Stannard,' she said. 'A friend of Ann's.'

'A suitor? Let me see him.' She struggled to raise herself again.

'Lie back, Mother. You can see him another day.'

'Another day I may be dead. Is that him?'

She was peering short-sightedly through the open door, her eyes narrowed, her head swaying from side to side. I sat in silence for a moment, rigid against the back of my chair, and then, judging acknowledgement of her curiosity to be less embarrassing than this absurd attempt at self-effacement, I rose to my feet and approached the doorway.

'This is Mr Stannard, Mother.'

'Let him stand where I can see him clearly.'

She beckoned me into the room and I entered, acutely aware of her control of the situation and determined to take matters back into my own hands. I stepped over to the bed and stood squarely in front of her.

'I understand from Mrs Rosewell that you've had an accident. Permit me to express the hope that you will soon be fully restored to health.'

She stared up into my face. I heard the coals shift and settle in the grate behind me.

'He's not from these parts, is he?'

'No, Mother. He's come to work on the church.'

'He speaks nicely. Annie could do worse.'

This was outrageous. I leaned over her, rigid with suppressed anger.

'Perhaps,' I said, 'you would be good enough to address yourself to me directly. And please refrain from making assumptions about the purpose of my visit and my intentions towards your granddaughter.'

The old woman's lips twisted in an enigmatic grimace, and suddenly, without apparent reason, she began to laugh, her head thrown back on the pillows, her gapped mouth wide open, her fingers clutching the coverlet; a series of strained, mirthless yelps ending in a spasm of coughing. Her daughter reached out and placed an arm across her heaving shoulders, pulling her forward into an upright position. The coughing subsided.

'I think Mr Stannard should leave you to rest now, Mother.'

'He's only just come in.'

'He came to see Ann, not you.'

She let her mother back down on to the pillows and motioned me away with a brusque flapping movement of her hand. I stormed out of the room and would have retrieved my coat and left the house without ceremony had Ann not gripped my arm as I emerged and, with an astonishing display of familiarity, pulled me away from the doorway and into the corner of the kitchen, pressing her mouth close against my cheek.

'You mustn't mind them,' she whispered.

'I do mind them. I mind them very much indeed. And I mind your presumption in inviting me, under false pretences and for reasons I now recognize only too clearly, into a household which appears to take a certain perverse pleasure in embarrassing and humiliating its guests. Your mother—'

'Please keep your voice down. Listen. You must believe me when I tell you' – she swallowed hard – 'when I give you my word that I thought Mother would be out of the house. It's years since she last missed market-day.'

'And what about your grandmother?'

'There would have been no reason for her to see you. I might have had to tend to her once or twice, but she spends half the day asleep. We could have talked in the quiet and warm. I wanted that. I wanted to be at ease with you.'

'How much does your mother know?'

Her fingers tightened on my sleeve and she glanced uneasily towards the parlour door.

'Nothing.'

'That's not possible. She was expecting me.'

'I mean, she doesn't know that we're . . .' She paused, pressing the palm of her left hand against her inflamed cheek. Her eyes reddened and watered.

'I told her you were coming to pay your respects,' she said at last. 'I had no alternative.'

'To pay my respects? You must have known perfectly well what she'd take that to mean.'

She stiffened and drew her body away from mine, but without lowering her gaze or relaxing her grip on my sleeve.

'It means no more and no less than you want it to mean.'

She seemed to consider her own words carefully for a moment, and then resumed with sudden fervour.

'Promise me you won't turn against me after this. Promise you'll still care for me.'

'What happened to your face?'

'Promise me. I want you to promise.'

Mrs Rosewell's return was felicitously timed. Ann broke away, moved over to the table and stood staring fixedly out into the garden. Her mother made straight for the hearth and lifted the kettle from the hob.

'A lot of steam,' she said briskly, 'but no tea. Ann, you might have seen to it while you were waiting. She's a dreamer, Mr Stannard, a good girl but a dreamer. Even as a child – but sit down, sit down. Make yourself comfortable again.'

'I'm afraid I shall have to leave, Mrs Rosewell. So much work to do, and the time I've allowed myself—'

'But not just yet, surely? The tea will be ready in a few minutes.'

She touched the back of the chair, lightly but firmly. It seemed unreasonable not to comply.

'Yes, even as a child she'd be lost in her daydreams for hours on end. Staring at clouds or gazing into the brook, making up tales about herself – oh, she was a saint, a fairy princess – you remember, Ann? – or a great lady robbed of her birthright and waiting to have her house and lands restored to her. John – my husband – would tease her: too good for us, eh, Annie? And do you know, Mr Stannard, sometimes I really felt it was so – I mean, I felt she didn't belong with us – she was that fine in her manners and her bearing, and her mind always straying off somewhere else. And I said when she was still quite small – you'll remember this, Ann, I said it in your hearing then and I've said it often enough since – this girl will rise in the world. And so she will, believe me. She's had offers – look how she's blushing, but I don't mind who knows it, Ann, and neither should you – offers of marriage from gentlemen who – but I don't need to tell you all this, Mr Stannard, I'm sure you can see –'

'Indeed I can,' I interrupted, anxious to stem the torrent, but aware at the same time of the dangers of saying too much. She simply ignored me.

'– can see what draws them to her. I'm not saying beauty's everything, but when a pretty face and a good heart are found together – no, I will say it, Ann – when a gentleman finds the two of them together in a young lady, you can understand why he should want to – not that she's ever accepted such an offer, of course, but she might have done, and on more than one occasion.'

She drew in a deep breath. Ann had lowered her head and was pulling her hair self-consciously across her bruised cheek.

'Look at her now. Here's a girl as fine-looking as any in the county. Sweet-tempered and biddable. Educated too. These' – she waved a chapped red hand towards the bookcase – 'are all hers, and she's read every one. But she's not spoilt herself with learning, Mr Stannard, she's not what you'd call bookish. Balance in everything is my philosophy, and she'd tell you the same if you were to ask her. Balance. Men like that in a wife. Oh yes, John used to say, though she was only a slip of a girl at the time, she'll be a rare find for any gentleman with the wit to recognize a good thing when he sees it.'

She stirred her tea slowly, picked up the cup and drank, smiling ingratiatingly at me across its rim.

'I should think you'd be the man to recognize such a thing, wouldn't you, Mr Stannard?'

This was distasteful in the extreme; but I was getting the measure of her now, I felt, casting about for a suitably noncommittal response.

'I'm sure she will make someone an excellent wife.'

She shot me a sharp glance.

'Someone? But I understood that you'd been addressing your attentions to her.'

Treacherous ground. I answered carefully.

'I've paid her such attentions as any man might reasonably pay a woman this side of courtship.'

Her face hardened suddenly. She set her cup clumsily in its saucer and leaned back in her chair, her eyes fixed angrily on mine.

'Which side of courtship would that be, Mr Stannard?'

'I'm afraid I don't quite understand you.'

'I'm speaking clear enough, but I can speak clearer if you need me to. Ann tells me you've fucked her.'

In the extraordinary stillness that followed, I heard the laboured breathing of the sick woman in the next room. I looked across at Ann, who was staring at her mother with an expression of such anguish, such helpless, hopeless misery that I could almost have found it in my heart to pity her. She caught my eye for the barest instant and then put her face between her hands and began to cry, her hunched shoulders quivering pathetically. Clearly I was under no obligation to prolong my own part in the absurd charade. I leaped up, snatched my coat from its hook and flung out into the wind and rain, slamming the door behind me.

I ran full-tilt down the hill to the village, careless of my own safety, burning with a savage, undirected fury and incapable of coherent thought. Back in my room, however, I sat and reflected more soberly on the afternoon's events, trying to construct from the fragments in my possession a plausible version of Ann's sombre world. What had happened to her since our last meeting? Under what barrage of questions, I wondered, under what hail of blows – and the thought entered my mind like a cold blade – had she betrayed herself and me? I suddenly saw with a horrible clarity the reddened knuckles connecting with the soft flesh of the cheek and Ann staggering backwards, one arm angled stiffly in front of her averted face, the other groping wildly behind her for support.

'Don't,' she cries as her mother draws back her fist to strike her again, 'please don't.' And then, so quietly that the older woman has to bend her head forward to catch the whispered words:

'You'll kill it. You'll kill the baby.'

21

I wasted a good half-hour the following morning in a fruitless search for my gloves, and it was well after nine by the time I reached the cottage; even so, Mrs Jefford looked as if she had just got out of bed, her hair unbrushed and her eyes vague and rheumy. Leaning weakly against the door-edge she seemed to droop like a cut flower. I stepped inside and made for the parlour, but she put out a hand to stop me.

'He's in bed,' she said. 'Hardly been out of it this past fortnight.'

She went ahead of me up the stairs and paused on the landing.

'Through here, sir.'

She pushed open the bedroom door and ushered me in. Jefford lay on a large iron bedstead, his back and shoulders supported by two large pillows, his head lolling back uncomfortably against the rusted bars. He looked towards me as I approached, his eyes so disturbingly dark in his hollow face that my greeting faded on my lips.

'I've been waiting for you,' he said. 'Mr Banks thought you'd be back last week.'

'That was my intention. I was delayed.'

He hooked his fingers round the headrail and pulled himself a little higher up the bed.

'I'll come straight to the point,' he said. 'I've got something for you. In there.'

He indicated a small pine chest in the corner of the room.

I found it difficult to imagine what Jefford might possess that could conceivably be of interest to me.

'In the top drawer.'

I hesitated.

'Go on. Open it.'

Mrs Jefford was hovering in the doorway as if uncertain whether to stay or leave.

'You'll be easy on us, won't you, sir? It was his illness, and his worry about me and the children. If it hadn't been for that, he'd never have—'

Jefford motioned her away with with a weak, irritable flap of his bony hand. She dithered a moment on the threshold before withdrawing. I heard the boards creak as she retreated across the landing.

'What's she talking about?'

'You'll see,' he said. 'Open the drawer.'

It was doubtless because I was so completely unprepared for it that I failed at first to notice the purse. Even when I eventually spotted it, lying at the front of the drawer on a thick pile of yellowed papers, it was a second or two before I recognized it as my own. I picked it out and turned to Jefford.

'Where did you find it?'

'In your pocket.'

I must have been a little slow to respond.

'Your jacket pocket,' he said. 'I took the purse that day in the church. When I was breaking up the pews.'

His voice was almost inaudible now, hoarse and feeble. His eyes brimmed suddenly and he drew a stained cloth from the sleeve of his nightshirt and dabbed at them.

'Thief,' he whispered. 'That's what I am. A petty thief. And as surely a sinner as if I'd taken twenty times as much.'

I opened the purse and tipped the coins on to my palm.

'It's all here,' I said. 'You've spent nothing.'

'Does that make any difference?'

'Perhaps. Why didn't you spend it?'

He shrugged helplessly. Mrs Jefford, I noticed, was back in the doorway, fidgeting uneasily.

'I don't know,' he said. 'I just couldn't do it.'

'Will's a good man, Mr Stannard. This looks bad, I know, but he's always been a kindly husband to me and a loving father to the children. He did this for us. But then he couldn't carry it through. It's not ours, he said. We'll keep it by in case we need it – though God knows we had need enough then – and return it later, when things get better.'

'And have things got any better?'

She looked at me as though she were about to cry.

'Better, sir? Just look at us. They could hardly be worse.'

'Then why return the money now?'

Jefford shifted uneasily in the bed, rucking the sheet beneath him. He tugged at it fretfully for a moment, then leaned back again, staring vacantly at the opposite wall.

'I'm letting in the light,' he said at last.

'Letting in the light?'

'That's how I see it. We've all got secrets. Some of them don't matter too much. But there's a kind of secret sits in your chest like a toad in a drystone wall. And instead of letting it out, you close up around it, hoping no one will notice it there. But it's there right enough, sitting tight around your heart and clogging your throat so you can't breathe or speak as you should. In the end, for all your efforts to keep it close, everyone around knows it's in you. They may not know what it is exactly, but they see it in your eyes, they hear it in the way you stammer or clam up when they speak to you. There's men go to the grave with such secrets, never letting the light back in. But not me.'

He seemed suddenly animated, edgily defiant, his eyes bright and a faint flush mantling his cheeks and neck.

'I had a dream the other night, Mr Stannard, Not an ordinary dream, not about the usual things. I was on a hill or mountain, very high, with snow and ice around me and the sky so blue it hurt my eyes. And my body – I looked down and I could see right through myself; clear as a window-pane, and the light pouring through me so that it was almost as if I wasn't there at all. But I was there, Mr Stannard, because I knew all this was happening. And just for a moment I felt as if – I can't get this quite right now, but it was so strong in the dream – as if there was nothing that couldn't be seen and grasped, nothing in this world or beyond it.'

Mrs Jefford gave a nervous cough. 'Mr Stannard won't want to hear all this, Will. And you should rest now.'

He showed no sign of having heard her.

'It was all so clear and bright,' he continued, 'that when I woke I thought it must really have happened. I mean, I knew I'd been lying in my bed all the time, but it seemed I'd been out there too. Out in all that light and space, though in here it was dark as the grave. Was it only a dream, do you think?'

'What else would it have been?'

'It would be a cruel thing to know it was just my mind fooling me. I call it a dream because I've no other name for it, but lying there in the dark that night I had a notion it was something more. Anyway, that was when I decided I had to see you, to give you back what was rightly yours. Mr Banks offered to do it for me, offered to explain things, but I wouldn't have that. No, I said, I have to see him myself, I have to say the word myself. Thief. Even now I find it hard to say. That's the weight in my chest, you see; that's the secret I've been holding so close.'

He fell silent, his eyes fixed on mine with such a desperate expression of – yearning, was it, or entreaty? – that I began to feel distinctly uncomfortable. I stuffed the empty purse into my pocket and held out the coins. 'Here,' I said. 'Have this.'

He shook his head.

'Take it.'

'I can't, sir.'

His features had slackened again and the colour was gone. He leaned forward, swaying unsteadily from the waist.

'It was a sin,' he said. 'No other way of seeing it. Circumstances don't justify it, though there's those would say they did. I spent a long time making excuses to myself. Now I've come to see it's not excuses I need, but forgiveness.'

I turned, suddenly tired of the whole business, and placed the coins on the scratched surface of the chest.

'Do as you like with this,' I said. 'I have to go now.'

Jefford nodded wearily and settled back against the pillows.

'Perhaps you'll come again when you have time,' he said. 'I need to know there's no bitterness between us on this score.'

Mrs Jefford seemed unwilling to move from the doorway. I pressed past her, rather more brusquely than I had intended, and began to descend the stairs. She pulled the door shut behind her and called after me in a hoarse whisper. I turned.

'What is it?'

'There's no point leaving the money, sir. Not so far as he's concerned. That's not what he's after.'

'I thought it might come in useful. I'm not insensitive to your predicament.'

It was as though a mask had slipped. She hung above me at the stairhead, one hand on the banister-rail, her neck grotesquely extended and her hair swinging loose about her contorted face.

'Not insensitive?' she hissed. 'Then why not let him have what he wants? He doesn't give *this* for your twenty-two shillings and bloody sixpence' – she made an abrupt, brutal gesture with her left hand – 'though you owe us that, and more.'

'Owe you? What do I owe you? I've no idea what you're talking about.'

Her anger appeared to subside as suddenly and inexplicably as it had erupted. Her face softened and she began to cry, the tears coursing freely down her thin cheeks.

'There's no need to come down,' I said. 'I'll see myself out.'

I had rather hoped to postpone discussion of my visit but Banks had obviously been on the lookout and, as I approached the church, he emerged from the rectory and came striding across the field towards me. I stopped just outside the porch and waited for him to join me.

'How is he today?'

'He seems to have lost a good deal of ground. I hadn't realized he was bedridden.'

'He's very weak. Listen, Stannard, this business with the purse—'

'You knew about that.' Something which had been burning dully in me sparked and flared. 'You knew when you asked me to call on him. You might have said something to prepare me.'

'Jefford particularly asked me not to mention the subject before he'd had the opportunity to talk with you. He was afraid you'd refuse to see him.'

'That might well have been my decision. I should have liked to have been in a position to make an informed judgement.'

It was, I felt, a fair point, well made, and I confess that I derived a certain satisfaction from Banks's evident discomfiture. It is not, after all, unreasonable for a man to want to see how the land lies about him, or to expect others to help him to do so. Banks had not proved a reliable guide.

'There's something else,' I said. 'I was misled by your account of Jefford's character. Scrupulous to a fault – those were your words. Yet the man turns out to be, by his own admission, a petty thief. I feel betrayed, Banks, and not by Jefford alone.'

'I'm sorry if that's so. But I spoke as I believed. Jefford's reputation in the village was borne out by everything I knew of him. I still believe him to be, as these things go, a fundamentally good man. You have to consider the effects of his injury, of his wife's sickness. You have to imagine the fears that kept him waking night after night – above all, the fear that his children would be left without any provision made for their future. When you can clearly visualize all of that – when you can *feel* it, Stannard – then you may be in a position to make an informed judgement.'

He had hurled my own phrase back at me with such extraordinary vehemence as to throw himself quite literally off balance. He reached out and placed one hand against the porch wall before resuming in a more measured tone.

'I can't tell you how my heart aches for the man. So much suffering there already, and to have compounded that suffering by a single impulsive act. And now that act, that sin as he insists on calling it—'

'You're surely not suggesting that the term's inapplicable to the case?'

'Not exactly, no. But in the long catalogue of human sins his theft seems to me to figure rather insignificantly. It's a question of proportion. We need to be able to distinguish between right and wrong – that goes without saying. But we also need to discriminate in subtler ways. Yes, Jefford's a sinner, as we all are; but so clearly deserving of our leniency – of our love, Stannard – that I'd have no hesitation, even in your place, in reaching out to him. The matter's pertinent: he attaches great importance to the idea of some kind of personal forgiveness. Your forgiveness. Did he speak to you about that?'

'He touched on the matter just before I left.'

'I hope you were able to respond appropriately.'

'I don't think my response was inappropriate.'

I could see him weighing this up.

'Have you forgiven him?' he asked at last.

'I've no intention of reporting the theft, if that's what you mean.'

He stared at me in silence for so long and with such unsettling intensity that I felt compelled to make a move. I stepped into the porch and raised the latch.

'No,' he said quietly. 'That's not what I mean.'

I pushed open the door. To my relief he made no attempt to follow me in.

22

I slept badly that night and woke before dawn, having dreamed myself indissolubly tied to a family of ragged children. They leaped and clamoured around me, one holding out her scrawny arms as though imploring me to pick her up. There's no proof, I remember thinking in my dream as I turned away, that the child is mine; but I lay a long time after waking, examining both the dream itself and the particular anxiety which had no doubt given rise to it.

By the time I left for work my unease had been augmented by a more immediate vexation: it had occurred to me over breakfast that my missing gloves must have been left behind in my flurried retreat from Ann's cottage. As good as lost, I thought, imagining the embarrassment of presenting myself at the door to reclaim them. And as if all this were not enough, I arrived at the church to find Harris gloomily preoccupied by the plight of the Jeffords.

'Will's no older than me,' he said without preamble, almost before I was through the door, 'though you'd not think it to look at him now.' He wiped his forearm across his face and leaned back against the wall. 'He's been dealt a rough hand, no doubt of it. And he doesn't deserve it.'

'Life doesn't deal fairly with us, Harris. The evidence is all around you.'

'Yes, but I never felt the unfairness the way I do now. Or the misery. I was lying awake last night thinking how Will might be lying awake too. I started to wonder, what's it like staring into the dark knowing there's nothing there for you any more, knowing you can't help yourself or the people who depend on you? And after a while I seemed to be suffering with him – not just thinking about the misery but feeling it deep inside me. I couldn't get clear of it. It was still with me when I got up, Will's sadness lodged in my own chest, so tight I could hardly breathe. It's not like me, sir, but I don't mind telling you I shed a tear or two on my way in to work this morning, understanding how it must be for him.'

'Understanding is one thing, Harris; a morbid involvement with other people's misfortunes is another. The best thing we can do, for Jefford as well as ourselves, is to get on with our own business, hoping to see him back with us before too long.'

There was a long silence.

'Will's dying,' he said at last. 'You do know that, don't you?'

'I can see that he's very ill. But remember what they say, Harris: where there's life, there's hope.'

He gave me a hard stare. 'There's precious little hope in the Jeffords' house,' he said. 'You must have seen that.'

'I've known men make the most remarkable recovery from serious illness. You'd be surprised.'

'Maybe so. But however I look at it, I can't see Will working here again. And I'd meant to say, sir, George is looking for something to tide him over till the spring. Bring him in now and we'll have the job done in half the time.'

He could hardly have made a less appealing suggestion. I could think of nothing more damaging to my authority than to have the two brothers working alongside one another on a daily basis.

'No,' I said. 'We'll manage. Just the two of us.'

'But all this rendering, sir. George was in the plastering trade until a few years back. You'll not find a better man for the job in the village, nor for thirty miles round about.'

'You told me you'd been in the trade yourself. It was one of the reasons I took you on.'

'Oh,' he said hastily, 'I can do it all right. Only I was thinking—'

'Leave the thinking to me, Harris. For the moment I consider it best to continue as we are. I'll let you know if my views change.'

That put an end to the matter and, indeed, an end to all conversation between us for the rest of the morning. His silence was clearly a form of reproach, and I was not unduly surprised when at midday, instead of settling down with his lunch in the usual way, he grabbed his knapsack and marched out of the church.

What did surprise me, however, was his failure to return. Whatever his shortcomings, Harris had proved himself a reasonably conscientious timekeeper, and by the middle of the afternoon I was sufficiently concerned – or perhaps simply sufficiently provoked – to set off in search of him.

I found him almost immediately, sitting on the wet grass by the roadside, his back against the churchyard wall. His demeanour had improved markedly, I thought, walking slowly towards him, faintly disconcerted by his bland, untroubled gaze.

'What are you doing out here, Harris? You should have been back at work an hour and a half ago.'

'I'm coming,' he said affably. 'Just give me a moment.' He rose awkwardly to his feet and stood with one hand on the wall, swaying slightly.

'What's the matter? Are you ill?'

'Never felt better,' he said, throwing back his head and drawing a deep breath. 'Never better.'

'Have you been drinking?'

His face darkened and he took an unsteady step towards me. 'Suppose I have,' he said. 'Doesn't a man have the right

227

to take a pint or two with his grub? And,' he added with sudden, disturbing vehemence, 'the right to give a lift to his spirits when he's down?'

I sized up the situation at a glance. Harris was not so far gone as to be physically incapable of returning to work, but I could see that he was unlikely to be in an appropriate frame of mind. There was, in any case, little more than an hour of daylight remaining.

'I think you should give yourself a holiday for the remainder of the afternoon,' I said diplomatically.

'A holiday? Very kind of you, sir.' He touched his cap, looking into my face with a curious mocking smile. 'Would that be on full pay?'

The suggestion that he might be paid at all was outrageous, but this was not, I felt, the moment to debate the point. 'We can talk about that tomorrow,' I said. 'You get off home now.'

He hesitated, just long enough to start me wondering whether he might make matters difficult for me; then he turned and moved slowly off down the lane.

I returned to the church and set to again with vicious energy, hacking away at the weakened plaster until the sweat broke out on my forehead and my wrist ached. How was it, I fumed, muttering like a madman as I worked, that I found myself time and again at the mercy of these people? – mocked, threatened, insulted, robbed, misled; held hostage among the teacups in a filthy hovel. And as I squatted there with the fragments flying around me, I felt rage harden into resolution: I should, after all, revisit the cottage. Enid Rosewell or no Enid Rosewell, I was going back for my gloves. A small act in itself, no doubt, but one with a certain symbolic value: I should be – and I remember phrasing it in exactly this way at the time – setting out to reclaim my own.

I emerged from the porch into pale sunlight, but the clouds

were thickening again as I climbed the hill, and by the time I reached the cottage it had begun to rain. I tapped gently at the door. No answer. I stepped over to the window, shaded my eyes with my hands and peered in. The fire almost out, no hint of movement in the room. My gloves, I noticed, were still on the table, apparently undisturbed since my precipitate departure. I tapped again, then cautiously lifted the latch and let myself in.

Retrieving the gloves should have been the work of a moment, but as I reached out to pick them up my eye was drawn to the battered book beside them – or, to be more accurate, to the handwritten sheet protruding from between its pages.

What was it about the discovery of my own letter that so profoundly troubled me? Not simply, I think, the fact that it had been used as a bookmark for what was clearly some twopenny-halfpenny romance, but also – and perhaps more importantly – the implicit suggestion that concealment was unnecessary. I had no doubt that the letter had been read by Enid Rosewell, and I felt my face grow hot at the thought.

I took the book from the table, opened it and removed the letter. And I should doubtless have closed it again immediately if I had not been struck by a passage underlined in pencil at the top of the left-hand page: *is unquenchable*, it ran, *and will blaze out through the present gloom, a beacon guiding you safely to the haven of my arms. I await, eagerly but without impatience, the realization of my vision. Ever your own – Alicia.*

I turned back to the previous page, scarcely able to believe the evidence of my own eyes; but there was no doubt of it. *I have been dreaming*, I read, *drifting in and out of sleep. And now the first birds are beginning to stir and sing. The fire is almost out, a heap of grey ash in the grate. But the love in my heart, my darling—*

I snapped the book shut, pocketed my letter and snatched my gloves from the table. As I turned to go I heard the old woman cry out from the back room.

'Is that you, Annie?'

I held my breath.

'Annie?'

I could hear the bars of the bed rattle as she turned; then the repeated knocking of her stick on the floor. 'Annie,' she called again, her voice shrill and raw. 'Come here when you're bid, girl.'

I stepped quickly out into the rain and pulled the door shut behind me.

If I had stayed in the house three minutes longer, Ann would have discovered me there. As it was, it was I who had the advantage, spotting her on the path ahead a moment or two before she became aware of my presence. When she saw me she started forward impulsively, almost breaking into a run before such decorum as she possessed reasserted itself.

'Had you walked out to see me?' she asked, approaching just a little more closely than seemed necessary. The situation, I realized, required careful handling.

'I thought we might talk,' I said.

She smiled up at me, and as she did so, some indefinable passion – grief, rage, desire, I don't know what – swept through me like a tidal wave, leaving me trembling and confused.

'Come back to my house,' she whispered. 'My mother's away.'

I shook my head. 'No,' I said. 'Not there.'

'But we can't stay out here. We'll be soaked to the skin.'

The skin of her thigh when she lay beneath me that night; the soft skin slick with rain.

'I don't expect our talk to be a long one,' I said.

Her smile faded. 'All the time I was waiting I kept thinking how it would be when you came back,' she said. 'I thought there'd be no end to the talking. If only my mother hadn't been there when you called . . . You've no idea how difficult things have been for me since your visit.'

'I should have thought your difficulties started rather earlier than that.'

'What do you mean?'

'Exactly what I say. Your mother had already struck you when I arrived.'

She stared vacantly at me, shaking her head a little from side to side.

'Struck me?'

'The bruising on your face. I thought . . .'

She touched her cheek gingerly with her fingertips and I experienced, for the briefest instant, as if through the tips of my own fingers, the warmth and density of the discoloured flesh.

'You thought my mother would have done that to me? If she hadn't scared you off the other day, you might have got to know her better. I suppose you see her as a hard woman, and in some ways that's true: she's been hardened by the blows her life has dealt her. But you're misjudging her if you imagine she'd harm me.'

'So the bruise . . . ?'

'An accident. I was reaching for a jug from the top of the dresser. The stool slipped. It was nothing, only I was embarrassed that you should have seen me like this.'

She took a step towards me. I was careful to make no answering movement.

'I was concerned for you,' I said. 'But I've been concerned for myself too. For my own health.'

'You've had good reason. Mr Banks told me there was a time he feared for your life.'

'I'm not thinking of the fever. Since then I've developed symptoms – nothing very definite, you understand, but . . . To put it bluntly, Ann, I need to know whether I might have contracted any infection from you when we lay together that night.'

She recoiled as though she had been struck, her mouth wide, her face and neck reddening furiously. For a moment she seemed to teeter on the verge of flight; then she squared up to me again, eyes blazing.

'What kind of a gentleman would ask a question like that? No one else has ever—'

Later, much later, I would come back to that abruptly truncated phrase, weighing the words, interrogating the momentary silence which succeeded them; but at the time, swept on by the sheer force of her indignation, I had no opportunity for analytical thought.

'Couldn't you tell?' she hissed. 'Didn't you realize?'

'Realize? What should I have realized?'

'That I was a virgin when I came to you. How could you have taken infection from me? Did I give you all that – did I give you myself? – for you to humiliate me in this way, for you to—'

'Keep your voice down.'

'There's no one around. And why should I care who hears me anyway? I've nothing to hide, nothing to be ashamed of except my own foolishness in giving you something you didn't even know you were being offered.'

I hesitated, disquieted by the vigour of her response but needing to know more.

'There's something else,' I said at last. 'Are you bearing my child?'

She averted her eyes, gazing down the hill towards the church. When she answered, her voice was calm again, her features composed.

'No,' she said. 'No, I'm not. You've nothing to worry about.'

I realize on reflection that my barely disguised relief might well have given offence, but she was evidently too deeply engrossed in her own thoughts to pay much attention to my reaction.

'What would you have done?' she asked. 'I mean, if there had been a child?'

'There's no need to discuss the hypothetical. The important thing is that we're free to get on with our own lives.'

I could hardly have expressed myself more clearly, yet she gave every indication of having missed the point of the remark, reaching out and twining her fingers in mine.

'It's as well it didn't happen like that,' she said. 'If there should ever be a child, I'd want everything to be just right for it.'

I disengaged my hand and took a pace backwards.

'I must get back to work,' I said.

'When shall we meet again?'

It was not clear to me whether her obtuseness was genuine or assumed, but either way she was making my task peculiarly difficult.

'I feel it would be better for both of us,' I said, 'if we were to agree not to see one another for some considerable time.'

'Some considerable time? What do you mean by that?'

'Simply that present circumstances—'

'Simply fiddlesticks,' she cried, suddenly back on the attack. 'Nothing's simple where you're concerned. You use words to confuse people, not to help them understand. Why can't you be straight with me?'

I was stung, of course, by the injustice of the accusation, but what angered me above all was to have it flung at me by a woman whose own position in this respect was so obviously assailable. My retaliation was perhaps ungentlemanly but not,

I think, entirely unjustifiable. I drew the letter from my coat pocket and held it up to her face. 'Do you know where I found this?' I asked.

She stared at it, frowning slightly.

'Of course I know. I used it to mark my page. What were you doing in the house?'

'Do you remember the page in question?'

'You've stolen that letter. You've no right to it.'

'I've every right. The letter's mine.' I crumpled it in my hand and thrust it back into my pocket.

'But given to me, treasured by me. There's a little of your heart in that letter. Can't you at least leave me that much to hold on to?'

I am not sure that I was not more irritated by the mawkishness of her appeal than by the preposterous accusation of theft. In any event, my response was understandably sharp.

'Treasured? Stuck between the pages of a third-rate novel and left lying around in the kitchen, where anyone might get hold of it. Where no doubt your mother did get hold of it.'

'No. She found the book under my pillow, and your letter inside it. I couldn't have known she'd go poking about in my bedroom. And the book's not what you say it is, either. Parts of it are so beautiful that I go on reading them over and over again.'

'And among its particular attractions, I presume, the passage you so shamelessly plagiarized when you wrote to me.'

'I don't understand all the words you use. But if you mean I copied the letter from the book, yes, of course I did. I wanted something nice to send you, something you'd want to read. How could that have been wrong?'

'You passed off the letter as your own.'

'I was trying to let you know what I felt.'

'Or what someone else felt. They weren't your words.'

She paused awkwardly before replying.

'I'd already tried to give you my words. You didn't want them. I might have taken greater pains, you said. And I went back that night wondering how I could find words that would please you and still be true. I must have written half a dozen letters over the next few days, but I couldn't send them for fear I'd said the wrong thing, or perhaps just said the right thing in the wrong way. You talk as if I'd deceived you, but that's not so. When I read that letter in the novel it seemed truer than anything I could have written myself – so fine and clear. As fine and clear as my love for you. Why shouldn't I have used the words if they told you what I wanted you to know?'

It seems to me axiomatic that a woman arguing in defence of her own dishonest dealings is unlikely to have anything very illuminating to say about either truth or love. I could see no point in prolonging the discussion.

'I'm sorry,' I said. 'I really have to go.'

At the turn of the path I looked round, to see her standing exactly where I had left her, quite motionless, her head bowed and her hands covering her face. She might have been crying, but from that distance it was difficult to be certain.

23

There was no mistaking Harris's bulky frame. As I made my way down the hillside in the failing light I could see him sitting on the gate, his head bent forward, his forearms resting on his knees. He raised his eyes at my approach, easy and unsurprised, and wagged the stem of a short pipe towards the slope behind me.

'That'll be a well-trodden path for you, Mr Stannard.'

I scanned his face carefully. His eyes gave nothing away.

'I'm in the habit of taking a short stroll in the evenings,' I said. 'This is as good a walk as any.'

He grinned suddenly, baring his uneven teeth.

'It's the scenery makes a walk worth taking, I always say. A man might go a long way to find scenery like that.'

There was something about his tone which made me uneasy: a sly, knowing mockery, perhaps the faintest hint of menace. I stepped forward and placed one hand on the gate but he showed no inclination to move.

'Do you smoke, Mr Stannard?' He was probing the bowl of his pipe with a small bone-handled clasp-knife. 'A filthy business when you come to think of it. Look at this.'

He tapped the pipe into his palm and held out the broken wad of dottle, half overbalancing as he did so, his heavy face almost brushing mine. I recoiled from the threatened contact, from the warmth of his beery breath.

'All that muck in there,' he said, recovering his balance and settling himself more firmly. He let the fragments fall and wiped his palm on his corduroys. 'All that muck, and a fool at the other end sucking away at it.'

'If you'll excuse me, Harris, I have to get back to my lodgings.'

He closed the clasp-knife with unnecessary care and slipped it, along with his pipe, into his pocket. Then he clambered down, lifted the bar and pushed back the gate, bowing me through with exaggerated formality.

'I'll walk back with you,' he said.

I set a brisk pace but Harris, though by no means entirely steady on his legs, had no difficulty in keeping up with me. For a few moments he maintained what I took to be a respectful silence; but as we stepped off the cart-track into the lane he veered towards me and, with a graceless familiarity which I attributed to his condition, grasped me by the elbow.

'How long have we been working together, Mr Stannard?'

'Working together? You've been in my employment for nearly two months.'

If he appreciated the point of my precise and deliberate phrasing, he gave no sign of it.

'Long enough for us to take a drink together, would you suppose?'

The suggestion was thoroughly inappropriate, and I was about to make my view of the matter as clear as politeness allowed when I felt his grip tighten. He leaned closer, speaking into my ear with a more overtly menacing intimacy.

'You'll come for a drink with me, Mr Stannard, and meet my friends.'

It was less an invitation than a command. I looked down the deserted lane.

'As you like,' I said cautiously. 'Perhaps I could spare half an hour.'

Thinking about it afterwards, I wondered what would have happened if, on reaching the door of the Black Dog, I had simply continued walking. Isolated and backward as it was, the village was not, after all, a lawless corner of the world, and Harris, even in his cups, would doubtless have recognized, had I chosen to assert it, the authority conferred on me by birth and breeding. But his hand was still at my elbow, and it seemed easiest, all things considered, to submit to its pressure.

The snug was full of smoke: smoke from the pipes of men seated around the battered tables, and from the sulky fire which, as we entered, released an acrid cloud into the room. Harris closed the door behind us and made his way purposefully, if a little unsteadily, to one of the tables. I followed, uncomfortably aware of being watched.

'There's room for you there, Mr Stannard.' He motioned me through to a small space at the end of the wall-bench before easing himself on to a high-backed chair opposite me.

'Two of the usual.'

He had hardly raised his voice and seemed to be talking to no one in particular, but two large mugs of ale duly appeared and were set before us. I reached for my purse but he put out a rough hand and laid it on my wrist.

'There's no need. I'll pay for these.'

'It's very good of you.'

'It's the least I can do after all you've done for the village.'

His face was almost expressionless, his voice neutral, so that I looked in vain for evidence of the sarcasm I suspected. Nor was there any response from those around us: all eyes were turned now towards the end of the table, where an old man had just begun to sing in a cracked, tuneless voice. Harris leaned forward confidentially.

'You'll appreciate this, Mr Stannard.'

It seemed hardly likely. The old man was apparently in the advanced stages of inebriation or mental decay and his song made little sense to me, though I quickly realized that it was of an indecent nature. His neck, thrust forward by some degenerative disease, swayed from side to side like that of a tortoise; his eyes were half closed in what might have been either ecstasy or stupor, and the words dropped slurred from his toothless mouth. Every so often the man on my left would take up the refrain, and then I heard more clearly.

> *Oh, she try to get up, get up, get up*
> *But he keep on pegging her down.*

I was drinking quickly, hoping to be able to leave as soon as I had finished; but as I drained the last of the ale, Harris raised his arm high in the air, glanced over his shoulder and called for more.

'Thank you, Harris, but I don't think I've time for another.'

The young man sitting next to him wiped his lips with the back of his hand and stared hard at me. There was something vaguely familiar, I thought, about the set of his mouth, his prominent cheekbones, the nervous challenge of his gaze.

'Arthur might take it amiss,' he said, 'if you were to leave while he was singing.'

The idea that I might have to spend the entire evening there out of respect for the old man's sensibilities was at once repellent and absurd, but this was clearly no time to voice my opinion. My mug was refilled; I lifted it and drank.

> *Whatever she do, whatever she say*
> *He just keep on pegging her down.*

The song came to an end at last in a burst of laughter and applause. Harris sat back ruminatively for a moment and then draped his arm clumsily across the young man's shoulders.

'This is Daniel,' he said. 'You'll like Daniel.'

His voice was thick now, the words indistinct. Daniel wriggled uncomfortably, his thin body huddled over the table as though the weight of Harris's arm were insupportable.

'Don't be fooled by his looks. He seems no more than a boy but he's got the heart of a man twice his size. Or even' – he paused, breathing heavily – 'the heart of two men twice his size.'

He laughed loudly, but I noticed that there was no answering laughter from those around us. The man on my left shifted his bulk uneasily on the bench.

'He knows what's right,' Harris continued inconsequentially, 'and he knows what's wrong. And when something's wrong . . .' He appeared to lose his thread; his arm dropped and he sat back, staring at the ceiling. 'When something's wrong,' he repeated hazily, shaking his head slowly from side to side.

'There's nothing wrong,' said the man beside me. 'You just drink up and let the lad alone.'

His words seemed to reanimate Harris.

'There's a difference between right and wrong,' he said. '*He* knows it' – he gestured slackly towards Daniel – 'and I know it. Do you know the difference, Mr Stannard?'

I could see that he was beyond the point of rational or even coherent discourse, but it was obviously important to keep matters on a more or less civilized footing. I bit back my anger and attempted a smile.

'I think we all know the difference between right and wrong, Harris. Whether our actions are invariably informed by that knowledge is another matter, but speaking for myself, I'm well aware of my moral responsibilities and I've always sought to discharge them to the best of my ability.'

Harris glanced sideways.

'What do you think of that, Daniel?'

'I think they're fine words, but . . .' Daniel faltered, flushing

deeply so that I noticed for the first time the wrinkled indeterminate patch of scar tissue above his left eyebrow, pale
against the surrounding skin. His mouth worked soundlessly
as though something were jamming his throat. The man at
my side leaned towards him.

'You be careful now, Daniel,' he said. 'Don't go getting
yourself into trouble again.'

'Let him speak,' growled Harris.

'No harm in that,' I said. 'I'm willing to hear what the lad
has to say.'

Daniel glared at me. 'I'll tell you what I have to say,' he
muttered, 'with or without your leave.' He was trembling
now, hunched into himself, gripping the edge of the table
with his right hand. 'What I say is, fine words come easy,
but you gentlemen are all the same. You talk so high and
mighty, but one sniff of what you're really after and you're
down here in the sty with the rest of us.'

Harris gave a snort of laughter. 'Is that right, Mr Stannard?
Has he got the measure of you?'

'I'm not even sure that I know what he's talking about.
You must excuse me, Harris. I have to go.'

I made to rise, but he lurched forward in his seat and placed
a blunt finger on the rim of my mug.

'You've not finished your ale yet,' he said.

'I'm afraid I haven't the time.'

'A man should always be able to make time for a drink
with his friends.' He looked round, as though for corroboration, before turning back to me. 'Or perhaps we're keeping
you from other business, Mr Stannard. From one of your
meetings. From one of your – how would you call them? –
assignations.'

I should have held my tongue; but in the taut silence that
followed, it seemed to me that the whole company was
waiting to hear me speak. I heard my own voice echoing

through the room, small, hard and a little distant, as though it came from someone else's mouth.

'I know what you're insinuating, Harris. I know what you think you've seen. But I can tell you, quite categorically, that there's nothing in it. Do you understand? Nothing at all.'

Harris might have been talking to himself. 'You hear that,' he breathed, almost inaudibly. 'Nothing, he says. He thinks it's nothing.'

The blow, delivered from a crouching position, could hardly have caused much damage even if it had connected. As it was, I saw it coming and jerked back out of range so that Daniel staggered against the table and had to put out his left hand to steady himself. His face, thrust towards mine, was a twisted mask of fury. His neighbour reached out to restrain him.

'Easy, Daniel, easy.'

'Easy be damned.' He drew back and lunged at me again but the man had him by the lapel and pulled him sharply down so that he fell forward on to the table among the pots. The fellow on my left leaned over and bore down on his neck with both hands, preventing him from rising. Harris was staring at me, his face lit with an extraordinary expression of exultant malice.

'You see what you've done now?' he shouted. 'See what you've done?'

I pulled myself to my feet with what I hoped was a degree of dignity, but the ale, drunk too quickly and on an empty stomach, had gone to my head and I stumbled clumsily in my attempt to negotiate the space between the table and the wall. Somebody sniggered. Face down in the slops, Daniel stopped struggling and began to sob like a child. As I reached the door I looked back, surveying the scene with a sudden dizzying sense of detachment; then I stepped quickly out into the night.

24

I had not expected to see Harris again, but the man's impudence evidently knew no bounds. I entered the church next morning to find him already there and hard at work, shovelling the scattered debris into a heap against the west wall. He looked up as I approached, acknowledging my presence with a perfunctory nod before returning to his task. It was, given the circumstances, an extraordinary display of nonchalance and I was tempted to imagine that over-indulgence had completely obliterated the events of the previous evening from his mind; but as I stood there debating how best to proceed, Harris himself brought those events into sharp focus.

'I suppose I should apologize for the lad,' he said. 'He'd taken a drop or two more than was good for him.'

That was, I realize in retrospect, the moment at which I should have taken decisive action. To have dismissed the man on the spot would have been the only appropriate response to a remark which, as I see it now, constituted an oblique and utterly inadequate apology for his own outrageous behaviour. But he led me off down some byway – Daniel's unhappy childhood, unspecified but damaging influences on his subsequent development, the restlessness and mental instability that had prevented him from leading a normal adult life – and I lost the initiative. I was in any case weary of the business – not simply of my dealings with Harris, I mean, but of the whole miserable project – and I had no stomach for any action which might prolong it.

'Get on with your work,' I said. 'I've no wish to discuss

this matter, either now or at any time in the future. Is that understood?'

I chose to interpret his shrug as a gesture of acquiescence.

'Once you've cleared this,' I said, 'there's another patch of rendering to be hacked away at the base of the wall there, just to the right of the door. I've marked out the affected area. I'll be in the tower if you need me.'

The timbers in the tower are fundamentally sound but I had noted in my original report that there was evidence of minor infestation on both floors and I felt it incumbent on me to carry out a more detailed survey, if only to reassure myself that the damage was as slight as it had initially appeared to be. I clambered up the ladder to the first floor and squatted down to examine the boards, running my fingers over the dusty surface, testing with my penknife for areas of weakness. No cause for concern there, I concluded, and I was about to climb to the second floor when I heard the south door grate open, the sound oddly distorted as it echoed up to me from the nave below.

Her voice was distorted too, its edges softened and blurred so that it was a moment or two before I recognized it.

'. . . thought I'd just look by and see how the work was going,' I heard her say. And then Harris's rumbling bass cutting in.

'You've no business in here, Annie.'

'Why not? I've as much business in here as anybody else. Anyway you can't keep me out. Nobody's allowed to close a church.'

'Just while the work's going on. The building's not safe.'

'I want to see Mr Stannard.'

'Better you don't, Annie.'

'Is he here?'

There was a long pause. I heard her footsteps move across

the flags and stop beneath the tower. When she spoke again her voice was clearer and harder.

'I said, is he here? I've a right to know.'

Harris again, paternal, cajoling: 'Listen, Annie, it's for your own good . . .' And then the girl crying out in sudden fury, sending the pigeons rocketing from the top of the tower: a sharp 'oh' – the flat of her hand striking the ladder below – followed by an angry tirade. It was hard to make sense of it all, wild and confused as it was, but the gist of it seemed to be that she was no longer a child, that she refused to be treated like one, that everyone had a right to a better life, that her own life had been lived in the shadows but that she was now, as she put it, going to walk in the light; and there was some vague threat, too, against those who conspired to cheat her of what she called her birthright. When she had finished ranting she began to sob.

It would be unnatural in a man to remain unmoved in the face of such a display, but it was clear that it would have been in no one's interests for me to have revealed myself at that point or, indeed, to have been discovered by her. It seemed best to distance myself as fully as I could from any such possibility, and with that end in view I began to climb the second ladder, testing each rung carefully before committing my full weight to it, listening for tell-tale creaks while the sound of sobbing dropped away behind me.

It was a different world up there. The first stage had been kept more or less clean, presumably by the bellringers; but up at the top of the tower, standing on a litter of scattered twigs and straw, white bird-bones and crumbled mortar, I had an overwhelming sense of isolation from the reassuring routines of everyday life. There were the bells, of course; but if they spoke of anything at that moment, it was not of human ritual but of their own monumental stasis. And there was the wind.

I have never experienced anything quite like it. I don't mean its strength – I have been out in worse – but the sound of it. Or sounds; because what struck me as I stood there was the range of contending voices – the shrill intermittent whine from the partially obstructed light in the west wall, a whirring or rattling from somewhere in the rafters above, the softer buffetings from outside. And behind all that and, as it were, on some other level, a more mysterious note: a sweet, sustained singing, like a child's treble but finer; not quite consistent in pitch but in some sense holding true against the comings and goings of those other, less ethereal voices, so that as I listened it seemed to foreground itself or, rather, to redefine itself as the delicate, inviolable centre of all that stir and noise.

It was brighter there than below, too, the light entering freely through three of the four apertures and only partially hindered on the fourth side by an arrangement of crude slats jammed into the aperture, presumably as a baffle against the damp westerlies. The device had not been entirely successful and the boards lying closest to the wall would need, I decided on closer inspection, to be replaced; but in general the timbers seemed to be in a surprisingly good state of preservation.

I took a few rough measurements and was just reaching into my pocket for my notebook when I heard the door crash shut below. I could see her in my mind's eye, stepping from the porch into the blustering wind, lifting her tear-stained face to the sky and tossing back her curls before setting off down the path. I pictured her fastening the gate behind her and hurrying away down the lane; and if I felt, as I confess I did, a pang of regret at what I took to be an emblematic resolution of the affair, I was able to console myself with the reflection that no other outcome could have been seriously contemplated.

And then I heard her call my name. Quite softly but

unmistakably, the sound rising unimpeded from the church-yard below; a long note, almost as high and pure as that mysterious resonance at the heart of the wind. I dropped my notebook and pencil, scrambled to the aperture on the south side and looked down.

She was standing among the gravestones, one hand cupped to her mouth, small and neat as a porcelain doll; I might, I felt, have reached out and taken her in my hand. As I watched she called again, this time more loudly; and her voice, purged by air and distance of its grosser undertones, seemed to prolong itself unnaturally, ringing round my narrow chamber like the chime of a struck wineglass. I leaned forward, and at that moment my body was convulsed by a wave of pain, a dark visceral pressure which, as I gasped for breath, surged up through my chest and throat. I almost cried out, but brought the unspeakable thing under control before it could betray me; before, I suppose I should say, I could betray myself.

There is a history of heart disease in my family and I remember having been deeply impressed as a child by my uncle's account of a near-fatal attack suffered in what most men would regard as the prime of life. It was, in the circumstances, natural that I should have experienced, as the pain receded, a momentary flutter of anxiety about my own condition. But as my pulse and breathing returned to something approaching normality, I turned back to Ann, now making her way diagonally towards the church across the wet grass, evidently still on the lookout for me but with a gaze so fiercely concentrated at her own level that I felt able, without fear of discovery, to lean forward over the sill and track her progress to the corner of the tower.

At that point she disappeared from view. I heard her call once more, from the far side of the building; but it was a good few minutes before she reappeared, moving more slowly now, her head bowed. She made her way to the path and turned to face the church, standing motionless for a moment, hands clasped before her. Then she gave herself a little shake, swung briskly round and moved towards the gate.

I still find it difficult to account for my reaction. I remember leaning my cheek against the cold stone of the embrasure in what I think of as an attitude of resignation, and I have absolutely no recollection of having made any decision to act; yet I was suddenly on the ladder and fighting to get down, my hands hot with friction, my feet slipping on the worn rungs. I swung myself through the lower trap and hit the floor running; and I should have been through the door and out of the building if Harris had not been blocking my way.

I realize in retrospect that his intervention functioned as a desirable check on my own uncharacteristically impulsive behaviour and that I have some cause to be grateful to him, but my immediate response was considerably less generous. I believe I swore violently as I tried to sidestep his ungainly bulk, and I am certain that I struck wildly at him as he reached out a hand and grasped me by the sleeve.

'Let the girl alone,' he said, drawing me firmly towards him. The action was threatening, but his tone was oddly gentle, unemphatic. 'Let her be, Mr Stannard.'

'This is none of your business, Harris.'

'I've watched Annie growing up over the years,' he said, 'and I care for her as I'd care for one of my own.'

'That doesn't entitle you to lay hands on me.'

He relaxed his grip a little and I tugged my arm free, taking a pace backward as I did so.

'I meant no harm,' he said. 'But Annie's not for you. You know it yourself. She'd be as miserable under your roof as a caged lark.'

'I've no intention—' I began, and stopped abruptly, suddenly and acutely aware of the implications of denial.

'Of marrying her? Then what kind of a game are you playing with the poor girl?'

The question was so far beyond permissible bounds as to release me from any obligation to continue the conversation. I turned on my heel and made for the door.

'You'll not follow her, Mr Stannard?'

'I'm going back to my lodgings,' I said. 'I've business to attend to.'

25

I had, in fact, very little business, and none requiring my immediate attention, but it was clearly impossible to remain in the church with Harris. I had it in mind to sit quietly in my room and write for an hour or two before walking out to pay my respects at the Hall.

I had been considering for some time the advisability of taking Redbourne into my confidence, and recent events had sharpened my thinking on the matter. I should be presuming, of course, on an acquaintanceship which was unlikely to ripen into anything more cordial, but I recognized a pressing need to talk with someone who might have knowledge of the girl and her family, and I naturally shrank from broaching the subject with Banks.

I was sitting at my table, beginning for the third or fourth time what was proving to be a peculiarly difficult letter to Aaron, when I heard Mrs Haskell's footsteps on the stairs. She knocked gently and poked her head round the door.

'There's someone outside for you, Mr Stannard.'

'Who is it?'

'Annie Rosewell. She says it's important.'

I am not certain that I was entirely successful in concealing from Mrs Haskell feelings which surprised me both by their force and their ambiguity. I laid down my pen and endeavoured to control the shaking of my hands.

'Tell her I can't see her,' I said.

'The girl's in a real state, Mr Stannard, dithering like a mad thing, and her eyes red and puffed up with crying. She said you'd know what it was about.'

'I'm afraid I don't have the remotest idea what it's about, Mrs Haskell, and I don't have the time to find out now. Tell her I'm busy.'

'She said she knew you'd be busy, but I was to tell you that nothing could be more important than this.'

'I've given my answer. Perhaps you'd be good enough to communicate it to the young lady and leave me to get on with my work.'

I thought for a moment that she might continue to press for a more favourable response: certainly she seemed reluctant to leave, and at one point she opened her mouth as though to speak. But I turned back to my letter, pointedly ignoring her, and after a while she withdrew and made her way slowly down the stairs.

My correspondence took longer than I had anticipated, and it was late in the afternoon before I reached the hall. Redbourne opened the door himself. He was visibly taken aback by my unannounced arrival and stood staring stupidly into my face as though unable to place me.

'I'm sorry to disturb you, Redbourne. I wonder if I might have a word with you?'

Even then, he made no move. I began to regret having called.

'You suggested that I might—'

'Of course.' He seemed to come to himself, throwing the door wide and standing aside to let me pass. He took my coat and led me down the corridor to a spacious but cluttered living-room.

'You'll have to excuse this.' He waved a hand vaguely at the litter of books and botanical specimens strewn across the floor. 'If I'd known you planned to visit . . .'

'I'm afraid there was no planning involved. I must apologize.'

'Please, Stannard.' He motioned me to sit down. 'You'll take a glass of claret?'

Two bottles stood side by side on a low table, one empty, the other evidently only just broached. He opened the door of an ornately carved cabinet, brought out a glass and filled it for me.

'A little early for you, perhaps, but as you see' – he indicated a full glass on the floor beside his chair – 'I've already begun.'

It struck me that he had probably begun some considerable time earlier and that discussion of the serious matter I had in mind might be better postponed, but the directness of his approach seemed to rule out that option.

'Now, Stannard,' he said, swinging his chair round to face mine, 'tell me what brings you here. You may have walked out for the sake of your health, but I fancy not.'

'Not exactly, no.'

'Nor for friendship's sake?'

There was the faintest hint of reproach in the question. I shifted uncomfortably under his gaze.

'Naturally our friendship—'

'Naturally. But that's not why you've come.'

'No. The fact is, Redbourne, that I appear to have created something of a problem for myself. There's a girl—'

'Ann Rosewell.'

'Yes. How did you know?'

'Don't be absurd, Stannard. The whole place has been buzzing with the affair for weeks. When an outsider such as yourself comes to stay in a village like this, he inevitably attracts attention. When he chooses to address his attentions to one of the villagers – a girl, moreover, who has already generated a certain amount of interest in her own right – gossip and speculation run wild. Did you imagine it was some kind of secret? Every servant in this household knows – or thinks he knows – what's going on. Hadn't it occurred to you how closely you'd be scrutinized? How widely the affair would be discussed?'

'I'm beginning to realize.' I sat back for a moment, flushed and awkward. 'What do you mean when you say that Ann has already generated interest?'

'Well, to begin with, there's her beauty, which has led to a feverish and not entirely good-natured scuffling for her favours among the susceptible young men of the neighbourhood. She might have kept herself aloof from that, of course; but what makes her so interesting to the village at large is the extent to which – you must forgive me, Stannard – she seems to have compromised herself in the bestowing of those favours.'

'How can you be sure that that's anything more than village rumour? She told me—'

'For heaven's sake, Stannard. I'm sure you know as well as I do that what a woman tells a man in a situation of this kind is unlikely to be entirely true, and may well deviate so far from the truth as to be unrecognizable to anyone familiar with the facts. You have to remember, too, that women of Ann's social class – well, let's just say that it's better to avoid involvement. This is *terra incognita* as far as you're concerned, and those who venture into unfamiliar territory risk error and ambush. This really isn't my business, but since you've evidently come here expressly to discuss the matter, allow me to warn you to be on your guard against the girl. In particular let me caution you against imagining that you're under any obligation to her. You're not the first to be snared by her charms, and you certainly won't be the last. My advice is simple: you should let her know, unequivocally and at the earliest opportunity, that you want nothing further to do with her.'

'Eminently sensible. But it might not be as easy as that.'

'Nonsense. She'll come round to it more quickly than you think. You'd have been quite a catch for her, admittedly, and she'll resist the assault on her dreams of social advancement as well as resenting your rejection of her. But women are more resilient than they'd have us believe, and Ann herself would have no difficulty in finding consolation elsewhere. I can think of half a dozen handsome and not particularly fastidious young men who would be delighted to step' – he smiled, intimate, collusive – 'into the breach.'

I flared suddenly with an intense and irrational anger.

'And if I don't wish to relinquish my own place? Have you considered the possibility that I might—' I hesitated, feeling on my tongue the weight of the word which had come so spontaneously to mind; testing, rejecting – 'that I might admire her?'

'It has occurred to me that you might be – that you must be – infatuated with her, yes. But you can surely see that the whole business is preposterous. How could you ever have thought of bringing the affair to any but the obvious conclusion? It may seem cruel to turn her loose now, but how much crueller not to do so. Imagine yourself shackled to such a woman, Stannard: what kind of happiness do you think there'd be for either of you?'

He refilled my glass and threw a thick wedge of pinewood on to the fire. We watched as the flames took hold.

'It seemed to me at one time,' I said after a moment's reflection, 'that I might make something of her. She has some natural assets – there's beauty there, undoubtedly, and a certain elegance of bearing and, for the rest, she might well have proved teachable.'

Redbourne shook his head. 'Not Ann,' he said. 'She looks the part, I grant you, but it's skin-deep. If you want to know what you'd be left with once the surface bloom was gone, take a look at her mother. And then there's the father—'

'Lost at sea, I gather.'

'Well, that's a convenient fiction. Certainly Thomas Rosewell was a sailor, and equally certainly he set off some ten years ago on a voyage from which he never returned. In that sense, he's undoubtedly lost, and it seems unlikely that the family will ever see him again. But the word in the village – and it's something more substantial than rumour – is that he has settled in Australia and simply refuses to come home. I can't entirely blame him for that – Enid Rosewell is an unstable and sometimes irrational woman and must have been almost impossible to live with – but his departure left the children vulnerably exposed to her unpredictable bouts of violence.'

'Violence against the children? There's bruising on Ann's face. She told me she'd fallen against the dresser. Is that—?'

'Another fiction. There's not a stick of furniture in the cottage against which that poor girl hasn't stumbled at one time or another. The answer comes pat: I fell and struck the table, the shelf, the bookcase. She's had enough practice. And the whole village, to its shame, colludes in the lie. Believe me, those children have suffered over the years, Daniel even more than Ann. When he first came to me, he was in a pitiful state, literally shaking with fear.'

'When you say he came to you—'

'He ran away from home. We had spoken occasionally, and my small kindnesses to him had perhaps encouraged him to see me as some kind of saviour. I wish I could have given him more of the love he so clearly needed, but I suppose it was too late. All the evidence pointed to a history of surprisingly savage beatings; and how do you undo that? You'd have been shocked, Stannard: the boy not yet seventeen years old, the delicate skin of his shoulders and upper back permanently marked by large patches of scar tissue, puckered and rough to the touch.'

'To the touch?'

'And what damage had been done to his spirit, heaven alone knows. A growing boy profits from firm guidance, perhaps even from occasional chastisement, but there's a profound difference between that and the sheer brutality to which he had evidently been subjected. He would sometimes wake in the night, crying out and sobbing, completely inconsolable. And all the time he was with me he remained tense, easily startled, always strangely hunched in his posture, as though he were waiting for the next blow to fall.'

'You took him in?'

'What else could I do? I offered him one of my vacant cottages and found him enough work around the estate to justify his presence there. I did what I could for him, but he seemed unable to settle to anything and moved on within a year. We see him back here now and again, drinking in the Black Dog or wandering through the meadows around the village, sometimes in Ann's company; but I don't believe he ever visits his mother.'

I thought suddenly of the young man with the scarred forehead lunging at me across the bar-room table.

'What is it, Stannard?'

'Nothing,' I said. 'It's a sad story.'

'Even sadder than you might think. Because, odd as this may sound after all I've just told you, I'm convinced that Enid Rosewell loves her children – loves them with a genuine if somewhat disordered passion. A few days after Daniel's defection, she appeared on my doorstep with Ann at her side, demanding to see her son. My first impulse was to protect him, but I quickly realized that she was quite capable of dragging my name through the dirt if it served her turn to do so, and I was left with no choice but to betray his whereabouts. I thought she would simply march in and haul him home and was pleased to be proved wrong, though I suspect that the vigour of his resistance owed as much to his not unreasonable fear of retribution as to any newly acquired strength of will. She, for her part, seemed badly affected by the business, and certainly she has never forgiven me.'

He swayed forward in his chair and rested his elbows on his knees, staring into his glass. I listened to the pinewood cracking and whistling in the grate.

'No,' he said at last with a little grimace, 'it's rotten stock, Stannard; and tend it how you will, rotten stock bears rotten fruit. I've given you my advice: take it or leave it, as you wish.'

He rose unsteadily and went to the window, squinting up at the sky through the misted panes.

'It will be getting dark soon,' he said, 'and it looks as though we'll have snow before the evening's out. I suggest you get back while you can.'

It was cold, certainly, the wind stronger now and blowing from the north-east. Redbourne walked with me as far as the back gate.

'I'm sorry,' he said.

'Sorry? For what?'

'I suspect that what I've told you may not have been exactly what you wanted to hear.'

'I don't know what I wanted to hear. The truth, I suppose. And I'm grateful to you.'

'The truth?' He leaned close, so that I caught the sour tang of wine on his breath. 'Is that what you thought you were getting?'

'Isn't that what you were offering?'

'Nothing so dignified, I'm afraid. Just the view from where I stand.'

A sudden gust whipped across the garden, throwing the straggling laurels at his back into a frenzy of agitation. He held out his hand.

'Good luck, Stannard.'

'Thank you. You must come and inspect our progress on

the church before too long. We're nearly there now: another fortnight should see us through.'

He hunched his shoulders and jammed his hands into the pockets of his smoking-jacket.

'I'm cold,' he said. 'I must get back to my fire.'

I turned up the collar of my greatcoat and set off into the wind. Redbourne's warning had been timely: a bank of cloud was sweeping in, dark and distinct, across the translucent blue of the evening sky. I imagined the hillside featureless under a mantle of blown snow, and quickened my pace.

A fortnight? Wildly optimistic, I reflected as I walked; an estimate based on nothing more substantial than my own desperate wish to be out of the place. Perhaps, with luck, a month, though even that was questionable. Quite apart from the repointing of the exterior – and the full extent of that work was still unclear – there were the new pews to be fixed in position, the stove to be installed and the base of the north wall re-rendered; and I should be obliged, of course, to make good the damaged plasterwork around the chancel arch.

Make good: that was the phrase in my contract. But supposing, I thought, there is no possibility of making good. What if the structures we inherit are fundamentally flawed or debased beyond redemption? Why should we take upon ourselves the burden of restoring what was never good and can never be made so? – a decaying patchwork of stone, wood and plaster, a world of damage and disease. Perhaps it was the claret or an after-effect of my illness, but I was suddenly buoyed on a wave of elation, lifted and washed clear of my moorings. The vision, if one can call it that, was not in any obvious sense either illuminating or consoling: on the contrary, what presented itself to me was a chilling and terrible immensity of darkness, formless and ungovernable. I have been here before, I said to myself; but now I let myself drift out, thrillingly aware of my own helplessness and knowing – yes, knowing, for however brief an instant, beyond any trace of a doubt – that all my actions, past and future, were sanctioned by that uncoercible emptiness. I can leave, I thought, leave with the new pews still cluttering the aisles, the rendering unrepaired, the floors unswept; no farewells, no explanations. As I walked down the hill towards the village I threw back my head and began to sing.

26

If I had seen her waiting there by the stile, I should have turned aside and cut down to the village through the woods; but the light was fading and I was not aware of her presence until she stepped away from the hawthorn trunk against which she had been leaning. She was, considering the weather and the hour, decidedly underclad, in a dark dress and a fringed woollen shawl, and I noticed as she drew close that her face was pinched and stiff with cold. She attempted a smile, a poor lopsided grimace, which she abandoned at once. There was no ceremony in her greeting.

'I wasn't expecting you from that direction. Where have you been?'

I was on the point of telling her that my activities were none of her business, but thought better of it. I sensed that she was in a highly emotional state, and I was anxious to avoid argument.

'I've been talking with Mr Redbourne.'

'About me?'

'Of course not. Why should we have spoken of you?'

I was aware that I might have phrased my denial more tactfully, but I was quite unprepared for the stream of vituperation that followed. It was difficult to make sense of it all, but I was left with the strong impression that she felt Redbourne might corrupt or mislead me in some way.

'I don't understand you. We've simply been conversing over a glass or two of wine.'

'Conversing?' She mimicked my own careful articulation

of the word. 'Say what you like, I know he's been telling you stories about me; about my family.'

'Stories?'

'Yes, stories. You're all story-tellers, you gentlemen – liars if you like. And you're the worst of all, using me as you do, making me and remaking me as you see fit. No, don't deny it. You make me, you force me – force me to be this thing or that. I'm an angel, I'm a demon, I'm the sweetness – yes, you said that – the sweetness you've waited all your life for, the infection blighting your future for ever. It's all stories with you. Why won't you see me as I am? Look me in the eyes! Why can't you look at me?'

She was hysterical, of course, and it struck me at that moment that what I was witnessing was the surfacing of some deep hereditary taint, she being perhaps as severely afflicted as her mother. It was, I suppose, partly with the intention of administering the verbal equivalent of a sharp slap that I turned her argument back on her, but I realized as I spoke that I was shaking with anger myself.

'What about your own stories? The way you made and remade yourself when you were a girl. What was it your mother said? You were a saint, a fairy princess, a great lady. And now? If it's true that I've failed to see you as you are, perhaps that's not entirely my fault.'

'I know what my mother said. But who is she, that little girl dreaming beside the brook? I'll tell you who she is: she's a character in yet another story, an imaginary figure called up by a foolish woman in the hope of impressing her daughter's gentleman visitor. I don't recognize her.'

Had I been entirely sober I should not, I think, have acted quite as I did, though I feel even now that my impatience was not entirely unjustified. Slippery, in every sense unstable, Ann had perpetually eluded my grasp, and perhaps I simply wanted to lay hold of her, to pin her down. At all events, I caught her by the arm and shook her, perhaps a little more roughly than the circumstances warranted but certainly not in a manner likely to cause distress. Even so, she winced and started back, twisting her head sideways with an odd jerky movement, as if to avoid a blow. Surprised but also encouraged by her momentary discomposure, I determined to press home my advantage.

'Here's another portrait: a girl who spends her childhood in fear of her mother's violence, who reaches womanhood without freeing herself from that violence, who constructs a series of more or less transparent fictions in a misguided attempt to conceal from the world what the world already knows – shall I go on? Is that a figure you recognize?'

'You're hurting my arm.'

I relaxed my grip. There was a long silence. When she spoke again, her voice was hushed and unsteady.

'Whose story is that?'

I realized I had already said too much. I hesitated.

'It's all right,' she said wearily. 'I don't need you to tell me.' And then, breaking my grip completely, flinging away from me, she suddenly cried out with the most extraordinary vehemence:

'I hope Redbourne burns in hell for what he's done to my family. And that's where he's bound, make no mistake. Next time you see your precious friend – next time you converse with him – ask him about my brother. Let him find a story to explain that.'

'Redbourne has already told me about Daniel. I'm sure that what he did was done with your brother's interests at heart.'

She gave me a brief incredulous stare. And then, without warning, she was crying, the tears streaming down her face, her mouth distorted. I should, I suppose, have pitied her; perhaps, to a limited extent, I did. But what I felt above all was embarrassment – embarrassment at a display of unbridled emotion which seemed at once to exclude me and to demand a response. I pulled a handkerchief from my pocket and held it out to her.

I believe she may have misinterpreted the gesture. She grasped my extended hand and, with a little moan, pulled herself towards me and laid her head against the lapel of my coat. I should not like it to be thought that such matters were uppermost in my mind at that moment, but I am naturally rather fastidious about my clothing, and as soon as I decently could I applied the handkerchief, wiping her eyes and nose carefully, firmly, as though she were a child. She pressed closer and slipped her arm around my waist.

'Take me away,' she whispered. 'Take me away from all this.'

The idea was unthinkable, yet I had once entertained it.

'It's out of the question.'

She strained my body to hers with a sudden vicious intensity, and I felt her breath on my throat.

'It's not just that you owe me this,' she said. 'It's what we really want, you as well as me. This closeness. This touching. Surely you can see that?'

'I can see no such thing. You're speaking like a whore.'

Intemperate words, and I immediately regretted them; but I noted with a certain disquiet that she scarcely flinched.

'I'm speaking the truth,' she said.

She threw back her head and fixed me for a moment with a gaze so direct and unintimidated that I squirmed beneath it.

'Why won't you admit it?' she asked. And then, with a sharp cry, she caught hold of the hair at the nape of my neck and pressed her mouth against mine, at the same moment reaching down with her left hand to touch the inside of my thigh. I recoiled, but her right hand tightened its grip while the left came up to grasp the collar of my coat, and she pushed her face against mine with the blind, desperate movements of a suckling animal. I ducked and twisted, trying to break her hold, but she clung to me in the darkness like one of the suffocating presences of my childhood nightmares, sobbing and sighing.

I am obviously not proud of my reaction, which I now recognize to have been informed by a degree of panic; but the circumstances were clearly so extreme as to leave me little alternative. Freeing my hands, I thrust her back from me and, as she stumbled, struck her smartly across the face.

If the blow had had the desired effect, I should no doubt have found it unnecessary to strike her again. I am unable to recall now the exact sequence of events or piece together all of the details, though I know that even when she fell to the ground she refused to relinquish her hold, twisting the fabric of my coat about her fingers and wrist as she lay at my feet. And if – as I hazily remember and as such evidence as I had seemed subsequently to confirm – I kicked out at her at that point, I naturally regret that; but I console myself with the reflection that my actions were a not altogether reprehensible response to behaviour so ungoverned and ungovernable as to constitute a genuine if admittedly indefinite threat. I will not say that I actually feared for my life, but I did experience in that girl's presence, out there in the biting wind, beneath the dark bulk of the massing clouds, a remarkable sense of menace, even of evil; of her possession by forces which might well, if I were to relax my vigilance for an instant, draw me into their ambit.

No doubt of it. I see her now, struggling to rise but momentarily frozen in an attitude so purely and primevally savage that it assumes for me, as I re-examine it, an emblematic or monitory force. Squatting among the tussocks, one hand extended to steady herself and the other clasped to the back of her neck, she glares up at me from under her thick brows.

Her left cheek is marked by a dark smear, and a hank of damp hair straggles across her mouth and sagging chin. The expression on her face might be one of rage or grief, desire or disgust, but what is unquestionable is the brutal energy which informs it. Yes, I am afraid to look at her; I am afraid to look away.

I must have made some movement towards her for I remember her dropping back on to her hands and knees and scrambling away from me with a wild scream, so shrill and raw it set my teeth on edge. 'Don't,' it might have been, or 'No' – her neck arched backward, her mouth wide. And then, quite suddenly, she was – as one might say – herself again. Simply and reassuringly herself: a gauche country girl snivelling into her muddied skirts in the middle of an open field. It was with a profound sense of relief, not unmixed, I should like to think, with genuine solicitude, that I reached out to help her to her feet.

She was, I thought, about to take my hand; but then, with a curious shrug or shudder, she rose unsteadily to her feet and began to stagger towards the beechwood. I followed at what I felt to be a suitable distance, calling her name softly at intervals. As she reached the wood's edge she appeared to stoop and fumble among the bracken stalks; then she half straightened and turned to face me. 'Let me be,' she said. 'I'll have no more to do with you.'

It had begun to snow, fine gritty flakes driven slantwise, stinging the side of my face. My lips and tongue were clumsy with cold.

'Let me see you home,' I said.

'I'll see myself home.'

She coughed convulsively, spat; seemed momentarily to lose her balance.

'Come on, Annie.'

'Don't Annie me.'

268

She eased herself back against a beech trunk, breathing heavily. I approached her as one might approach a frightened animal, cautious, placatory. As I closed on her, I slowly extended my arm and placed my hand on her shoulder.

'I'm sorry,' I said quietly; and I imagine that at that moment I really meant it. 'I'm sorry.'

I think it was the surprise of the attack as much as its force – her sudden duck and swing, the heavy stick catching me under the ribs as I stepped hurriedly backward – that brought me to my knees, but the pain was by no means negligible. I curled forward, pressing my face into the cold leaf-mould, both arms raised to protect my head and shoulders – though there was in fact no second blow. When I looked up she was still just visible, a hunched, graceless figure stumbling away between the trees. I fancied I saw her look back at me over her shoulder, though it was hard to be sure; then the darkness closed around her and she was gone.

She must have delivered the letter while I was at the Hall. Mrs Haskell had wedged it against the catch of my living-room door, doubtless to ensure that I would see it as I reached out to let myself in. There was, I realized, little point in reading the thing – whatever Ann might have had to say earlier had obviously been superseded by our recent exchange – but I was understandably curious. I lit the lamp and spread the crumpled sheet on the table beside it.

The letter offered further proof, if any were needed, of the woman's true nature. Scrappily written, confused in its arguments, decidedly unbalanced in tone, it confirmed the fundamental wisdom of my own response – of actions which, though apparently unbalanced themselves, could hardly, given the circumstances, have been carried through in any other way.

Dearest,
Mrs Haskell was kind when I called this morning, she could
see how it was with me. But you would not come down.
When I got home I was raging but now I am quieter. And
I ask you again. Please let me see you, please let me speak
with you. I shall go out at dusk to the usual place.

   I beg you do not ignore this letter. It is not for my sake
only that I write, but for yours. Did you think when we
lay in the dark with the rain falling on us that that was the
end? I know you did. But it need not be so. Before that
you loved me. Tipping my face to the moon you loved me
and earlier too, looking up as I stood watching you in the
churchyard. I know it and you know it. And why not again?
Did I disappoint you in some way? I think this but I do not
know your thoughts. And I want to know you better and I
want you to know me better for that is where love really
begins. In knowing people as they are. My mother says you
should marry me and so you should but not for her bidding
and not even because I ask it but because of your own need.
I am sad when I think of you. And sometimes I am sorry
for myself and sometimes for you. Can you see that you
hurt yourself too? I mean you will not take what you need
even when it is offered. I offer it now.

   I am thinking of you. Of your hand on my breast when
you loved me. We could be like that again if you wanted.
I can not give you all you want but I can give you more
than you think. Why should I hide this longing I have for
you? Why should I be made to feel ashamed? I am not in
the wrong in wanting you near me. I am not in the wrong
in wanting to spend my life with you. You have no right to
treat me badly, I have done nothing to deserve your content.
I am angry again when I think of this but still your loving
                                                         Ann

I think she must have meant contempt. I knelt down beside the hearth and raked up the fire; then I set the letter edgewise among the turned coals and watched as the flames took hold.

Long after the embers had cooled I was still sitting in my chair, staring into the grate, listening to the hollow sobbing of the wind in the flue. It was not indecision that held me there through those leisurely hours; it was, rather, the assurance of a man whose decision had already been made and who, knowing his path to be clear, had no need of haste. I was leaving. That night. Nothing could have been simpler.

Called upon to account for that decision, I might have invoked in my own defence the ingratitude of a community, the duplicity of a woman, the sheer futility of the task which had brought me to the village in the first place. Reason enough for the world, I should imagine, but falling short of some essential truth. How should I have explained the rest? – the emptiness glimpsed behind or at the heart of things; that absolving darkness which, even as I sat there in the lamplight, continued to ripple over and through me like a tide, washing me clean of obstruction. Who would have understood? And to whom, in any case, was I accountable?

I must have resisted Ann's advances with rather more vigour than had been apparent to me at the time, for the upper surface of my right boot was flecked with blood. I took a sheet from my notebook and dipped it in the ewer, dabbing the leather as clean as my inadequate means allowed before squeezing the paper into a ball and dropping it into the grate alongside the filmy residue of the letter. Then I packed my valise with all I wished to keep or needed for the next day or two: my plans, instruments and notebooks, my toilet-case, a change of clothing. I felt a little light-headed, oddly detached from my own actions as I threw the remainder – shirts, breeches, even my tweed shooting-jacket – into my trunk and snapped down the clasp.

Jem Poster

The note I left for Mrs Haskell, along with what was actually a rather generous sum of money in settlement of my debts, instructed her simply to sell both trunk and clothes and to use whatever she could get for them as she saw fit. I might have given more specific guidance on the last point, and certainly the Jeffords were in my mind as I wrote the words; yet the plain truth is that I found it impossible to take any serious interest in what might happen in that godforsaken place after my departure.

And that, I thought as I let myself quietly out of the house, was that. I walked the eight miles to the station through the narrow lanes, arriving shortly before dawn. I remember very little of that part of my journey, but a few details stand out with preternatural clarity: the shrilling of the wind in the leafless hedgerows; my boots scuffing the powdery snow on the deserted platform; the dim carriage, the familiar smells of polish, leather and horsehair; the sky just beginning to lighten as I unbuttoned my greatcoat and settled back in my seat.

27

I tell myself that this, or something like it, has happened, though I am careful, with each fresh recapitulation, to leave intact some essential grain of doubt. A boy is walking with his dog on the fringes of the wood above the village when the animal suddenly bounds forward, yelping. The boy follows, treading down the bracken, pressing into the gloom, and almost stumbles over what he takes at first to be a heap of abandoned clothes.

The girl is lying on her side, her cheek resting on the grey beech-roots. She has covered her face with her right arm as a sleeper might; but the fine snow lies unmelted in the folds of her dress, on her dark hair and in the hollow of her left hand, and the boy knows at once that she is dead. He turns and, with his dog at his heels, runs down the slope towards the village.

The boy reappears, now at the head of a small group of men. They climb the hill, briskly but without haste. One of the men carries over his shoulder a roll of stained sailcloth. The dog capers around the group, leaping, lunging, nosing the frosted tussocks. Nobody pays it any attention. Nobody speaks.

The landscape has the luminous clarity of a Dutch painting. A cold blue sky without a cloud. Not a breath of wind stirring the trees or the brittle grasses. A covey of partridge huddled where the ground-cover thins at the wood's edge. The roofs of the village below lightly dusted with snow, shining in the pale sunlight. A woman stands in a doorway, shading her eyes, looking up; but she does not move.

Suddenly the partridge rise, rocketing from the ground with a whirr of wings, skimming away across the sunlit hillside as the men enter the wood. The boy hangs back, holding the dog hard against his leg, his fingers twisted in the coarse hair at the back of its neck. Both are tense, the boy leaning forward, staring into the shadows, the dog quivering with suppressed energy.

They have found the girl. One of the men turns away, burying his face in his hands; but the others cluster around her, one leaning down to touch her cheek softly with his knuckles. There is no hurry. The sailcloth is unrolled and spread flat on the leaf-mould, and I see now that each corner is provided with a padded loop of rope. The body is stiff, but with something of the calm grace of a memorial effigy. They manoeuvre it awkwardly, with a kind of clumsy reverence, until it lies in the middle of the canvas. Her skirt has ridden up her calves to the knee; and now someone squats down and rearranges the rucked fabric, pulling it gently over her ankles.

I can feel the pressure of the loops on the palms of their hands as they carefully lift their burden; my own shoulders are taut with the strain. I know with what anxiety they hold her clear of the ground, avoiding the gnarled tree roots and the fallen branches, easing her towards the light. I understand their absurd solicitude for the insentient flesh and feel with them, for her, each jolt and bump of their slow descent through the frozen pasture.

Others have gathered by the gate at the foot of the hill, shivering, subdued, expectant, their breath clouding the still air. They gaze out and upward, tracking the progress of the returning party. The clouds are massing again on the horizon, the light beginning to fade from the sky. Someone lifts the bar and the gate swings wide.

There is more, I see that now. Almost impossible to make out at first, but the details sharpen as I examine them. It is night. The body is stretched naked on a deal table in the middle of a sparsely furnished room. Firelight; a candle burning in a chipped saucer at the girl's right shoulder, a brown earthenware bowl at her left. The kettle on the hob begins to steam gently and a woman steps forward out of the shadows, carries it over to the table and fills the bowl. She has draped a sheet over the back of one of the chairs; and now she takes this in both hands and, with an abrupt, angry movement, tears off a strip of the coarse fabric. The sound rings out like a cry in the appalling stillness of the room.

The woman puts both hands to the nape of her neck and tightens the soiled blue ribbon which binds her thick hair. Then she sets to, plunging the strip of linen into the water, wringing it out and wiping the small white face from brow to chin. She does this for some time, gazing down as a woman might gaze at a newborn child; and as she works, her actions become increasingly delicate, increasingly tender, the cloth itself seeming to soften as she dabs it into the corners of the closed eyes, runs it down the sides of the nostrils and across the fine, downed contours of the upper lip. I see her wince as she presses it to the yellowish patch of bruising on the girl's left cheek. It occurs to me that there may be other injuries, but the room darkens suddenly as I look, and for a while I can see nothing.

Her hair, then, what about her hair? Someone will have to see to that. And of course the woman does so, picking out the brown beech leaves and smoothing back the tangled curls as I smoothed them back that night in the moonlight. She makes no sound, but the tears begin to fall, lightly at first and then more steadily, wetting her lined cheeks and dropping on to the vacant, upturned face.

She has reached the neck. She draws the cloth with a long,

slow movement down from the jawline to the collarbone and then round to the nape, damping the soft hair there, registering with a sharp spasm of bewildered love the knobbed contours of the skull behind the ear. And on down the body, painfully engrossed, swaying a little from side to side, caught up in the rhythm of the work until, quite unexpectedly, her legs buckle beneath her and she crumples and sags, flinging the cloth aside as she gropes for support. She steadies herself against the table and then, bending forward, lays her head on the girl's cold belly, sobbing a little now, but quietly, her hands beginning to wander aimlessly, unhurriedly across the smooth surfaces.

So vivid, the stark candlelit interior, so sharply delineated; but not that, surely? Stories, she said, all stories; and if I ask myself why that story rather than another, I find I have no ready answer. This, then? Scrubbed white walls, a marble mortuary slab, a faint smell of carbolic. The drip of water into a ceramic trough. The body lying unattended in the chilly half-dark, awaiting the indignities of forensic examination, the disclosure of injuries more terrible than I have yet dared to imagine.

Is that it? Perhaps so; but in that case whose are they, the hands still moving with such unspeakable tenderness over the white flesh, brushing the ribs below the breasts, minutely responsive to the nuances of the sunken flanks and the soft skin on the inner surface of the thighs? Whose is the wet face pillowed on the belly? – the face suddenly lifted in an attitude of anguish so immediate, so intensely and irrefutably real that I start up from my chair like a madman, my own mouth framing a silent cry of pain.

And it strikes me that, plagued by unnameable terrors and disorientated by lack of sleep, I may indeed have become a little crazed. Certainly anyone might be forgiven for thinking so, stumbling into the curtained gloom to find me slumped in my greatcoat beside the cold hearth or pacing the floor, stubbled and unwashed, lips working soundlessly, my valise unopened and my clothes unchanged since my return.

I have gone backward and forward over the whole business, and I am little the wiser. What am I to make of them all, the recollections, the impressions, the elaborate inventions to which I return incessantly like a singed moth to a candle flame? Even the smallest detail seems questionable. A glance, a phrase, the faint sigh breathed from a kissed mouth: how should I interpret any one of these?

Or this, glimpsed yesterday from the window of the train? An isolated farmstead – brick-built house, thatched barns of local stone; late-morning sunlight reflected off the buildings and the white waste of snow around them; and in the yard, three figures, their faces turned to watch us pass. The man and the woman standing side by side with an easy familiarity, her head tilted slightly towards his, exposing the pale skin of her neck above her brown fur collar. Her right arm reaching down, hand resting on the shoulder of the small boy at her skirts; the man, mirroring her gesture, resting his left hand on the child's other shoulder.

Nothing remarkable, you might think, in any of that. But I was struck by the delicate interalignment of the three bodies and by some related notion of the way lives might fuse and flourish in worlds unshadowed by my own preoccupations. Yes, and just for the barest instant I was swept up and outward by the force of my own perception, knowing it all as though I were part of it – the texture of the glowing brickwork, shared warmth of flesh and breath, the eloquent geometry of love.

And as I stared, the train swung round on the curve and the sun blazed through the window, filling the whole carriage with light. The landscape beyond the glass shimmered and dissolved. I craned forward in my seat, knowing they must still be out there somewhere, those three interlinked figures, at the heart of all that glare and dazzle; but my eyes, unused to such intensity, began to smart and weep and I was obliged, not without reluctance, to reach out and pull down the blind.